For David

Chapter 1

It was dusk and squally. A stall-owner packed away the day's news of world revolutions and tossed an old sandwich into the road. Two pigeons fought over it. Several taxis passed in a row, heading West, seats empty, lights on. One taxi slowed, the driver peered in his mirror at a couple, walking out of step under a tattered golf umbrella. They didn't hail him. Or even notice him. He accelerated, turned into the right-hand lane and lost sight of them.

Angie was regretting wearing heels. The paving was uneven. She tugged at Ted's arm, almost dragging him towards the embankment. He seemed more absorbed in keeping control of his wretched umbrella, rather than getting anywhere. Infuriated, she pulled free, teetered on, sliding to a halt at the water's edge. He was still lagging behind. Getting her breath, she tucked her cleavage back into her too-little black dress and tried to smooth down her damp hair. Without success. It always frizzed in the rain.

She scanned the wharf, where three barges were moored in a row. The first two pulled darkly at their ropes; the third spilled light, music, laughter from its portholes.

"It's still here," she told him.

He tamed the umbrella into an arrow pointing downwards before joining her.

"That's the one!"

"Let me check." He held out his hand for the invitations.

"No, not now."

"Yes, come on."

She let him have his.

The barge was rocking, its engines turning. She broke into a canter to reach it, heard his voice behind her:

"Lord and Lady Beaverwood?"

The envelope might not have been addressed to them, exactly, but it had, quite definitely, been left on their doorstep. It promised a ride on the Thames, 'cutting edge' food – whatever that was – and an exotic home as a prize for entering some competition. In Angie's opinion, owning something exotic would come close to being something exotic. "Never mind that."

"Angela?"

The boat edged forward, its engine revving. A boatman was already untying the mooring rope. Gauging the distance between the wharf and the boat, Angie kicked off her heels and jumped. She found herself sailing between land and boat, her breath trapped in her throat like a plastic bag on a bare branch. Eventually she landed, scrabbled to regain her balance on the wet deck. The boatman muttered something. It could have been Polish, or Glaswegian for all she knew.

"Hello," she said to him. "Bring my shoes," she yelled to Ted.

The engine drowned out his reply as one shoe plopped into the Thames. Catching light from a bridge lantern, it righted itself, and bobbed gamely towards Wapping.

"Jump!"

Ted didn't.

The boatman heaved the ropes on board and steered the vessel free of its mooring. It gained speed, leaving Ted mouthing something on the quayside.

As she watched him downsize, her bag began to vibrate. Rummaging amongst old Kit-Kat wrappers, some anti-histamine cream, her bargain book on Mongolian sourdough recipes and Dusty's awful end-of-year report, she found her phone. It flashed Ted's insistent ringtone at her as the barge sailed towards Waterloo Bridge and he disappeared completely.

She switched it off.

They were now approaching Gabriel's Wharf and the Oxo Tower, all lit up in neon, misty, beautiful. She drank in the damp spring air, shook her curls loose, letting her head drop backwards. Stars winked at her. A jumbo jet sliced through a watermelon moon.

From inside the boat a live band burst into Cuban salsa. With her bare feet, she kicked open the door, stubbed her toe, swore, and entered the party.

"Lady Beaverwood," she muttered to the doorman, handing him her invitation. He ticked off a name on a list, handed her a gilt-embossed nametag, and let her through.

The wave of perfumes made her sneeze; a blast of trumpets made her ears ring. For a moment she couldn't see anything other than candlelight flowing like a silk ribbon through a room connecting eyes, sequins, diamonds. It was hard to pick out any individual people amongst the bobbing heads, or define the genders of the glittering bodies that heaved around a makeshift stage upon which musicians were playing salsa with faraway expressions. A tall waiter in a tuxedo handed her a drink. It tasted of peaches; bubbles went up her nose. She looked around for someone to talk to.

"...Died of nothing at all,' said a woman in green silk.

"In oil, wasn't he?"

"Gas."

It was like entering a dream in damp stockings. Would anyone notice if she removed her tights? Before she had a chance to experiment with standing on one foot and tugging, a waiter handed her another drink; she wanted to laugh loudly and would have done so, but the musicians softened their pulse to a patter of drums that blended in with rain on the roof, and a spot highlighted a tall, spindly man with greased-down hair and a well-cut suit.

"Hi, I'm Ray Brebington." He gave a little bow. "Giving you a once-in-a-life-time opportunity…"

On a screen above their heads floated the golden domes of Florence, the turquoise canals of Venice.

He must be referring to the competition. If she won an exotic home perhaps Ted wouldn't cancel coming on holiday like he normally did. Last year they'd managed to reach Gatwick before he had to race back to deal with a fallopian tube emergency. This year they hadn't made any plans. Another waiter refilled her empty glass and she knocked it back in one this time, trying to look at home.

"…To fully experience Venice, Vienna, Lvov, Vladivostok…"

Any of them would do. She waited for him to outline the rules of the competition. She liked rules. But the room was beginning to go in and out of focus. Her lunchtime Slimline soup had left her hungry ten minutes after eating it. She rose onto tiptoe; dinner was hidden under silver covers.

"We take the time that you can't spare to ensure your timeshare is exactly…"

Her empty glass was whisked away and replaced with red wine this time. She gulped that down too.

Ray applauded his audience's good taste by clapping. Hoping to blend in, she cheered, waved.

"Because time is the precious commodity we are giving you.' He appeared to be directing a regretful smile at her. 'So, if you're too busy before you board that plane, we haveour specialists in all of our locations, ready to…"

He reached for a canapé, tossed a large pink prawn into the air, catching it with open lips where it settled, feelers waving. One swipe of his handkerchief and his teeth were flashing again.

"...Do your wishing for you."

Ray seemed to single her out with his gaze.

"Do you have any questions?"

He loomed towards her. She could smell his aftershave and came out in a sweat. What if he asked her to sign something? She was backing away, when she thought she heard a female voice to her right:

"Angie!"

Was this directed at her? Oh no! Had she been rumbled? Was she swaying or was it the boat? Rain was now pounding on the roof overhead. A fog seemed to have descended on the room.

"Angie Riley!"

Nothing else for it! She would have to hold her ground. She was Lady Euphorbia Beaverwood. Who was daring to challenge this? She squinted at the bobbing heads and located the voice's owner: a tall woman in a zebra-striped ball gown, crowned by an orange and black-feathered hat, her face half-obscured by a sequin-peppered veil. The woman was weaving an unsteady path towards her. Was everyone sozzled?

"It's you, isn't it?" the voice insisted, in a tone which she half-recognised, but couldn't place.

"No, it's not."

She was about to be named and shamed as an impostor, and unceremoniously dumped, or worse, escorted onto a dinghy, and left to row herself back to central London.

The hat's veil was tossed backwards, snagging on a startled man's cocktail stick. Angie found herself gazing at flecked brown eyes, glittered cheeks, a long, almost transparent nose shading plum-coloured lips, until, with a tightening of the heart, she recognised the owner.

"Fiona?"

It was a lifetime since they'd huddled together in the Holy Trinity Convent, in the freezing dormitory, where a North Sea wind threw them together, making them share secrets, a single bar heater, eye-liner, and a world of strict rules that they made up and swore to.

"Is that you?"

"Who else would I be?"

Angie's bare feet were being scrutinised.

"But you…"

"I'm afraid I'm not on the list."

"…Aren't wearing any shoes."

"No, they're…"

Fiona didn't appear to be listening; she was staring at the stage where Ray was helping a short, bouncy man in a chef's apron and hat onto the plinth.

"Let me introduce you to the world's maestro of cuisine… the Guy (*Ghee*) de Borzoi!"

The man gave a grand bow, the effort bringing beads of sweat to his bald spot and a hum of approval from the throng. Angie thought she recognised him from 'Dine with Me' on Sky.

"Trotters in snares," said Fiona.

Angie assumed that was the name of the minuscule morsels he tendered towards them all like a sacrifice.

The crowd plunged forward like a herd of wildebeest sighting a waterhole. Angie was too polite to join its thrust. In a second, the tray was empty of anything but toothpicks.

"My husband," hissed Fiona.

"Your what?"

Fiona sighed.

He was certainly a change from the upmarket but gormless escorts from Eton with trust funds and titles. Angie noticed the invited guests now held plates and napkins and were gathering into two queues. She itched to join them.

"He looks cuddly."

"Daddy hates him."

The spectre of a whiskered Papa Gregoyan, with bulging eyes, thin as an exclamation mark, emphatic as an autocrat from another century, sailed into Angie's mind, much as he'd sailed up the drive to the convent school parlour in his powder blue De Dion Boutin coupe with gold-plated mirrors.

"How is he – your father?"

Behind them, the band was tuning up again. A moustachioed man from the military, carrying his laden plate, passed mouth-wateringly close. Angie had to restrain herself from grabbing his stuffed mushroom.

"Indestructible."

"Your mother...?"

Fiona pointed heavenwards.

"So sorry, you never told me..."

"You were too busy being a socialist, remember? Didn't want me around, embarrassing you with Daddy's money."

They were at the buffet counter, finally. Angie pointed at all the available dishes. Her plate scantily adorned with tiny samples of food she didn't recognise, she steered a path around a few sharp, silk-suited elbows and several perfumed bosoms towards two empty seats, Fiona bringing nothing with her but a bread-stick.

"I had to build up Guy from scratch, you know. It wasn't easy. He was plain old Gary Barker from Brum until I set to work on him."

The breadstick searched out something that could have been fish pate; Angie never found out. Apart from a few carrot sticks and some lettuce, the plate was looted. It was all coming back to her. Fiona always wanted what Angie had. Angie thought of Ted left behind on the wharf and wondered if he'd reached home yet.

"You're still hiring and firing for your father?"

"No. He fired me. Or got my replacement to."

"So, what do you do now?"

"I make hats. Famous ones. Global ones. 'Crowning Glories' is mine. You have heard of 'Crowning Glories'?"

Angie could only shake her head.

"God. Look me up."

This explained the creation on Fiona's head. Must be some sort of promotion.

"What about you? Did you marry the animal-rights activist – it was Craig, wasn't it?"

"No, Craig got God and..."

"He never looked that healthy."

"Actually, I married a doctor."

"I suppose someone has to."

Angie felt oppressed by the feathers. Abandoning the cramped seat, she lunged towards a porthole. Rain smeared neon colours against the glass. The boat thudded as it hit waves. Had they passed the Tate yet? Was that the wobbly bridge?

Fiona was right beside her, feathers and all. She grabbed her hands, studied them. "You haven't managed to grow your nails."

"No."

"You still bite them."

"I don't."

"I like that."

"Like what?"

"Oh, never mind."

Angie saw her own reflection in Fiona's eyes – auburn curly hair framing an even, round face and snub nose, undistinguished by anything asymmetrical. Not young, but not old. Her head was clearing.

The music struck up again. A quickstep on bass and drums.

"Does he… you know, this doctor husband of yours… still…?" Fiona pointed downwards.

Angie felt her cheeks inflame. "Of course."

"Ah ha! You twitched your nose." Fiona was snorting in triumph. "You always do that when you're lying."

Angie turned away to stare pointedly at Guy de Borzoi, aka Gary Barker, who was repositioning a gooseberry on a pale green blancmange. "Is that who you are now – Fiona de Borzoi?"

"Nice name, don't you think? Let's dance."

The sun was high over next-door's roof when Angie sank into bed next to Ted, every part of her body aching. She wasn't used to dancing the salsa with anyone, never mind Fiona Gregoyan. She certainly wasn't used to staying up that late. She claimed her part of the bed, mirroring Ted's body with hers. She loved his tan-coloured back with the well-carved torso dimpling in at the waist. She listened to the rhythm of his breath: long, short, long long, short, short, snore, start, then again, long...

A 'touch of the Levant', her father had said, when Ted had braved the first Sunday lunch, along with an Anglican bishop from Guyana. Her mother made all sorts of nervous jokes about anthropology and inter-faith worship.

"Ted's Jewish," she had said.

She touched his shoulder. He stirred.

"Did you play Lady Beaverwood the whole evening?" he mumbled.

"You should have jumped," she said.

"Doctors don't jump."

"You'd never believe what happened..."

"Hmmm."

"I met an old friend from school."

"S' nice."

"Wouldn't call her nice, exactly."

"Hmmm…." He let a snore loose, then a few more. His breath returned to its natural rhythm: long, short, long, long, short, short.

Chapter 2

Fiona woke from a dream to the sound of the smell of strong roast coffee and an angelic choir in the room – '*All things bright and beautiful...*' She flicked the radio off, tugged her eye pads back down, and pulled the duvet over her head.

"Babe..."

"I'm asleep."

"I've brought you breakfast in bed."

"What on earth for?" She emerged from the deep, kept her eyes covered and felt for the table next to the bed. Her fingers located the coffee pot and a warm cover. She lifted it, moved the eye pads and peeked. Her favourite. Poached egg on toast. Coffee and a fresh tomato juice to cure her hangover. What a nice husband. "Why, thanks."

She plumped the cushions, sat up, and tucked into the egg.

Guy placed himself on the corner of the bed. He was freshly scrubbed and ready for work.

"You're up early. When did you get back?" she asked.

"Not long after you."

"I didn't hear you."

"You looked as if you'd died and didn't want anyone to know it."

The egg was perfectly poached. She was beginning to feel

better.

"It went okay?"

"Ray couldn't be faulted. Or the food. Or the band. And the guests were definitely gold-chipped. "

She didn't have the heart to point out that at least one of them wasn't. "Oh, good."

"But the orders didn't exactly come flying in."

"Don't worry. I'm sure they will." She opened both eyes wide and blinked at him. He was looking rather pale. "Just have faith and hold onto your nerve, Guy." She chomped into the second piece of buttered toast.

"We needed someone to buy something, Fiona. Urgently."

He slumped own onto the side of the bed. He was panting slightly. She hoped he wasn't going to have one of his anxiety attacks.

"You have taken your pills?"

"You might need to help tide us over for a few months."

"Certainly not. The bank's the place for loans."

"The bank won't answer my calls, never mind lend me any money."

"Let Ray schmooze it out of them. He's the man for that job."

"Ray's maxed out on his credit, Fiona."

She drained the last of her coffee. "I'll talk to him."

She pushed the plate away, threw off the covers, kicked some clothes out of the way and stood up. Outside the window a watery sun lit the opaque glass of the offices opposite. It was windy. Clouds promised a deluge. She found the phone under last night's hat.

His voice was gruff yet cheery.

"Hello, Ray," she said.

Fiona liked the look of Ray's new apartment. His last flat was in a dingy basement just behind Klburn station. This penthouse overlooked Regents Park and the Zoo. If she craned her neck to see past the tropical plants on his roof terrace, she could make out the aviary and the giraffe house. How enticing to be so close to the wilds. The décor was marvellous too. Unlike her own flat, filled with all the junk she could never throw away, this room was bare of features. Unless you counted a chandelier constructed from glass balloons. Oh, and some grey buttons dotted around the white walls. And, also, a stylish sideboard, which protruded from the wall and had nothing on it.

All this must have cost a bob or two. What was Guy on about? She stretched out on the sparkling white sofa.

A smell of dark roast and 'Sauvage' cologne and Ray reappeared, bright-eyed, clean-lined.

"Nice place."

"It's the company flat."

"Hmmmm."

"Look." He waved his arm in the air. "Table."

The sideboard lit up, a crack in the wall opened, ejecting a strip of Perspex which unfolded into a coffee table. She wasn't sure what this was supposed to prove.

She looked around for a sign of strings. There were none. Was he a ventriloquist?

"It's a Piers Fettucini."

"Sorry, who?"

"The second of his *Mood Installations*. It's called *Aspirations*. Arthur is what I call it. His *Desperation* is in the Tate Modern. It came with the flat. You do know who Piers Fettucini is?"

"Of course I do." Fiona had no idea what he was talking about.

"His ideas are so *recherché*."

"Of course they are."

"Higher," he said.

It sounded like a command. It was a command. The table raised itself a further inch, wobbled a bit and kept on rising.

"Stop!" he said.

It didn't until it crashed into the ceiling. They both stared as it stayed there.

"Down, Arthur," he called to it, more cautiously this time.

The coffee table descended rather haphazardly. Fiona moved her legs out of its way. It reached a position in front of the sofa and seemed to settle.

Fiona kept her distance. "How does it work, exactly?"

"Actually, I don't know. Luckily I haven't had to. Arthur knows."

It took her a moment to remember Arthur was the installation.

Ray poured the steaming hot coffee into transparent, shining clean, hourglass-shaped vessels, then topped hers with cream from a tall silver jug and handed it to her. "Guy's told you about his shortfall?"

"His? Aren't you business partners?"

"Yes, but he's the label on the tin."

"Guy?"

"Don't you believe in him and his conquest of the world's palate?"

"Of course I do. It was me that made him who he is."

"Yes, yes, we both know who he used to be."

A wind shook out wet leaves. Fiona looked out of the window where the sun attempted an entrance.

"So, what about helping him? You've got plenty of credit."

She made a point of looking around Ray's flat very appreciatively.

"I could make it up to you."

"How, exactly?"

"Don't be vulgar, Fiona." He smirked. "I could give you a timeshare in apartments anywhere in the world."

"What for?"

"Fun. Heard of that?"

"What sort of fun?"

"Well, that's up to you. But if it was me, I would tango in Buenos Aires, sky-dive in Tenerife, burn driftwood by the Caspian Sea, then fly to Sydney for an opera via Fiji at sunrise."

Fiona hated journeys. She'd made too many of them as a child, trailing after Daddy on his quests to conquer the world. "Ugh!"

"Are you too old for romance?"

"I'm not in slightest bit old and I'm fanatically romantic."

Ray snorted. "You could take a friend." He winked.

Fiona rounded up her acquaintances mentally, and came up with couples, hat-customers, an ostrich farmer, a fabric dealer, several shrinks and a tarot reader.

"You do have someone, don't you?"

"Bucketfuls, but...."

"There's a loft in Liverpool, next to Albert Dock if you don't want to be too far away."

Fiona poured herself more coffee, ripped off a big piece of croissant, dunked it, and lost it. Like her toothbrush on a trek with Daddy to some desert fiefdom where she brushed her teeth by a well. Even more like her fur gloves on a school skiing trip – they disappeared down a bottomless crevasse. On the top of that mountain in a blizzard, Angie had lent her one of her own hand-knitted woolly gloves. Sedate, safe, old Angie was a friend. But Fiona wasn't taking any wretched journeys with her, however trendy.

"How about here?" she said, tapping the coffee table. It shuddered so she took her hand way.

"Here? I live here."

"Okay, then forget it." She fished for her sunken croissant with her finger.

The birds were singing their hearts out beyond the window, with sweet, shrill voices.

"Why here?"

She looked around, shrugged. "I could get away from Guy's cooking, for starters."

Ray looked as if he was beginning to regret his offer. Good.

"It's a company flat, remember? I could drink your wine, eat your leftovers, watch your old DVDs, and play..." (She looked about for the art installation controls. All she could see were small grey buttons dotted around the walls. Were they switches? Or sensors? She reached over and tapped at one. Nothing happened. She brushed the sideboard. It glowed and the room was suddenly decked in flock wallpaper.) "...with Arthur."

"Just you and Arthur?"

"No." She searched for something that would wipe the smirk off his face. "Me and a friend."

His smirk gave way to something cunning. "It would have to be when I wasn't here."

Give him a taste of his own timeshare medicine. Angie had told her she had one afternoon a week off. "Thursday afternoons, from one till six," she said.

"Every Thursday?"

She smiled sweetly at him.

"Well..." His voice was croaky. "...What about a hundred thousand as an interest-free loan..."

"What?"

"Keep your hair on! It's small change for you, Fi." He took her empty cup. "Of course, if you don't think you can help, I could approach an investor I know."

She tried to imagine Ray pawning his art installation on the high street... 'It rises when you ask it and sinks when you don't.' "Yes, why don't you."

He arranged her cup and his on the tray. "But they'd have their own ideas about the catering. Of course, I'd fight for Guy. I'm doing that right now."

The bloody man; words dripped out of him like oil.

"But my hands would be tied, if the bailiffs walk away with the food mixers. Guy will be back making shepherd's pie at Lee's Diner on the Old Kent Road.'"

He went to the window, and leaned out, letting a breeze ruffle his thick hair. Then he flaked croissant onto the window ledge, for the birds, she supposed. He kept his back turned towards her.

Fiona hated backs. Her whole life had been punctuated by people having more important things to do than present her with their faces. Maybe that was what she liked about making hats – people always faced you, however outlandish the result. She watched birds flutter down next to the crumbs, chirruping. Others lined up on a potted cherry tree branch, setting off a wave of pink blossom, as if on cue.

"A year of Thursdays then," she said.

He turned, walked back towards her. "Alright," he said and whipped a document from his jacket pocket. "Sign this."

He'd had it there all the time. He'd known she'd agree to a deal of some sort. Well, at least she'd got the flat out of him. Even if it was only on Thursdays. She peered at his pocket to see if there were any other documents he might spring on her. Her last will and testament, perhaps?

But no more surprises. He smoothed out the paper, on which were rows of blurry figures, all ending in zero.

She should use reading glasses but there was no way she was going to admit to any weakness in his presence.

He pointed to the place for her signature.

"There are three copies."

"Is the timeshare for this flat on here?"

"I'll give you the entrance code and..." He snatched back his pen, packed it carefully away in his pocket. "...I will be discreet."

From the pavement, Fiona gazed back up at the penthouse imagining Ray on his roof terrace pacing backwards and forwards among the potted topiary, talking into his cellphone. The bastard was probably broadcasting his triumph over her to the world. Well, let him. She was a hundred thousand pounds poorer. But at least she'd wheedled something out of him. Daddy wouldn't approve. In fact, he'd be horrified. Thinking of the devil, she felt her phone vibrate in her pocket.

"Daddy?"

"Who's that?" he barked.

He must have pressed her name by mistake.

"It's Fiona."

"Who?"

"Your daughter, Fiona."

"It can't be. I want my plumber. It's cold."

She worried about his memory. But the thought of trying to persuade him to have carers or move into a care home gave her hives.

"Yes, it is. I was hoping to pop over…"

"What do you want?"

"To see you."

"Is that all?"

Daddy could sniff out any insecurity. She kept her voice steady. "Yes, of course."

There was the sound of pages turning. She struggled to contain her childhood fear of being banished to an island that only allowed visitors in leap years.

"When can I come?"

"Between seven thirty and eight o' clock on Tuesday evening."

"I'll be there," she replied, but he'd gone. She tossed the phone back, rolled up her sleeve, ripped off a nicotine patch and rummaged. From the recesses of her bag she extracted a battered Silk Cut cigarette. She lit it, and with one long drag, reduced it to a stub.

Relaxing, she admired a cyclist as he passed by her on the pavement. He flaunted his tattooed biceps and his angular chin at her as he stopped at the zebra crossing.

"Cheer up darlin', " he said, grinning, before taking off again.

'A friend', Ray had said. And smirked. She had a sudden flash of Sid Budgen from the grammar school, whom she and Angie had ravished ruthlessly behind the kitchen garden wall until he fainted. She saw his pale spotty face lit by the moon as he creaked away, leaving behind his bicycle and one boot. Yes, Angie was going to be her new best friend.

She shook her hair free of her brow, stubbed out her cigarette and added a new name and number to her phone.

Chapter 3

Under the brilliant light of the white-tiled restaurant, Angie was trying to keep her chrome stool from wobbling. The high ceilinged, pillared restaurant was haunted by wafer-thin diners picking at their seafood salads with long forks. It was a vision of vertical lines where she felt rather like an exhibit, perched between a marble counter upon which equally marble-eyed sardines lay and a tank in which lobsters brooded. Feeling uneasy, she tapped at the tank. The nearest lobster raised his claw. She noticed a name tag: 'Cedric', it said. He was giving his partner, labelled 'Angelique', a brittle hug. Angie shuddered, turned her back at this watery death row, gazing instead at the steel-capped kitchen, a place of tall hats and shouting, where flesh steamed and fires flared. She decided she'd be a vegan for the evening and looked at the menu.

There was a luminous photo of Guy de Borzoi above the entrees, looking fresh-faced, enthusiastic, his whole life ahead of him. The special lunch menu was 'Plateau de Fruits de Mer de Borzoi' followed by 'Sole de Borzoi avec pomme frites', followed by 'Basil Sorbet Borzoi'. There were no prices on the menu. Angie ordered a glass of sparkling mineral water and let it glitter.

After what seemed like an age, the glass swing doors

whooshed open, letting through a blast of spring air, a rustle of bags and, eventually, Fiona, who tossed her shopping into the arms of the nearest waiter as she wobbled, recovering her balance the moment he took the burden from her. Angie watched her scan the room, nodding grandly at various hands lifting forks, until she followed the waiter over to Angie's table, baggage cresting beside them, overturning a fruit bowl, and crashing a knife onto the tiles as she passed. She aimed a kiss at Angie's nose and plonked down, the parcels coming to rest in a heap by her feet. The waiter sighed, pulled a notepad free of his striped fish-market apron, and waited, pen poised.

"Dearest…" Fiona waved her arm at the décor. "…What do you think? Daddy paid for it." She downed Angie's water. "What are you having?" she asked.

Feeling suburban and shabby, Angie studied the menu, as if she hadn't seen it before. She opened her mouth to say, "Vegetable soup…"

"We'll have grilled lobster for two." Fiona pointed to the tank.

"Angie and Ced?" asked the waiter.

Angie cast a last glance at her namesake.

You'll love the way Guy sets fire to them."

The waiter nodded a man with a net towards the lobsters.

"And a bottle of Epinard."

Fiona snapped shut both menus, handing them to the waiter, who glided away, tidying up her debris as he went. Then she fixed her with an unsettling smile. "So, how *are* you?"

Angie wanted to tell her that she'd had a trying week and that her job was going nowhere. There had been one death, three noisy arguments at tea, Sid the goldfish had eaten his mate, the lawn needed mowing and the magician's escaped rabbits were demolishing the flowerbeds. They'd obviously been breeding again. "Great," she said. "How are you?"

"Marvellous, fine, wonderful."

Angie found both her hands clasped in Fiona's grasp.

"You see, I've had this brilliant idea."

Angie could see their table-neighbour's eyes fixate on them like those of a locust trapped under glass.

"Guess what it is."

It was difficult to know what could excite her. Whatever it was, it would be expensive. She shrugged.

"It involves *you*."

"Us? We don't have any money! I've got kids." Angie could sense the silent diners crackling disdain.

"We're not involving Todd in this."

"Who?"

"Your boring husband."

"I never said he was boring."

"And we're certainly not involving Guy."

"We?"

The waiter was sailing towards them bearing a silver bucket, champagne and glasses. Behind him the fish tank attendant poked at Angelique who was resisting visibly. Angie tried not to watch.

"It's not going to cost anything."

"What isn't?"

"A timeshare. I can't do every week."

"Timeshare?"

"On alternate Thursday afternoons."

"You've lost me."

"A timeshare just between us – on Thursday afternoons."

Fiona's face hovered motionless in front of her, pale, heart-shaped, insistent.

"Sorry?"

The attendant was heading for the kitchen, his hands clamped around the claws of Cedric and Angelique.

"A lover, of course."

"A what?"

"You get him one week and me, the next. We alternate, like we did with Sid Budgen."

"Sid Budgen, you..."

"God, not with him, he's in the House of Lords now. Making laws. Or blocking them. Someone much younger."

"What are you talking about?"

"We'd pick the candidate together and share him, equally. You know, with rules."

"What rules?"

"And we've got a super flat with a view, and masses to catch up on. All safely confined to Thursdays."

"But how will we catch up with each other if we are there on alternate Thursdays?" Angie had at least managed to work that out.

"Yes, it's perfect." Fiona was desiccating a bread-roll. "This way, when we do meet we'll have something to catch up about."

Angie remained confused in a way that only happened with Fiona's schemes.

Fiona poured the vintage bubbly into Angie's glass, then her own, which she downed in one gulp. "Have you got a better idea?"

Angie tried to remember what she usually did on Thursday afternoons. This week she had to do her fortnightly supermarket shop, and call somebody back with the phone number of a plumber. Last Thursday? Nothing came to her. She had a flash of Ted microwaving something from the freezer she'd labelled 'single left-overs'.

"No, no, no, Fiona. Absolutely not." She shook her head as well as her index finger. You couldn't make it clearer than that.

Then that old delicious panic came blustering in from a

grim brick school building in Norfolk and torched all her careful schedules.

"I can't be involved in anything like this. Definitely not. Absolutely not."

The waiter arrived bearing two chargrilled lobsters. "Is the flat nice?"

"Gorgeous," said Fiona. "The only drawback is some mechanical problem. But that's going to be fixed, so don't worry."

"Sid Budgen in the House of Lords?"

Angie was a little hazy about the journey to Fiona's place. "It's only round the corner," was what Fiona had said. It wasn't. There was an expensive ride in a mini cab with a long stop on double yellow lines at the Nicolas off-licence in Shoreditch, the cab driver lamenting in a language that seemed to blow in from the Central Asian steppes. Fiona had finally emerged from Nicolas, carrying two purple-tis-sue-wrapped bottles, heading in the wrong direction. She'd only turned back after Angie shouted, the cab driver hooted and a passing police-car blared its siren.

Once they were at Fiona's apartment block, Angie had had to pay the driver with all her small change and help Fiona turn out her bag for the key to the door. She would have left then but Fiona insisted. And Angie was worried what Fiona might do if left alone on the doorstep. The apartment block was stylish enough to have an antique lift. It wasn't modern enough for the lift to actually work. Fiona trailed up the stairs ahead of her, singing 'Roxanne' so loudly and tune-lessly that Angie found herself worrying about the terms of the lease. Several times she managed to prevent Fiona from sliding backwards; even the magenta-papered walls seemed to be swaying.

When Fiona pushed open the door to her apartment, Angie was struck by the smell of cinnamon and the sight of gilt-framed oil paintings featuring a long faced robed gentleman. There were so many, she thought she was hallucinating.

"Saint Gregory," said Fiona, handing the two bottles to Angie. "Our namesake. My father gives me a new painting of him every birthday."

They both stared up at a particularly forbidding pair of eyes that seemed to be regarding them with suspicion.

"Let's have some fun." Fiona waved for Angie to go on ahead of her. "Take these upstairs. I'll find the corkscrew."

Angie sneaked a wink at the nearest St Gregory, armed with a staff and a papal hat, tucked the bottles under each arm, and mounted the spiral staircase.

"Room at the end of the corridor," called Fiona from the kitchen.

The first-floor corridor also boasted gilt-framed paintings. In these, Renaissance angels replaced the fierce frown of St Gregory. Angie wondered if Papa Gregoyan had gifted those too. At Easter, perhaps?

She padded to the end of the corridor and stepped into a bedroom hushed by tapestries and cushions; the walls were hung from floor to ceiling with fleshy nudes, also gilt-framed, but certainly not provided by Fiona's father.

She turned her attention to the mantelpiece, upon which were several framed wedding photos of Fiona in various outrageous frocks and hairstyles, each with a different groom. Had she married that many times? Angie was taking a closer look at the Fiona and Guy wedding special when Fiona appeared.

"Here, catch," she said, and threw her the corkscrew.

It was one of those pump, puff, turn, and pray-for-deliverance stainless-steel gadgets that only worked when Angie gave up.

Fiona opened the belly of a plump, plaster cherub on the mantelpiece and produced two stained glass beakers. She grabbed the open bottle and filled both glasses.

"To us," she said and downed hers.

Dropping her handbag, Angie sank down onto the nearest soft cushion and sipped at her full glass.

A bottle and a half later, they were sprawled out on the rug.

"We need to write a few things down," said Fiona in a slur. "Paper, that's what we need."

She began to open drawers, rummaging furiously, feathers and lace flying, until she managed to extract two stubby eye pencils.

Angie located her handbag under the bed and pulled out the pad of Post-its she always carried.

"We can use these."

Fiona lurched then stared at the pad suspiciously. "Don't you have any other colour but grey?"

"Sorry."

Fiona tore off most of the paper for herself, and threw the remaining sheets and a pencil to Angie. Then she sprayed her part of the pad with perfume before attacking it with her pencil.

Angie smoothed out her single Post-it note, poured the last of the wine into both glasses equally, sipping hers from the glass with the least lipstick. "Right..." She dusted glitter off the tip of her pencil, hiccuped, and then wrote: 'Two women.'

No, it was important to point out they were sophisticates, not scrubbers. And leave out the two. It sounded desperate.

'Ladies' – yes.

'Are looking for...' No, 'seek a man...'

Mind you, it couldn't be any sort of man.

A hunk? A youth? A gentleman? Angie thought 'gentle' was an important quality; they weren't looking for a bit of rough. Or were they? Finding her glass empty, Angie dabbed at her lips. What could they possibly offer the man? They weren't young or gorgeous. In fact, they could be classed as 'older'. Was there a way of turning this to their advantage?

'…interested in gaining a full experience…'

The promise of intimacy in a discreet sort of a way.

'…of mature women. Only serious offers considered.'

That gave the enterprise a modicum of dignity.

She looked at Fiona, who was on her belly, with her head cupped in her left hand, her brow furrowed in thought and the pink tip of her tongue showing, surrounded by discarded Post-its. Pen held high, she mused over each word like some sort of intellectual. It reminded Angie of when Fiona had tried to emulate Simone de Beauvoir – right down to the scowl and chain-smoking. It lasted until Fiona discovered French cinema, and pouting, and found she couldn't frown and pout at the same time. Also the Gauloises made her cough uncontrollably. Pouting was replaced by the half-closed-eye-lid stare she learned from Julie Christie. Fiona always made things her own. Even now. She was hogging the stationery. Was so much waste paper really necessary? They weren't trying to rewrite *War and Peace*.

"Do you want to hear mine?" Angie asked.

"No."

Angie felt as if they were seventeen. Maybe this time around she could learn some of Fiona's tricks – how she got people to answer her letters, agree to her ridiculous requests, and not shout when she jumped queues or was late and forgot the theatre tickets. Mind you, when they'd both written love missives to Cliff Richard, Fiona received a magnificent signed photo, whereas Angie's letter came back unopened, and mouldy as if it had been left out in the rain.

What was it about her? Did she exude a chemical attractant like female moths? An electrical charge? Or was it simply that she was fun to be with?

Now Fiona was emitting small grunts, while staring straight ahead, into the dark recesses under the bed. Was she looking for inspiration there?

"We've got to bloody well seduce them into taking the bait and..." Her voice was even more slurred.

"You haven't said that, have you?"

Sunlight was edging down the bare bottoms on the wall above the mantelpiece. It must be late. Alex and Dusty would be back soon. How was she going to extricate herself when everything in the room was spinning?

"What's this?"

Angie realised Fiona was opening her – Angie's – handbag. "Stop that."

Fiona reached inside it and drew out Dusty's school report.

"Stop rampaging through my things."

"That's the word!" Fiona dropped the handbag, sat bolt upright, seized another Post-it and pencil, and wrote it down. "Now listen to this!" She read out: "Two sirens on the rampage want to share a bloke. No strings attached. Thursday afternoons. Replies: Box 7455."

"What are we going to do? Tweet it? Put it on Facebook?"

Fiona gave her a contemptuous stare. "The internet? Don't be ridiculous!"

Angie felt an old panic rise. She'd agree to anything if she could get her handbag back and escape out of there. "You win," she said.

Fiona lay back on the mountain of Post-its, looking smug.

"Let's see yours, then." She grabbed it and snorted. "God, it's something from the last century." Fiona tossed it back to Angie.

She dropped the Post-it into her jacket pocket, where it stuck against the lining, its edges curling and reached over for her ransacked bag. "I must get going."

"Let's keep this just between us," Fiona said.

"God, of course." Angie set the glasses and empty bottles straight, and headed to the bathroom where she dipped her face under some cold running water. She hoped she wouldn't see Fiona again for a very long time.

"I'll see myself out," she said as she stumbled downstairs.

On the street she remembered she'd forgotten to buy Ted an anniversary present. Not sure where she was, she hailed a passing taxi and told the driver to drop her off at the nearest Sainsbury's. She'd be able to find a cashpoint there and roses and breath mints, and get directions to the nearest Underground station.

Chapter 4

Ted found it difficult to sleep through Angie's sharp, rhythmic snores. She'd been in the bath when he'd got home from a bloody awful day at work, and in bed when he came upstairs, complaining of a terrible headache. She'd had lunch with an old school friend, she said. He suspected the lunch of creating the headache, but what the hell. Alex made dinner. Not bad, if you like tomato sauce. They all watched the Arsenal Liverpool match; there'd been no squabbling, no interruptions. Resident Liverpool mole – Dusty – had a cold. Peace. Couldn't stop thinking about the court case though.

Her snores mutated into whistling; he gave her a little shove. Silence. Then a muttering. Her breath smelt like vinegar.

The Courts of Justice gates loomed. With a great creaking sound they opened, then closed. He thrashed about, sweating. He'd never been an expert witness in anything before, never mind court. Pull yourself together, man. The case could open doors. It was flattering to be called in as an expert witness. Even if it was because Nick Brewer was away. This would define his standing as an IVF specialist. Yes. He tried tugging the duvet back from Angie, then managed to roll her away from a small corner of it.

There was only one slight problem – Ina Endicott. Of course, he had no option other than to support her. She was his client. He shuddered. The woman had a ferocious bark whenever she disagreed with anything, which was very frequently. The unearthly sound burst light bulbs and penetrated your temporal lobes. He'd never had face-to-face, high intensity conversations with his patients when he'd been a humble gynaecologist.

Angie was stirring, muttering; she threw off the duvet altogether. He pulled it over himself before she changed her mind. Rather magnificent – his wife. Viewed from these angles, she was beautiful – all those curves. He tucked some of the duvet round her.

His eyelids grew heavy. He was emerging from a murky violet sea of fertilised eggs when his BlackBerry made its morning bleep. He snatched at it, turned it off. Let Angie sleep it off.

He didn't put on the light, but slipped out of bed very quietly, opened the cupboard, took down a white shirt, then stretched a little higher to reach his dark suit. Not wanting to brave the drawers for his boxer shorts, he picked up yesterday's shorts. They would do. As he pulled them on, he felt a piece of paper stick to his leg. It must be one of Angie's eternal Post-its. She had a mania for writing lists on them. He tried shaking it free before drawing on his trousers. It seemed to have disappeared. It would turn up eventually. Now, where could he find matching socks without making a noise? The wash-basket! Shoes in one hand, socks in the other, he went downstairs, snatched a coffee, and then took the no. 24 bus.

Angie heard the phone ringing, and reached out for it.

Ted's patch of sheet was empty and the red roses were wilting in their cellophane by his side of the bed. God, she must smash the stems and put them in water. By the time she found the receiver, the answer machine was flashing and receiving Fiona's breathless message. She heard the last of it:

"…And you're not to chicken out."

Angie picked up the receiver, cutting out the answer machine.

"I'm here."

The line crackled. Fiona's voice distorted. "It's on its way."

"What is?"

"The advert."

"You want me to read it?"

"No point. I've sent it."

Angie had a nauseous memory of Post-it notes and white wine. "Where?"

"To the *Times* and the *Ham and High*."

"You've what…?" Angie leapt up. The room spun, the phone dropped, disappearing under the bed. When she reached it, the line was dead. She dialled 1471 to learn the caller's details were withheld. She tried replaying Fiona's message. Instead there was another message in the weary, over-articulated voice of Mrs Willoughby. The last person she needed to hear from in her fragile state.

"I have been due to go off duty since 8 a.m. but can't leave my position as contrary to the rota, you don't appear to be here. Could somebody please ring through to say where you are, or indeed if something untoward has happened?"

The overturned alarm clock had its face to the floor. 8.15! Angie flew from the bed and ran round the room grabbing clothes randomly. She had to get the others up!

"Dusty? Alex? Hello?"

No reply.

Where was everybody?

Oh, God, Friday! Dusty had an early trombone lesson. She must have gone on the early bus. And didn't Alex say something about a morning football practice? Yes, that must be it. They'd travelled together. Stop worrying. They were both old enough to get themselves ready, mix their cereals with milk, and travel to the bus stop without her. Dusty was going to leave home, anyway, soon. That's if she did any work to get into Manchester.

Hadn't they missed her?

Hadn't they thought of waking her up?

Yes, she vaguely remembered hearing, "Hope you're better soon, Mum," while her eyes were shut.

Gingerly, she poked her head into the corridor. No sign of life. Holding her head steady with both hands, she peered over the banisters to see that the coat rack was empty of anything but a muddy football scarf and one ragged pink ribbon, and that the morning junk mail was attempting to cut off the route to the front door. She slid down onto the top step and hugged her knees.

She seized a Post-it note, a pencil and wrote – must not spend any more time with Fiona.

What was it they'd agreed to do? She tried not to laugh; her head hurt too much. Honestly. Then she saw the note from Ted.

"Happy Anniversary. See you later."

Oh, no. It was today. She'd have to book the cinema; she supposed they'd have a curry afterwards. That's what they always did. It was what they'd done the evening he proposed. They didn't have any money then. With his going out on his own, the school fees and the wrong mortgage, they didn't have any money now.

Exactly what was she going to tell him about Fiona's plans? And how was she going to square her absence with Mrs Willoughby? She needed coffee.

Chapter 5

Jake nodded at the security guard and entered the corridor leading to Court Twelve. He was under-dressed for the cold draft nudging his trouser legs and shivered violently, sending the *Resolutions* file flying. Damn, damn, damn. Late again. And for the judge's preliminaries. All he could think of was Rosalba, and her extraordinary eyes. And where would that get him?

Why had he even gone to the Embankment Underground Station that day? Why hadn't he saved the dosh and future heartache and walked home like every other day? Once he'd knocked her over, it was as good as over. Of course, he'd scrambled to help her to her feet. And enjoyed the way she clung to him, as she tugged her dress back down.

He wanted her there, then, in her clothes, or out of them, whatever she preferred, and however long it took.

"Will you marry me?" was what he'd said. Hard to believe.

She hadn't looked surprised or anything. Just grinned. "We can do, love, if you like. I'm Rosalba."

Love. No one he knew mentioned love.

But that's what she delivered. After work, he'd wait for her stilettos to clip-clop down the alleyway to his front window. Every night she wore another hair-colour, outfit, smell. Her perfumes were awesome. Mind you, he used fewer inhalers when she stopped using them. That's when he got the real thing – a famished, scorched, ticklish, bored sort of a smell.

End of story.

He looked down at the words on his phone screen – for the twenty seventh time that morning – *Gone home 2 marry Pascal. Saturday. Love R.*

He didn't notice Max motoring towards him until it was too late to avoid him.

"Yo! Jakey!" Jake felt Max's hand grip. "How's tricks?"

Jake made a meal of sighing.

"Not still moping over the dago bimbo?"

"Take your glasses off... so I can..."

"Cool down, it's been ages, bro."

"Max, do..." Jake couldn't think of what he wanted Max to do. He began to walk away.

"'Cos, see, I've got this plan..."

"Not now, Max."

Max ran after him, blocked his way.

"I've found just the thing. Divine intervention, I call it."

With a grand gesture, he produced a Post-it note.

The guy was trying. Jake galvanised himself into showing some sort of interest. "Divine what?"

"Read it, boyo!"

Jake peered at the end of the jabbing index finger: Ladies seek a gentleman interested in gaining full experience of mature women. Only serious offers considered. "Damn you, Max." He handed back the Post-it.

"Found it in the loo." Max was grinning. "Worth the once-over. Come on man, you owe me one."

Jake tried to think of anything he owed Max. "No."

"I covered for you. If Carruthers had known you were sniffing into your sleeve when you should be listening to him roar, you'd be guacamole."

Max had a point. Jake needed his compliance.

"What exactly do you want from me?"

"Answer the ad."

"If you're so interested, why don't you?"

"Look man, I'm giving you a gift here. I'm looking out for as I always do. Looking after your best interests. And see the thanks I get."

Jake felt guilty like he always did when Max got worked up. "Okay, so I answer the ad for you, then what?"

"Nothing."

"Nothing?"

"Nothing."

"Swear on nothing."

"If it's the real McCoy, I'll take over."

Jake grabbed back the Post-it note and stared at it. "Normal people use the internet, not the men's loo."

"Want a bet?"

Jake stared up at the baleful Queen's Counsel, painted in oils in 1799, who lorded it over Room Thirteen, eyebrows bristling with prohibitions. One day he would take his place on this wall. Only his expression would be wise and benign, rather than a permanent bleeding injunction. He never won bets.

"No." Disengaging his arm from Max's clammy grip, he dodged round him and headed up the stairs towards the second floor.

It was warm enough to open the windows of Vetchling Grove, and let a breeze loose amongst the dozing residents. This brought the smell of cats, and a single white feather which drifted for a while before settling on the back of Norma Samuelson's neck as she bent down to search for her teeth. Angie was on her knees, helping, when the mobile in her pocket vibrated.

"You are not going to believe the responses we've had...." shouted Fiona into her earpiece.

"Fiona! Where have you been? I've been trying to get hold of you to..."

"...To our advert."

Angie sank back onto her haunches, bumped her head on a ledge, bringing down the lost set of teeth and some dust. The unthinkable must have happened. In a sea of lonely hearts, dating agencies, massage parlours and dog-training classes, their advert had been noticed.

"You've got to come over and see for yourself. Oh, and could you pick up some sesame rolls and slimline tonic water on the way."

On the 134 bus, Angie counted fifteen men with copies of *The Times* or *Ham and High* newspapers. Okay, so maybe the City gent using the sports section as an umbrella didn't count. So, that was fourteen.

Could any of them notice the crazy ad? Surely not. A sombre-eyed tweed-coated man caught her eye outside Kentish Town tube station and she felt he knew. Her cheeks blazed. She got off at the next stop and walked.

At Mornington Crescent, she stumbled into a bakery. There was no queue.

"Six sesame rolls please."

Adonis put down the paper he was reading and gathered up her rolls in his big hands. Was he winking at her? Or having a stroke? She could feel perspiration drip down her neck. Get a grip, she told herself – even if he had read the ad, how could he know it was anything to do with her?

"Thank you, thank you."

Outside, she hailed a cab because it was driven by a woman and had her drop her at Trafalgar Square. She walked along the Strand, keeping a safe distance from all men bearing newspapers, even the freebies.

42B Fleet Passage was in a tiny side street off the Strand. The 'Crowning Glories' sign was in the shape of a gilded harlequin hat and was hand-painted. The striped awnings were ochre, magenta and sky blue. In the windows sat bare, identical stylishly sculpted heads set at sharp angles, stark against thick canvas curtains on which celebrities in hats were printed randomly as a multi-coloured montage.

There was no possible doubt. The shop was Fiona's.

Angie pressed the gold bell. There was a blast of opera. The door twinkled open; she stepped inside.

The interior was stiflingly close, smelt of straw, cloth and wool, and didn't present a single straight line. What the window lacked, the interior of Crowning Glories made up for in spades: every surface bloomed hats like the monstrous manifestations of strange tropical plants. There were tall hats, squat hats, fat hats, floppy hats, stiff hats, hats in the shapes of animals, fruit, flowers, famous buildings, hats of all shades of all colours, urgent, combative, clashing.

She located a feathery bird's nest of a hat under which Fiona was ensconced. In front of her was a pile of papers.

"Sit. I'm nearly done."

Fiona screwed up a piece of paper and tossed it onto the parquet floor where there was the now familiar pile of bunched up rejects. "These are ludicrous." She opened a fresh envelope with a long turquoise hatpin.

Angie felt around for a place to sit. Stupidly, she chose a stack of boxes, and sank a few feet, embroidered felt closing in around her.

"What do they think we are? Hookers?"

Angie reached for one of the discarded paper balls, smoothed it out.

Staring back at her was a photo of an erratically bearded

man. Lonely eyes loomed beneath stormy eyebrows. The words read: 'hobbies – sailing, knot-tying, drinking, outdoor sex….'

"You mean all these…" She stared at the rest of the pile.

Fiona tossed another ball across the room.

Angie caught it and opened it. The tiny print ended in a wild splodge of a signature - 'See you soon', said the postscript.

"…Are replies?"

"Phwah." Fiona swiped the table clear, and stood up, clutching a slim stack of papers, which she flapped at Angie. "But here are our six possibles."

Angie pulled herself up, which was difficult. "Let's be clear about one thing, Fiona. We are not taking this any further." It was impossible to be vehement at floor-level.

"And they're not bad."

"You're not listening."

Fiona turned to stare at her, her big dark eyes oozing out two large tears.

It took Angie back to a cupboard at school, where they shared a battered biology book and a torch.

"You don't seem to be appreciating the effort I've put into this."

"Yes, I do. Of course I do."

"It's taken hours and hours. And I've done it for us."

"Don't cry. I am grateful. Of course I'm grateful."

"It's just a laugh, Angie. Something we can share for old times' sake."

"Can't we share something else? We could go to the theatre, or see an old movie? You know how we loved West Side Story."

Fiona snorted derision.

"Okay, we could arrange a school reunion. You'd like that. Let's do that."

"I would not like that. I've found you again after all this time, Angie. And I want to share something just with you."

"Fiona, this could be…" Dangerous – was one of the possibilities.

"All these years you've stayed out of touch."

"Not intentionally."

"So, humour me and come do a little harmless window-shopping before we're too old, mad, or dead."

Angie looked around the room for excuses and only saw hats. "Do any of these candidates have a beard?"

"Why?"

"I don't like beards."

"Okay, no beards."

Were these men really interested in the availability of two middle-aged women with husbands? Angie thought of her own father's fiery Sunday sermons, delivered to a row of elderly Norfolk ladies with hearing aids, in which he forbade pleasure, sin, and voting Labour. He'd never bothered to mention sex to them. He must have thought they were past it.

"We'll need to set some rules, Fiona."

"Okay." Fiona uncrumpled one of the discarded letters, turned it over, and unscrewed a felt-tipped green pen. "Rule number one: whatever happens, it must be fun."

"That's not a rule."

"It is now."

"Then, rule number two has to be that we keep everyone happy."

"Course." Fiona wrote that down too. "Anything else?"

"The most important rule of all is not to fall in love."

Fiona looked up, made a face. "That's bloody obvious."

Chapter 6

For the first time in ages, Fiona found herself alone in her kitchen. Honestly, she could hardly recognise it from the place she once toasted cheese sarnies. It was stuffed with gadgets, pingers, pots the size of China, jars and jars of spices she'd never heard of. She looked around for something to actually cook on and, after finding a freezer, dishwasher, and something from Zanussi that whirred with menace, she located a space shuttle type apparatus that had the word 'oven' on it.

Why on earth did Guy need all this? Weren't great cooks supposed to be able to make heavenly soufflés with no more than a wok and a butter knife?

She placed her shopping on the granite worktop, decanted each premade meal carefully into copper casserole dishes and popped them into the oven. Then she scrunched up the containers and buried them deep down in the dustbin. She took out a couple of carcasses the butcher had given her. Now, where were the knives?

When he was still Gary Barker he hadn't had all this equipment. He only had a motorcycle helmet, a pizza in a box and a Brummie accent. What with that and the rain cascading round him, it took several repetitions for her to understand he needed the loo.

"Oh, is that all? Come in then."

He was shivering so much she had to carry the box and his helmet. He squelched upstairs after her. When he came out of the loo, she thought it only fair of her to ask him to warm up the sodden pizza.

His accent made everything such a mystery; it was only later she discovered he was complaining about her oven.

She remembered him using her favourite silk scarf to dry himself. Then he sat down to share the pizza with her. She didn't remember asking him to. He probably couldn't understand her either. They'd chatted away though, quite happily. If only she knew then what she knew now. She was much too impressionable. She had an awful soft spot for dreamers. And somewhere in all his mumblings, he told her he dreamed of being a great, world-famous chef.

"Not with that accent."

He'd looked hurt.

"You've got to be French. Or Italian. And I can't speak Italian, so it's French."

"Will you teach me?"

That's what she thought he said. He smiled so winningly. "What's your name?" she asked.

"Gary. Gary Barker."

"Ooh. No. No, no, grrrolll your rrrr's… as in gggrrre-nouille."

"Grrrraree Barker."

"No. Forget Gary."

"But…"

"From now on, you're…Guy."

"Guy?"

"Ghee. And the Barker's going to have to go." She went through the names of her customers… "Du Pont? No. Du Mare? No. De Spair? No no. De Beere? Hmmm." A dog bounded into her mind - Barker, Barking. Yes, that was it.

"De Borzoi."

Music had chimed up on the sound system next door. Something foreign crooned to a guitar. They'd ended up smooching. He got the zip of his leather jacket caught in her hair. But he was warm by then. Very warm.

The oven timer was pinging. She switched it off, put on oven gloves and took out the dishes. She sniffed at them. Nice, but ordinary. She took down the last spice from the rack. Wattleseed. It smelt funny. She shook a generous helping over the shrimp chowder.

It hadn't been easy, but Daddy's secretary found him a job at Browns. So the next time she was hungry at breakfast time, she took a taxi to Mayfair. And *Guy de Borzoi* gave her an extra helping of her favourite game pie, strengthened her coffee, and asked her out on a proper date. Sweet really.

A sound interrupted her reverie. There was a kerfuffle on the landing outside the flat. She heard the door slam and keys hit the marble top hall table. Guy was back.

"Surprise!" she shouted. "*Entrez!*"

He didn't seem to hear her. She could hear him banging things about in the hall cupboards. Moments passed before the door to the dining room squeaked open.

"Guy!"

Time passed slowly until his head appeared in the hatch, and hovered there, his eyebrows glued to each other as he surveyed the state of the kitchen, his mouth open.

"See what I've done for you my dear, sweet, under-appreciated husband, all by myself." This was just a small white lie.

"Are you feeling alright?" was all he said.

"Don't be silly. Sit down." She pointed at his place at the dining table.

He stayed where he was, staring at the carcass of the rabbit she'd draped on the draining board.

"But, Fiona, I've eaten."

"Don't be silly, Guy. Come and tuck in!"

She didn't mean to sound threatening.

He stopped protesting. She could see him through the hatch, perched high on his chair, sliding his napkin in and out of her mother's silver ring.

"Da da!" She skipped with the shrimp chowder, swooshed the bowl down in front of him where it wobbled, grey waves bashing against the sides of his bowl. She used his napkin to dab at the splashes, then smoothed it onto his lap. Then she colonised a chair opposite him.

He was peering down at the soup.

"Aren't you having any?" he asked.

"I've been tasting it for hours. Go on…"

He scooped up a spoonful, letting it steam, then sipped, all the while eyeing her balefully.

"Well?"

"Mmmm," he said. "Great. Absolutely delicious," he added.

"Don't have a second helping because there's rabbit in pomegranate to follow, then roly-poly rhubarb custard, chocolates, and…" She rummaged in the dresser, ripped open a packet, shook it so that the aroma was released. "… Brazilian coffee ground for you personally by yours truly."

He looked as if he was about to say something, but seemed to decide against it.

"And then, darling… I think we should have an early night."

"Oh my God – I mean, sorry."

He seemed to be staring at her with alarm.

"What's the matter, Guy?"

"Has the doctor changed your prescription?"

"Bah!" She wasn't having any talk about her mental state. No siree. Sidling up to his chair, she put both hands on his shoulders, tugged at his taut muscles with her fingers.

"Now do try very hard to relax."

Angie booked two seats at the Everyman for 'The Dog Basket', a Finnish film, advertised by two women standing back-to-back, with guns to their own heads. Not her sort of thing really; it was a treat for their anniversary. Ted loved films he could read rather than watch. It relaxed him, he said. He'd better not be late. She could hear Dusty on the phone upstairs. Alex was quiet though. Working, Angie hoped.

What a day! She poured herself a small glass of his Chianti and waited. The wine smelled of mouldy raisins. She took a mouthful.

Rules indeed. Scores of them, like clashing colours. Fiona was crazy.

'A marriage is like the twinning of towns' came to Angie's mind. Melanie, their couples therapist, only ever addressed Ted, and hardly ever glanced at Angie. It was infuriating.

She picked up the Chianti bottle and poured herself another glass.

Last time they were on Melanie's couch together, she had devoted the whole session to comparing despair to a traffic jam. Ted swallowed it hook, line and bumper. Perhaps she shouldn't have got the giggles. But then, it was sex aligned with the National Grid. She couldn't be serious.

On the third glass, Angie decided to let Ted go alone. See if he and Melanie noticed she wasn't there.

No sign of him. She could hear Dusty's television now upstairs.

"Dusty!"

"Yes, Mum?"

"Switch that off and get on with your essay."

Dusty's door slammed.

What was the point in telling her? She was either going to get those grades or she wasn't.

No sound from Alex's room. What was he doing?

She checked her watch. There was still time to get to 'The Dog Basket'. She corked the Chianti and tried to concentrate on BBC News 24.

Terrible things were happening to the world, to the City and to the weatherman's hair which seemed to be receding before her eyes. It must be the effect of wine on her empty stomach.

Her phone made its cicada chirp. A text from Ted: Held up at court. Don't wait.

Nothing about their anniversary.

She tramped upstairs, pushed open Alex's door. There he was, in the dark, the light from his computer streaking his fiery red hair. She felt like pressing kisses into his forehead and holding him close, like she did when he was a baby.

"Hello, poppet," she said.

He turned, glowered at her, and quickly turned the screen away.

She glimpsed a chorus line of bare breasts.

"Aw, Mum, I wish you'd knock."

"Sorry, darling. But I was just wondering if..."

"I've done my course work, Mum."

"Because I thought that if it was English literature, I might..."

"Naw."

"Hungry? There's Chinese with pineapple..."

That seemed to interest him. He switched off his computer.

"Yawl, ssokay then!"

"I'll warm it up, then."

She didn't travel on to tackle Dusty's telly-viewing habits.

Screams and creaky music continued behind her closed door. She was tramping back downstairs to the kitchen when the cicadas chirped a second time. She didn't hurry. 'Shall get a bite on the way home', it said.

Angie reopened the Chianti, poured some of it into Chinese pineapple beef and the rest into her glass. She put the dish into the microwave and sat down in front of Newsnight.

Chapter 7

Morning arrived, sharp, acid-bright, jingling with bird-song. Angie groaned, reached for Ted. There was only a warm dent in his pillow and, beyond that, on his bedside table, a half-drunk glass of water and an open packet of aspirin. A headache. Serve him right for not remembering their date. How late had he been? At least the roses were now in a vase of water, even if they were papery and brown already.

She peered at the bedside table. For a note, or some sign he was sorry. Nothing. He'd forgotten.

Strangely, she felt relieved.

She would have had to tell him all about Fiona and the timeshare craziness.

It was his fault she hadn't.

And today was the day.

They should abandon the whole idiotic scheme.

Would any hopefuls turn up for the audition? Surely not. It would be nice to be a fly on the wall.

She threw back the covers, snatched at some clothes, drew a comb through her hair, scurried downstairs. Half-way down them she panicked. She must be mad. She went back to the bedroom, found her cell phone and pressed Fiona's number. The voicemail told her to leave a message. She didn't. Instead she went down to the kitchen.

Dusty and Alex were at opposite ends of the kitchen table, on iPods, chomping their cereal together like synchronised swimmers.

"Seen Dad?" she asked.

She may as well have been talking pidgin; neither of them responded.

"Fire!" she shouted into Dusty's ear.

Dusty shook her head free of her ear-set, and peered at her with some concern.

"Are you feeling better, Mum?"

Ignoring both of them, Alex poured milk onto a second helping of Frosties.

"Yes, thank you, darling."

Feeling scrutinised, Angie opened the fridge, not really knowing what she was looking for. Whatever it was, it wasn't there.

"Are you here later, Mum?"

"It's my day off."

"Oh, great. I need you to help me with the Civil War."

"That's lovely darling. I'm always happy to fight them off. But, I might be a bit late." Feeling uncomfortable about what she was keeping back, Angie pulled out half a lemon and poured hot water over that.

"Why?"

Angie felt herself blushing. "Just a few things I need to catch up on." Her life for the last twenty years came to mind.

"Can I come too?"

"Er, not this time, darling."

"Oh."

Alex ripped out his earphones. "There's no bread, Mum," he said.

"It's okay. I'm on diet."

"Really? Isn't it too late for all that?" Dusty looked even more concerned.

"Well, thanks a lot." Angie sipped at her sour hot water.

Dusty began to load the dishwasher.

"Don't worry. I'll do it." In an effort to distract attention, she snatched a cup from Dusty's hand. It fell onto the tiles and rolled a few times. A chip broke off but otherwise the cup remained intact. "Damn."

Dusty swooped down to reclaim it.

"Did Dad forget your anniversary again?" asked Alex.

Oh, God, why had she also trained them to be so forthright? "He's got more important things to remember," she said.

"Yeah, right, like his test tubes." Alex gathered up his bag.

"Shh, Alex, let her be."

"See ya." He was gone, the door slamming after him.

"Sorry about Dad, Mum." Dusty was reaching for her coat.

"Wait! I'll come with you." Angie lunged to catch the door before it closed and raced after Dusty up the path. She caught up with her at the gate. Alex was further down the pavement. The 24 bus was rounding the corner. There was no time to say anything else. The bus stopped. Without a backward glance, Alex jumped on board. Dusty gave Angie an embarrassed smile and followed.

"Bye, darlings." Angie waved madly. Neither of them looked back from inside the bus. A guide dog barked at her instead. Feeling ridiculous, Angie put her arm down and watched the bus pull away. It was as if, without her noticing it, her children had gained maturity in mysterious, secret increments and left her behind.

She trudged back to her front path and noticed that green moss had filled cracks in the bricks and winter had killed the white rose bush. She kicked the root; it snapped. The house loomed over her, seeming taller than usual, bigger somehow. In five years it would be too big for two people.

In the hallway she realised she was still in her dressing gown. No wonder the kids had looked so uncomfortable at the bus stop. God, where was she supposed to be? She found the piece of paper Fiona had given her. Reptile house—10.00 —candidate one, man from Birmingham. Aquarium—10.45—candidate two, opera-singer. Gorilla House—11.30——candidate three, barrister's pupil. Pig enclosure—12.15—candidate four, recently-divorced man. Penguin pool—1—candidate five, man who lives with his mother. Tiger cage—1.45—candidate six, foreign student from Belarus. It was late. She unbuttoned her dressing gown, and, uncertain as what to do with it, loaded into the washing machine and set a low-temperature wash. Then she ran upstairs.

Exactly what was the right apparel for auditioning lovers? May as well enjoy the joke. She tossed the contents of her wardrobe onto the bed. A vermilion blouse with a cream skirt? A magenta jumper with short sleeves? Viridian green might terrify the animals. Shocking pink might frighten them. She tried several skirts and dresses, a trouser suit, then settled finally on a plum-coloured top, tighter than she remembered around the bosom, matched with some flattering black trousers. She topped the arrangement with a black cotton cap to cover her hair. That didn't look quite right. She discarded that, using sunglasses, instead, to conceal her eyes. In the mirror it reminded her of someone in a spy movie. A femme fatale. Don't be idiotic, she told herself. Fiona's going to be better at that.

Fiona was a little puffed when she arrived at the zoo entrance. It was a stroke of genius to plan their rendezvous here. It was safe – they would be surrounded by the public. It was intellectual – the place was teeming with zoologists.

And there were plenty of signposts – to avoid muddles.

"Twenty eight pounds?"

She tried pouting her pink-glossed lips at the ticket-seller to get a reduction in the price, but was met with an icy look that could be Stalinism or misogyny or ageism, or all three. Okay, she would make him suffer. She made a meal of counting out the eight pounds in small change, waving aside the sighs arising from the queue behind her. Then, just as he was turning his attention to the next customer, she decided to buy a map and brochure by credit card, cancelling the last transaction and demanding her coins back. She also took her time gathering up her bag before languidly vacating his counter.

Some primary-school kids in green blazers were just behind her in the queue. What were they laughing at? She looked down to see if anything had attached itself to her. Okay, okay, so perhaps a see-through dress of black chiffon wasn't normal zoo attire. And it was possible she had over-done it with the diamante butterfly kirby grips. She tried smiling. The school party just carried on sniggering.

She turned away from the little blighters to buy a giraffe balloon.

Now, where was Angie? Armed with a map, brochure and ticket and with a string bobbing up to the clouds, she steered a course to the reptile house.

Jake was early. Idiotic idea. Bloody Max. He was always putting someone else on the firing line while he hid in a trench. The Post-it promised an older, married woman with no strings attached. The sign said: Gorilla gorilla, largest of the apes, indigenous to Equatorial Africa. These are non-aggressive creatures but please do not shout, scream, feed or compete with them.

Was the man really that desperate? And, anyway, what was the matter with the Internet?

Jake cleared the bench of crisp packets, sat on it, and stared into the greenery of the glassed-off enclosure in front of him, trying to spot the gorilla. A pair of eyes stared back, blinked, and a fist swiped a bluebottle from their neighbouring nose. Jake gave it a nod. The creature actually nodded back. Ha. Jake kept still. So did the gorilla. So, okay, it was peaceful – them gazing at each other. A fly came and went. Hard not to swipe at it.

Three school children in green blazers poked at the bars in front of him, before being dragged away by a teacher. Clouds thickened, spat a few drops.

If no one showed up, he could go with a clear conscience, and say it was a no-brainer.

Two foreign nuns carrying a green crocodile balloon appeared and stopped in front of the gorilla, the balloon blocking Jake's view.

Was the zoo was the right place for this blind date? It would be just like Max to get the wrong end of the stick.

A bruiser of a man, covered in tattoos and piercings, plonked down next to him. He spat, emptied his pockets, rearranged a wad of banknotes, draped his leather jacket over his arm, rummaged, jostled, and blew his nose a few times, before launching himself back onto the walkway.

Rosalba. Her torrent of hair. Now was the time to tear up the tiny photo he carried in his wallet. He felt in his pocket.

The wallet was gone. He felt for the notes he kept in his trouser pocket – thank God, they were still there. He shook out all his pockets. No wallet. No photo. No Oyster card, and no typed instructions from Max. Bloody hell – the tattoo man?

He got up. Where should he report the crime?

Angie was late, flustered. She ran down the walkway to the Reptile House where she skidded to a stop in front of a sign – No entry: cleaning in progress. Her chest was heaving uncomfortably under her tight top. Go home now, she told herself, before you are recognised by a school kid, one of the mums or even by one of the candidates.

Derek Spriggs thumbed through his morning's pickings – a pencil case masquerading as a purse, a cheque book with no cheques, a single ten pound note, an out-of-date credit card, the membership of a gospel church, an almost-empty wallet with an Oyster card and a note, folded – something typed on legal-headed notepaper. What a way to make a living. Enough to send him into a job centre. He was about to toss the lot into the bin, when he felt something go up his nose, making him sneeze. While searching for something with which to wipe his nose, he had another look at the note: 'Blind date rendezvous – 11.30 – The Gorilla house – she's called Angie'. He took a quick look at the time on one of his prized, stolen fake Rolex watches.

Fiona scoured the Reptile House for Angie and candidate number one. It was dimly lit and empty, apart from a group of large children, and a woman with a mop. She couldn't remember how they were supposed to recognise the man from Birmingham and wished Angie would turn up with the rules and the notes.

Then she saw him. Tall, straight, pale, with the sort of hair that answers to a comb by lining up stiffly over a white scalp. He looked well dressed, had roving, intelligent eyes and a nose that protruded into the room, bristling with attitude.

Also, there was a briefcase bulging with papers at his side. This was all very promising. Time to get the thing on the road. She was about to walk over to greet him when she noticed he was using the tip of his flapping black umbrella to tease something black and long in the reeds behind the glass. She peered at the sign: Venomous snake – Black mamba. She looked to see if she could see it more clearly. There it was – puffed up against the glass, spitting. The man wasn't backing off. He twisted and flapped his umbrella at the fangs and spat some comment at the thing. Then he stood back, satisfied, turned and showed Fiona his teeth. His canines were long, pointed and yellowing. She felt paralysed as if by venom.

"Hi, doll," he said. "Are you Angie?"

"Angie?" Fiona shook her head frantically. "Certainly not." She kept her eye on the umbrella as she backed away.

Angie couldn't believe Fiona was moving so fast. She marched her past the snack bar, past the toilets, forced her into trotting round the back of the aviary, the penguins, and the llamas, in a very circuitous route to the aquarium. Fiona seemed breathless, giving nervous backward glances, giraffe balloon bobbing after her.

"What happened?"

"Nothing."

It began to pour, drowning the squeals of children, screeches of cockatoos, craaaks of monkeys, and the rise of umbrellas. Fiona dived into the aquarium as rain thundered down. Angie followed. The place was cool and quiet. Golden fish glided past. There was a strong smell of mould and chlorine.

"So…" Fiona grabbed the list. "Is it the newly divorced man now or the…?"

Before Angie could answer, a baritone voice intoned:

"Rudolfo Miranda, opera singer."

They both turned. He was a curly-haired older man with soft, doe eyes.

"…Enchanted to meet you," he said.

"How lovely." Angie put out her hand.

Rudolfo ignored it and took Fiona's.

"Here you are." This was directed to Fiona as if the two of them were alone.

"It is for this moment that I have left my home in Argentina. In the hope of meeting you have I sung in the opera houses of Milan, Paris, Venice, Moscow, Berlin."

The way he let his voice roll out the consonants made the places sound encrusted with gargoyles and culture from which Angie felt utterly excluded. She peeked at Fiona, and found her open-mouthed, only closing it to coo in response to his cadences.

Fiona sank gently down on the bench in front of the turtles' tank. Rather like a swan, Angie thought. Rodolfo settled down beside her.

There was nothing for Angie to do but perch on a railing opposite them.

"My mother didn't take me to the opera," Fiona was saying. "She was so anaemic you could see through her."

Rudolfo was nodding, whilst patting Fiona's hand.

She appeared spellbound and didn't seem to notice the obvious. Rudolfo was enormous, Angie thought. Exercise might kill him. And this could happen in their timeshared flat. She could hear the sirens, the feet of the paramedics pounding up the stairs, see the stretcher carried past grim-faced members of the residents' association. There would be paparazzi flashing cameras in the street outside, her face in the *Daily Mail.* How would she explain all that to Mrs Willoughby? Or Ted? Or Dusty and Alex?

"They wouldn't let me sing in the choir at school. I had to stand in the back row and mime the words," Fiona was saying, tearfully.

Angie had to extract her. "We're running late," she said, tapping her watch.

Fiona waved her away.

"You could take down Mr Rudolfo's phone number."

Rudolfo moved so that Angie couldn't see Fiona anymore.

Okay, if that was how they both wanted it. Angie stood. "We'll be in touch, Mr Rudolfo."

"You go on ahead," said Fiona.

This was not on. Fiona was flagrantly violating rule number five restricting each auditioning candidate to twenty minutes.

Determined that she, at least, kept to the rules, Angie marched off into the thunderstorm. "I'll be with the gorillas," she shouted.

Chapter 8

Fiona tried pointing at the sign: Please don't sing, shout or wave. It frightens the fish. Rudolfo didn't appear to notice.

"Tum tee tumm tee tumm teeeeeee….secondo… quando," he sang. His voice travelled out of the aquarium only to bounce bounced back again. Resoundingly. Rather like his tummy which pivoted over one leg then the other as he continued to warble.

Why on earth had she asked for a sample of his work? It had been perfect when he'd listened to her. Even in the cool blue of the near-deserted aquarium, she was feeling awfully hot and bothered.

"Quando pando... isssimoooo secondo..."

He was nodding meaningfully at her. Was he expecting her to join in? Was this an aria? A fugue? And what was the opera? It could be Puccini, or Verdi, or anyone, actually.

She tried squeezing his hand to stop him.

He seemed to take this encouragement, and added a trill at full throttle.

She lowered her face to be level with his, and shook her head violently.

He didn't understand. He smiled right back at her and launched into throbbing, light-bulb-swinging delivery of, "Nana trala lala... Americanaaa..." that had all the tanks vibrating dangerously. Two fish labelled 'Mississippi Paddle-fish' make a dash for cover, their fins glooming like taillights of a misty traffic jam. Even the terrapins dived off their rocks and hid in underwater crevices.

She decided to take the Paddlefish and terrapin route.

Mouthing, "Bye bye, see you later," she ran for the exit.

Ears ringing, she stepped outside and gulped in the rain-cleansed air of the great outdoors. Children. Mothers. Queues. The normal world. A parrot flashed its colours behind bars, repeating the tone of a mobile phone. A little boy in battle fatigues tugged at the giraffe balloon still bopping from Fiona's bag. She scowled back. The boy's mother turned, menaced over her. The boy grinned. The voice from within the aquarium carried on soaring. Would he notice she was gone?

She rummaged in her bag, extracted the list and a pencil and scratched out the first two candidates. She peered hazily at number three, fished for some glasses and gave up the search. Then she tied the giraffe balloon to a location notice board and hurried off in the direction of the Pig Enclosure and the newly divorced man.

While passing the Reptile House she almost fell over the foot of a police officer who had his binoculars trained on something in the distance. Had some animal escaped? She stopped to peer at what he was looking at and saw the group of green-blazered primary school children in his sights.

"Pervert!" She hurried on.

The storm eased. Angie gave her umbrella a shake, rolled it up and looked around to see if she was in the right place. There was a ripping sound in a bush and she saw him – a large gorilla savaging a corncob. Yes, she was.

Minutes passed. The walkway was deserted. If the third

candidate didn't turn up, then she would be perfectly within her rights to pin a polite note to the railings, and go home. She could always meet Fiona in ten years' time for a more civilised chat and a coffee.

The gorilla came closer. Scratch scratch, he went, his eyes closing. He didn't seem to have anyone to talk to, either. Feeling sympathetic, she gave him a polite nod. He seemed to like that.

She waved.

At which point he went bananas, roared, hurled himself at the glass wall which shook violently but, thankfully, held.

"Wouldn't like to get on the wrong side of him, now would you?"

She jumped, turned to find a man grinning at her.

A smile flashed gold in a face lined like a bulldog's. The man was rippling with muscles, tattoos, rings and intensity.

Could this be the third candidate?

"You waiting for someone?" he asked.

His voice sounded as if it had to scratch its way out of his throat.

"Well, yes. Are you?"

"Could be."

She wiped the condensation from her watch to check the time.

"Eleven thirty-five," he said. 'Name's Derek. Like my Dad. And his Dad before that. And the old bugger before him. A long line of Dereks."

She couldn't remember a Derek in the list. "Look, I…"

"Mind if I?" Not waiting for an answer, he plonked down next to her. "Pleased to meet you."

"Are you training to be a barrister?" He didn't look like a trainee barrister. Perhaps she was simply out of touch.

"Straight out of the Law Courts and into your life."

He thrust out his hand. It had a red and blue serpent

tattoo curled around it.

Flustered, she took it in hers. It was hot, dry.

He took a Lion Bar – what else? – from his inside pocket, ripped it into two perfect halves and tossed one onto her lap. Realising she was hungry, she nibbled at it, staring ahead into the enclosure where the gorilla was glaring at them both. It was a little unnerving. "Thanks. Sorry, I'm Angie."

"Well, hello, Angie."

He looked her up and down, whistled through his teeth.

"That's the kind of figure I like."

She found herself tucking in her tummy. "Since we're both here..." Her fingers trembled as she unfolded the list of questions she and Fiona had so drunkenly prepared. "I could begin by asking you a few questions."

He gave her a sideways glance.

"Are Thursday afternoons good for you?"

"I'd invent a new day of the week for you, Angie, darlin'."

She ticked a 'yes'. The ink ran. "Have you..." She felt herself redden. "...Any preferences..."

"That depends. What do you have in mind?"

Quickly, she turned the page. "Are you a vegetarian?"

"They wouldn't have me."

He moved closer.

She noted down a question mark, scrolled down.

"Are you energetic?" God this was embarrassing. "Er, resourceful..."

Ted could never be called resourceful. Her flushed face was contrasting her lower limbs. She was getting cold feet, then realised they weren't her own. Derek's steel toecaps were chilling the arches of her exposed feet. He was that close.

"Oh yes," he said. "When do I get to prove it?"

"When my friend gets here."

"Your what?"

"My friend. Didn't you-?" Hadn't he read the advert?

"This friend a man?"

"No. You see, we're sharing everything equally..."

After a pause he said, "We are, are we?"

His breath was warm, his laughter deep. It had a precision.

"So we have to agree on everything."

"I see. What, you mean both...?"

"Yes, but she has to agree too."

"Is she anything like you?"

Angie was distracted by some shouting just to the right of the gorilla cage where a group of men were running towards the Cat Pavilion.

"Look, I'm sorry, do we have your details?"

Derek stood. "No-one has my details but..."

The group of men had changed direction. They were now running towards the gorilla enclosure.

"...I'll take yours." Derek leaned over and – before she could stop him – he extracted the purse from her open handbag.

"Derek?"

"Hey you, stop..." someone in the group shouted. The gorilla roared. Derek jumped over the bench and disappeared into a hole in the hedge.

She looked around in alarm.

Two uniformed police were running right at her. There was a wild-haired man at their helm, waving, shouting: "That's him."

It was all so quick. "He's taken my purse," she said.

Both policemen vaulted over the bench in turns and disappeared into the hedge.

"Bastard," said the young man.

Was he also about to disappear? He was pale, dressed in a wet woolly jumper and had fervent dark eyes. Hadn't she seen him somewhere before? Was he on TV?

"I'm an idiot," she said.

"He picked me clean too, if that helps."

"He didn't look like a barrister, not even a trainee." She was jabbering now.

"A barrister? If he's a barrister, I'm the Docklands Light Railway. I should know. I'm a barrister. Well, I will be."

Of course, she'd seen those eyes and that hair before – in a photo sent in the post. *This* was the third candidate. Divorced? No, that was the other one. "Oh God, it's you I'm supposed..."

"I had a meeting here scheduled for eleven thirty, but all this and I'm late and..." He looked at his watch, then at her. "I'm Jake, by the way."

"Jake? Are you...?" She smoothed out the list.

At that moment the first policeman reappeared from the hedge, a pair of binoculars swinging dangerously from his neck.

"Er, madam, there are a couple of questions I need to ask you. Would you please accompany me?"

Fiona stared at the square-jawed man dressed in a camel raincoat with a matching Burberry attaché case at his feet. He had the sort of looks that could appear on the cover of a knitting pattern or a DIY manual. This must be the second candidate, or was it the third? Whoever it was, things were looking up.

He hadn't noticed her, however; his attention was entirely on the occupants of the 'bearded pig' enclosure. In the pen four energetic small animals were playing follow-my-leader around a muddied ground strewn with several torn purses and handbags. They seemed to be playing a game involving squealing, sniffing and mud-slinging. Ugh! She adjusted her blouse and stepped forward.

"Are you Francis?" His smile was warm, his teeth even. She liked that and took hold of his outstretched hand – which was smooth, the grip decisive. "I'm Fiona." She retrieved her hand with a sharp tug. "My friend will be coming soon."

The man dusted his hand on his trousers and looked up the path expectantly.

Fiona decided to conduct the interview herself. She sat down on a soggy bench, crossed her legs, and tried to look welcoming.

"We can start if you like."

"My ex-wife," sighed the man, "loves pigs."

"Does she?" This was a failing Angie might understand, but Fiona felt a tad put out. "I'm sure she'll get over them, now that you've gone." She uncrossed her legs. "You must have a few passions of your own."

He wasn't to be distracted. "We often came to the zoo, with the kids. And it was the pigs that we all... look at that."

She did. All the pigs were now in the ditch together. Their small tails were wagging; their snouts were mostly in each other's private parts, apart from the leader, who was now spitting out the confetti he had made of his lunch.

"Aren't they the most wonderful creatures?"

Fiona wondered what she was supposed to be admiring.

"Are they?"

"You've got to be a special sort of person to get them. That stumpy grey hair, those long dear heads, their small piggy eyes."

"Absolutely magnificent," she said, with more conviction than she felt.

She ironed out the list of candidate questions and hoped they could get on with the interview. "Now. You wrote that wildlife was your passion." She couldn't help wrinkling up her nose at the smell coming from the pigs. "Are there some other creatures we could view?"

"Other creatures? Did you know that these seemingly unintelligent creatures will migrate hundreds of miles to find a single randy female?" His voice was breaking with emotion.

Was this man Angie's choice? Fiona fished a mascara-stained tissue from her bag and tried handing that to the man. But he was waving at the snouts, as if directing traffic. The strange thing was they seemed to be responding to him.

Perhaps he needed a reminder. "Your divorce must have been messy."

She imagined Guy in the divorce court, the judge's final decision – I declare you divorced – and the two of them driving away in separate cars. Apart from a small worry about parking restrictions, that possibility didn't seem too distressing. She then thought of her father's likely response to the news; his invocation of the Psalms, Genesis, Job. That wouldn't be the end of the world. What she did fear was something else. The annulment of her trust fund. That was truly terrifying.

"It wasn't me that wanted it. I loved the way she cooked, bent down and filled the dishwasher. I loved lying in bed, hearing her shouting when she took the kids to school. I loved the way she couldn't park, or fill in forms properly, and I could take over and feel superior. I loved her in shorts, even though her legs were stubby. I loved her in trousers, even though her tummy stuck out. I loved her cold pink nose, her short hair. I loved her moods, especially her bad moods. I wanted to spend the rest of my life with her."

Was it a woman or a Scottie dog he'd been married to?

She had to get this man away from here. She took his arm. He didn't flinch, protest or even seem to notice. She guided him away from the things that squealed, marching him towards creatures that growled.

Angie was not enjoying herself. So this was what 'being brought in for questioning' meant.

There were three of them crammed into the zoo office. The large policeman stood. The smaller meaner officer leaned on the desk. They both towered over her. She sat on a low, green plastic chair, feeling somewhat at a disadvantage. The office walls were covered with animal feeding time-tables and employee sickness records. There was a framed photo, slightly blurred, of a smiling zookeeper perched up a tree, dangling a rope-tied cow's thighbone to a tiger on the ground below. The inscription read: We'll all miss you, Wally. Angie shuddered.

"Exactly what were you doing there?" the large officer asked her. Not unkindly.

How was she to answer that? "I was meeting someone."

"So why did he run away?"

"Er..."

"We've been watching him," added the smaller officer.

"He stole my purse."

"He did, did he?" The smaller officer wrote something in his notebook.

"Did you know him?"

"I've never seen him before in my life," said Angie quite honestly.

The large officer's eyes narrowed. "This person you've never seen before in your life? Was he the person you were meeting?"

"No."

"But you appeared to spend a certain amount of time with him."

"Five minutes and twenty two seconds to be exact," added the smaller officer.

"What?"

"We have our ways of knowing," he added, tapping the top

of his binoculars case with his pencil.

"And we saw you entice him," said the taller officer.

"I beg your pardon?" Angie was horrified.

"Yes, we both were witnesses to that."

Furious, she rose to her feet, knocking over the plastic chair with a clatter. "I'm not having this," she yelled. "You've got it all wrong. I didn't know that that man wasn't the man I was meeting."

The taller officer righted the chair. The smaller one indicated she should sit down. She stood upright defiantly.

"We all need to calm down," said the taller officer.

"Yes," said the smaller one.

"I am calm," she yelled, even louder.

"Didn't you know who you were meeting?'

"Er, no. Well, er, yes." They were both staring at her. The tall officer was frowning. The small one was smiling in a creepy sort of way.

"Could he have been this person?"

The smile on the small officer's face was looming closer.

Angie recoiled. "But what about my purse?"

"We'll get to that." The large officer tried taking a turn around the room, and banged into the filing cabinet.

The small officer closed down his smile. "So this gentleman," he said, "this man you'd never seen before that you were so familiar with…"

Had she been recorded on CCTV as well as surveyed through binoculars?

She slumped back onto the chair. "The whole thing was a case of mistaken identity."

"It was, was it?" Keeping his gaze on her, he made a note. "Would you recognise this gentleman if you saw him again?"

"He had a tattoo on his wrist."

The smaller policeman had his pencil poised. His eyes bulged.

"Of a snake or something wriggly."

"Was he a bit foreign?"

"Oh no, not at all."

Angie stared out of the grimy window at the figure of the real third candidate. He was sitting on a bench, throwing the contents of his sandwich packet at some pigeons.

"And what was the stated nature of your meeting?"

"It was a business meeting."

"What business?"

"Old people."

The large officer examined the tips of his fingers. "At the zoo?"

Droplets of sweat dripped down her back. Get a grip, she told herself. She stood. "Could I have an incident number since it was me who had my purse stolen? Please."

The large officer broke the silence with a sigh.

The small one snapped shut his notebook.

Chapter 9

"You'd have thought I was the criminal," said Angie.

She had left the tiny room and found herself in the world she'd been gazing at through the window. The man she should have been meeting at the gorilla enclosure was on the bench, his sandwich wrapper empty. He looked terribly young – just a few years older than Dusty. She felt like making him another sandwich.

"Did they caution you?" he asked.

It was sweet of him to care, and to wait. She felt they knew each other already.

"Sort of. What about you?"

"They're closing in on some guy they suspect is a pickpocket."

"You mean that man with all the tattoos?"

"Yes."

Angie pulled out a tissue and blew into it. A stray spotted, long-necked balloon passed over them, heading for the City. Wasn't it the one Fiona had been carrying?

"Are you going to be alright?" he asked.

His eyes were cautious; his jacket smelled of wet sheep and reminded her of family holidays in the Dales. He seemed lonely. Meeting him like this made her very uncomfortable. "I think so." She turned away and looked back at the office window.

The larger police officer was now waving at her from his steamed-up spot behind glass. He must have been watching her. Flustered, she turned back to the young man.

"Yes. I'm Angie, by the way." She tried to laugh. "You know, the..."

"I'm Jake."

"I know – a friend put me up to this."

Was it possible that he winked? The last time a man had winked at her she thought he was having a stroke.

"So what's it going to involve?"

She hesitated, for a moment lost for words.

The tiger cage appeared to be empty, apart from a desiccated bird and some bloody paw prints. Using the railings to lean her bag against, Fiona found her glasses, put them on her nose and checked the list of candidates. The next one was a student from somewhere called Greifswald. She hoped he wouldn't be too young; she didn't want to be called a cradle snatcher.

"Hello," said a voice behind her. She spun round.

"Are you Fiona?"

This young man was freckly, his ginger hair smoothed back from a wide, puckered brow.

"I could very well be," she said, looking him up and down.

"My name is Frederick…"

It was a funny accent, Russian, possibly. But he appeared keen, healthy, uncomplicated; he didn't seem attached to paddlefish, pigs or ex-wives, or about to break out into song.

"I am studying the English language and customs."

"You answered our advert?"

"Yes. My professor advises me to do fieldwork. I will be having sex with two English ladies."

"Excuse me?"

"He approves of this procedure."

"Your professor?"

"He is a stickler – that is the word, I think – for accurate data."

"Well…"

"At exactly what hour on Thursday will we be – 'in the sack' – don't you say?"

She tried not to notice the raised eyebrows on the teacher herding the green-blazered school party.

"Shhh," she said. "Just because you see an apple tree, doesn't mean you can go and pick an apple. Not right away, anyhow." That should impress the schoolteacher and the professor.

"No apples? What will we do then?"

She could see he needed coaching in English manners, never mind customs. She'd been taught them herself in cheerless dormitories and on holidays with the parents of her friends who didn't want her there – don't cry when you're heartbroken, or shout when someone's standing on your toes, or speak at all unless 'spoken to'. "We will begin by me giving you a class in English manners. That's what."

"What time will this begin?" he asked, taking a notebook computer out of his anorak pocket.

"Yes, well."

His fingers were poised over the keyboard.

"First, Frederick, my friend has to agree to all this."

He looked up with a frown. "The other woman?"

From Frederick Chizhevsky – fchiz@hotmail.com
To Herr Professor Schnitzel –Schnitzelprof@universitygreifswalt.fleishnet

Herr Professor, thank you for your inquiry. I can assure

you I am working on my English language practice and field research. I am gaining traction on a close study of an emerging trend. I will document my methods and findings thoroughly and look forward to your comments. Your student, Frederick Chizhevsky.

"There aren't any rules." Angie felt herself blushing.

The rain had stopped. Birds perched high along a wire fluttered their wings, scattering her with droplets.

"No rules?"

Actually, she was breaking rule number three right now: 'choice of candidate to be taken jointly'. Or was that rule number four? "Let's meet next Thursday. Two o' clock at…" She rummaged for the address Fiona had given her and couldn't find it. Of course, it was in her stolen purse. Well, never mind, she could remember it. She found a pen and wrote what she remembered on a page of her small notepad. She tore out the page and handed it to him.

He took it. "Wow! Does it cost anything?"

"The flat? Oh, no – as far as I know, it's free."

"Cool." Jake beamed. "I'll be there." He gave her another wink, or did he have a twitch?

He pocketed the wrapper, got up, and strode away with his head high, clearly more confident than he'd seemed at first. His mass of hair bobbed over the heads of some school kids, like Fiona's balloon, and disappeared.

A bit dazed, she drifted towards the pig enclosure. After a few forays into some leafy cul-de-sacs, she found herself in the butterfly tent where it was awfully hot and steamy, butterflies quivering on every leaf. Careful not to crush any fragile wings, she tiptoed to the exit, nearly tripping over the two police officers outside. They appeared to be back on surveillance duty with binoculars. Luckily, they didn't notice her. She hurried on, still a little aimlessly, thinking all the while of Jake's mane of hair, his shy smile. She worried what he had made of her choice of make-up, outfit and new perfume. She also wondered if Fiona had missed her yet, or even noticed her absence. On locating a notice board map of the zoo, Angie stopped, blinking at it until her heart slowed a little. One mode of anxiety gave way to another. Where was she? She felt as if she was in two parallel worlds at the same time – the one before the barge timeshare evening, and the new one since.

Talking of barge evenings, how was she going to voice this Jake development to Fiona? Never mind, if Fiona didn't agree, she could keep Jake to herself.

Anyway, rules contradicted themselves. How could 'keep everyone happy' work? Feelings were lining up against each other somewhere in Angie's stomach.

She'd leave explaining all this to Ted for a few days yet.

Okay, she would give Fiona the option. It was only fair. With that firmly planted in her mind like a flagstaff on a new administration, she marched off in the direction of the big cats. Fiona was perched on some railings in front of the tiger's cage. When Angie got closer she couldn't decide whether Fiona or the tiger behind her was looking more interested in a young man in a duffel coat.

"Meet Frederick, our front-runner," said Fiona.

Angie tried to give Fiona a kiss in greeting.

Fiona accepted it while keeping her smile trained on the young man. "He's a bit young, but he's clever, attentive, pliable, and foreign," she hissed. "And so far, he hasn't shown any signs of abnormality. And, anyway, where have you been all this time?"

Chapter 10

"Yo. How's Casanova then?"

Jake didn't want to talk to Max. Not now that he'd met Angie. It would be like discussing the sweetness of cherries with the person who planted the tree; it seemed both clinical and irrelevant.

Max put down one of the coffees, removed the plastic lid, and made a meal of blowing at the froth.

Jake prised the cup away from him, gulped at the scalding liquid. It was too sweet.

"She got good tits? Arse? – The facts, boyo."

Jake pointedly turned towards the barristers who were bustling past, their calm heads carried along on scurrying feet, white papers fluttering as if attempting flight. Would he and Max end up like these creatures? Would it happen in small increments, like old buildings flaking paint until the British Empire brick showed through, or would professional excellence surprise them in their Shreddies one morning when they would wake up to find themselves fully-fledged, competent barristers, starchy, yet finely tuned to the nuances of argument? He was so busy trying to imagine this that when a man stumbled over Max's outstretched foot, and fell heavily to the floor, he didn't see it coming. Had Max done this on purpose? It was the sort of random thing he would do when crossed.

With a glare at Max, Jake helped the man to his feet and reassembled his files. The victim had receding hair, a full dark round brow, and a direct gaze.

"Edward Gold, MD, expert witness," he said. "I'm looking for Court Five."

This was the expert witness on their case.

"Pleased to meet you,' said Jake. "We're here to help you."

"Excellent," said Edward Gold and smiled.

As a teenager, Jake had been fostered by a vet with a smile like this. The honeymoon lasted until Jake shaved the Persian cat so as to cure it of fleas, and he was back at the barred small window of his Barnados bedroom. "Court Five is just over there."

"Endicott versus Endicott," said Max, loudly, behaving as if he knew the bloke.

Max was always assuming friendships with people he'd never met before. It was horribly embarrassing.

"We're with Carruthers," announced Max. "On something we call the spunk- ownership trial."

Jake wished he could put a disclaimer on his colleague, or have the authority to send him down to *Filing*. "In a very minor capacity," he said. "I'm Bollard. Jake."

Max held his hand out. "Max Creighton."

"See you soon." The doctor disappeared into Court Five.

"What's she like?"

"Dunno."

Max blocked Jake's passage. "You did make contact, didn't you?"

Jake tossed his cup into a bin. "Next time, no sugar, remember."

"Come on, tell me."

"Tell you what?"

"Did you shag her for me?"

Idiot! "Why don't you give her a call?" Jake said.

"What?"

"Go on, give it a go, Max…" Max was trembling and had gone pale. "No, you won't, will you… 'cos she's a bloody tigress. Eat you up and spit you out."

Max was backing away.

Okay, if the blighter was going to stay in his open cage and wait for goodies to be passed through the bars, Jake would titillate him. "She may ring me, she may not."

Max pecked his head up and down like a woodpecker, united with a choice tree. "Either way is okay with me."

Max seemed to collapse inwardly, a man condemned to solitude.

Jake would have to put off helping him get over his terrors until some other time. He stepped into Court Five. There he was met by that confusion of paperwork, arcane language and bad temper that surrounded Carruthers QC. Jake slid into his place behind his master and the newly arrived expert witness.

"Where the God-damned hell is the Court Order?" growled the wigged bulk of his master, releasing a storm of papers as he searched.

"Here, sir," said Jake, producing it. "Hello again, Dr Gold."

The doctor turned to smile at him. "Call me Ted."

Chapter 11

It was a beautiful day. The sun shone brightly through the open doorway, picking out the gilt in Fiona's mirrors and revealing the dust on her winter hat collection.

She stared at her mobile. No missed calls. No one had called her since Guy accused her of hiding his terrine recipe books. What would she be doing with them? He always blamed her if he lost anything. It could be anything – his wallet, his direction, his appetite. Daddy was the same. No, she would resist calling Angie to see how it was going. Instead, she would clear the shop-front of all the greys, browns, blacks, wools and tweeds and replace them with the chiffons, feathers, fruit in the brilliant colours of the season, leading to Ladies Day at Ascot. Fiona tossed her phone aside, and started sorting.

Angie felt cold in the shade of the apartment block looming high above her. Perhaps her only linen dress suit wasn't the right choice for the weather. She buttoned up the top of her jacket, untangled her necklace, tucked the marmalade biscuits and bottle of Ted's best red wine into her shoulder bag and walked up the brass-trimmed swing doors of the apartment block. She pushed them. They didn't budge. They remained immobile, however much she elbowed them. She looked around for some advice.

The street was deserted apart from a man on the other side of the road taking photos. He looked familiar. But she couldn't place him. Probably an estate agent.

She smoothed out the scrap of paper Fiona had given her, to check the code – 1397. She tapped in the numbers very carefully.

The entrance remained gleaming-clean, but shut.

She scanned the date-palm-fronded foyer for signs of life; silent black-and-white tiles ended at a ruby-carpeted staircase. Chandeliers lit affluence with a haughty contempt. The twenties clock pointed its gloved hands at one forty-five. Fifteen minutes before Frederick was due. She was sure he'd be punctual. In fact she was depending on it, so as to head him off at the pass before Jake arrived. If he did arrive. She couldn't remember hoping more intensely for something since wishing she was pregnant. She banged on the glass, shouted and waved at the same time, rousing a cat from a laurel bush, a flock of pigeons from a balcony.

Something in the enclosed landscape moved. She spotted a capped head at a desk in the far distance, facing away from her. The cap rose, turned, revealing its occupant, a man with a haughty long face. He regarded her for a moment, then spoke through the intercom in a voice crackling with disdain:

"Good afternoon, madam. And a lovely afternoon it is. If you mean to gain access, you would need to impress your finger on the digit sign above the numbers."

She looked above the intercom. An arrow pointed to a small-framed box bearing the picture of a fingerprint. She pressed her index finger onto the image, and the doors flew open soundlessly. She was in.

"Has something taken my fingerprint?" She thought she

should be told.

"Yes, madam."

She must have looked a little rebellious, because he added:

"This building houses several important personages," – his stress of the 'purr' made it clear he wasn't including her – "so, in case of anything untoward, we need all visitors' fingerprints for our records."

This was no time to argue. She looked round for the lift. The voice followed her:

"First left after the reading room. You'll be wanting the seventh floor, flat number 73."

Fiona's friend must have told him to expect her. "Thank you very very much." She drew a deep breath. "The thing is, I'm expecting two gentlemen to call."

"Indeed, madam."

"A foreign student and a gentleman from the legal profession."

The porter's left eyebrow was rising.

"Could you please tell the student I'm ill, and let the lawyer up to see me."

"Do these gentlemen have names, or attributes, or do I have merely their accents to go on?" he asked, with only the slightest frosting of irony.

The Cock and Bull was crammed with even more City barristers downing Cote Du Rhone than Jake could remember applying for pupillage to. On the one hand, he was flattered that the expert witness was buying him a drink; on the other, he had a date with Angie of the zoo.

"Red or white?" asked the doctor, making his way to the bar.

"A half pint of bitter, please."

The doctor was now at the counter, where Max perched,

making a meal of indicating the overhead clock to Jake. Jake made a furious gesture that he could see what the time was. Was Max going to go on like this for the rest of his life?

The doctor returned with the beers, flushed from the crush. "…Seminal emissions?" He was continuing the conversation from before. "…Body corporates? Contractual corporeal exchanges? I have to say, I didn't realise there were so many obscure descriptions of the sexual act, and I'm a specialist in the field. All I want is a simple answer to the question – does my patient have a chance of winning this case?" He loomed very close to Jake, his eyebrows locked in inquiry. "Does her husband's sperm belong to its progenitor or – or to the person who possesses it: her?" He settled down next to Jake, toasted the air, gulped the bitter, and made it clear he expected Jake to know the answer.

Jake felt gauche, shabby, and found himself trying to conceal two holes on his own jacket where his shirt was herniating through, its colour an unhealthy grey. He tried to remember what he'd read late the night before, while working at his Wednesday evening off licence job. Quick! He'd have to come up with something.

After knocking off from the off licence, he'd gone through the 2002 case in Guyana of the Amerindians versus a US drug company. The drug company had patented the DNA in the Amerindian sperm, to use some of the genes for developing new fertility treatment. But, according to the Amerindians, their sperm was theirs; they'd created it. They won.

"Well sir, the ownership of sperm…"

"Yes?" The doctor sat straight-backed, away from the wall, gracefully toying with his drink, at ease with the world. "Meaning?"

"The husband made it and so, technically, he owns it."

"How did she get it?… Apart from in the normal course of… Hasn't he indeed *given* it to her, and she to me, her consultant, for use in her IVF programme? Isn't it therefore, her, our, property?" The doctor appeared to be settling in for a long argument.

Jake glanced at the clock again. "I can't stay, I'm afraid."

"Oh?"

"It's possible we could sue him – the husband, that is – for breach of promise. It's just possible. I'm no expert."

Around them, guffaws were replacing conversations. The noise level was growing. Max was bearing down on them. Jake stood up, flustered – he hoped the doctor didn't think he was working for the other side.

"It all comes under the general category of intellectual property copyright law," he said, grabbing his coat. "I… I've got to urgently get Carruthers some data from the Law Society Library on this very subject."

The doctor didn't look convinced.

Jake tried to remember what lie he'd served Carruthers. He just hoped the two wouldn't cross-reference. All this talk about semen when he was heading off for an afternoon with Angie from the zoo. Guilt gripped him. "Look, don't tell the old boy I said this, but you should, maybe, try dissuading your client from going through with this case. If hubby wants his sperm back, can't you get her someone else's? There are banks for that sort of thing, aren't there? Or more could be obtained – from men at large in field conditions, so to speak."

The doctor looked round, baffled. "You surely can't mean Hampstead Heath?"

Jake had to get out of there. "Thanks for the drink." He seized his battered briefcase.

"My client feels she's invested a lot of herself in the relationship, Jake. She's not going to let go of this last part of him without a fight." The doctor put a hand on his arm. "You're not married, I take it?"

"No, no, not at all." Feeling intensely uncomfortable, Jake made for the door. He gave the doctor a nervous glance before leaving and saw Max settling down opposite him with his customary draft Guinness. *He* would answer the doctor's questions. What he didn't know, he would make up. Good luck to him – he was heading for high office.

Jake ran along the Strand, past the Savoy and Charing Cross looking for a cab. Why was he so keen to do this mad thing? He'd had lie to his boss, which was like short-changing God. And he'd made an inexpert excuse to the expert counsel, a dodgy strategy. What if they found out where he was really going? It wasn't as if he owed Max anything. And it wasn't as if there weren't women all around him, just for the taking. There was no logic to it; he felt compelled. What was it, then? Perhaps it was simply that she was an older woman from another sphere who'd make no demands on him – someone with a gentle face and a soft body. Since when had a woman seemed so tremulous in his company? Well, go for it, boyo. He was jumping into a cab, which he couldn't pay for; and worst of all for a lawyer, he couldn't keep his own counsel.

The cab juddered a few steps, then stopped, its progress strangled by traffic. Cycles moved faster than they did. Joggers motored past. Couples sauntered by his window, arm in arm, luminous pale parts of their bodies exposed. The taxi driver did a U turn and drove down a small side street, honking madly. There the cab had to slow to a crawl behind a rubbish van. Jake sighed, allowing the sunlight to warm him, determined not to see the fare building. Instead, he gazed at the nearest shop-front. It was called 'Crowning Glories' and was filled to the rafters with heads bearing amazing hats of every shape and colour. He started when one of the heads under a hat moved. It was a woman. A pale, dark-haired woman. She was peering intently at her own reflection in a mirror as if she had never met herself before. Then she replaced that hat with another.

The rubbish van moved, the taxi lurched forward, leaving the image of the woman behind.

Chapter 12

Angie took a quick look at herself in the hall-mirror. The suit was better without the jacket. Was the necklace too much? She removed it, then fastened it on again before applying a fresh coat of her new 'Relentlessly Ruby' lipstick. The doorbell rang. She jumped, dropped 'Relentlessly Ruby', hunted for it, couldn't reach it, then stood up, peered through the door peephole.

It was him. Her heart raced. What was he searching for in his pockets? He pulled out a tenner.

Oh, God, perhaps he thought he was going to have to pay her. She flung open the door.

"Hi, come in," she said.

He didn't move. "Sorry, but I don't have enough…"

"You don't need to pay for anything…"

"But he's waiting."

"Who?"

"Downstairs."

"But why?" He shifted his weight from one leg to the other as if he was itching to get away.

She shouldn't have worn the necklace. It was definitely overdoing things.

"His meter is running."

"Oh." He must be waiting to see if things would work out,

before letting his taxi go. "Of course." What should she do now? Invite him straight to the bedroom? Fiona expected her to play hard to get on the first date. Panicky that she was losing his interest, she grabbed his hand, the one holding the tenner and stroked it. No, he didn't like that. He brushed her away and began waving towards the lift. Was he suggesting they rip their clothes off right there while letting the meter run on?

Then something dawned on her.

"You don't have enough cash for the taxi?"

"Yes, God dammit," he said.

"I didn't… so sorry," she said. She raced into the flat, found her purse, came back, grabbed his hand and closed it over a twenty-pound note.

He hesitated.

"No, no, take it, please."

"Thanks." He raced to the lift. "I'll be right back."

"Of course, that's only if you want to." She felt ridiculous.

The doors were closing. "Yes."

The lift descended. She thought she heard a door click shut down the hall, footfalls making a muffled exit. A radio programme began somewhere, but she couldn't work out what was said. Was it in Japanese? A lone goose flew past the window, honking. She leaned back against the hall wall, the door to Ray's flat still wide open, her heart pounding. Was he really going to come back? Of course not. It was clear he was merely humouring her. By now he had jumped back into his waiting cab and was riding away as quickly as the speed limit would allow.

What was she going to tell Fiona? Nothing, she decided. This was hardly an auspicious start to her stupid idea.

What if he did come back, though? She grew breathless, hot. How did 'this sort' of thing kick off?

She imagined herself doing a strip-tease act while he ate

he marmalade biscuits she'd baked, leaving crumbs on the pristine sofa. Or, perhaps, she should ask him to get ready for her while she boiled the kettle. She took a deep breath, fanned herself and undid her top button.

Fiona was standing in the street outside her shop, admiring her window. She'd pinned crêpe fruit and flowers to the tops of the starched linen and straw hats and had arranged pink and lemon-tinged chiffon to ripple away from the crowns in waves. Somehow the effect was missing something. It looked too worthy, when it was supposed to be frivolous. She needed something to jazz it up. She went back inside, found some wire and a box of plastic insects and started pinning them on at strategic points. A butterfly here, a beetle there. She was just pinning a green striped caterpillar to the crown of a red bowler hat when the bell sounded its tune from *Madame Butterfly.*

"Aren't you supposed to be at my flat?" a familiar voice said.

Startled, Fiona rose, scattering dragonflies in every direction and bumping her head.

He was lounging against her doorpost.

"Ray!"

He smiled, sloped in, pulled the door shut behind him, and turned the sign around to 'Closed'. Then he perched himself on her only comfortable chair, and pulled fluff from one of the winter trilbies, the lemon yellow one.

"Just passing," he said, trying it on. "Does it suit me?"

It was absurdly small for his head. But somehow he could carry it off. He could carry anything off.

"No," she said firmly. "It doesn't."

He picked up another, a few sizes bigger, in shocking pink and put that on.

"Business is very tough right now. Apart from the double-dip R word, people are frightened to travel. When you don't get jihadis, you get earthquakes, or tidal waves or spring uprisings. People need to feel secure. So we need something to help engender that very feeling. Something greater than money." He pulled the pink hat over his hair, smiled at her, sad as a clown.

She brought him a mirror.

He gazed. "I need the name Gregoyan on my letterhead."

"What?"

"It's a good name."

Daddy drifted past her consciousness, in an executive hot-air balloon. He wore a tuxedo, and an air of contempt. "No, no, certainly not."

"It suggests a long, reliable tradition."

"What's the matter with Brebington?"

"No, it has to be Gregoyan."

"Daddy would never allow it."

"You could persuade him to fly to Pluto and back. You're his princess. Being on the board will cost him nothing."

"Daddy on the board? Board? What are you talking about?"

"It would ensure you get your money back."

"It would what? I…?" Speechless, Fiona imagined Daddy's expression when she tried begging this favour – the loan of his lofty Armenian name. A name which had spawned a thousand generations of silk traders and diplomats, a name kings and caliphs had favoured. She tried seeing herself requesting that those eight letters be permitted to glorify the notepaper of Ray Brebington, timeshare salesman from Plaistow.

Ray grinned at her. The cheek of the man. What made him imagine this was possible? Compared to her father, he was a spiv. Not only had she survived forty-five years of Pater

Elijah, she had his blood coursing round her right now, making her furious.

"When I say no, I mean it!"

The door rattled. The woman on the doorstep was dowdy, dressed in ill-fitting charity-shop clothes, didn't look as if she could afford anything in Crowning Glories; but she was hatless. Fiona turned her back on Ray and went over to let her in.

It seemed like an aeon for Angie as she waited. Would or wouldn't he return? Her heart skipped a beat as she heard the distant whirring of the elevator beginning to ascend. The lights noted the floors of the building, as the lift climbed. One, two, three… It stopped at the fourth floor. Was someone else getting into the lift? Next week it would be Fiona's turn. That was if they stuck to rule four – candidate to be shared equally.

Bert, from school days, flashed into Angie's mind, with his crew cut and brogues. He preferred hunting and fishing to girls, he told her. Fiona was fine with that; she preferred the shops to anything he had to offer. But Angie fancied Bert. Stupid really, but she did. And she managed to wangle her way into a clay pigeon shoot she knew he'd attend. So cruel, that sport. The guests were insufferably posh, the gunshots gave her tinnitus, the tea burned her throat, and aiming high gave her backache for a week. But Bert had shared his flask of cocoa with her. Then Fiona arrived on the scene. Thinking clay shooting was bird watching, she'd bought a pair of binoculars and some wellies. And at the next clay-shooting competition there she was, situated in a bush, notebook on her knee, binocular lenses glinting. Instead of being affronted, Bert was flattered. Within days, Angie was no longer invited and Fiona was. Hmmm.

Chapter 13

Angie could hear the kettle switch off in the kitchen.

"Cup of tea?"

They were stuck on IVF and child adoption. He seemed to be an expert on them. Time was ticking away.

"Or wine?" She pulled Ted's bottle free out of her bag, unwrapped it and placed it on the table between them, along with the corkscrew she'd brought, just in case. "Why don't you open it?"

"This is nice."

He wasn't an expert with the corkscrew. He grunted and pulled and managed to break the cork. She took over, stabbed at the cork, losing it inside the bottle.

"I'll find glasses." She brushed past his knees to the kitchen. It took several cupboards to find some elegant long stemmed flutes in neat rows. She took two back to the other room and placed them carefully on the table. There was awkward silence.

"Shall I?" He pointed at the empty glasses.

"Oh, yes, please do."

He poured. They both sipped. The wine tasted of old raspberries.

"Well," she said, "this beats family holidays." Oh no, why had she brought up her family? "Of course, when I was eight or nine."

"I didn't have any family holidays."

"Oh." There was another silence. "Well, never mind. You didn't miss much. There was always a cold wind blowing sand into our sandwiches. And if it wasn't windy it was misty or rainy and miserable. What did you do with your family?"

"I didn't have one."

"What, no family?"

"No. I'd rather not remember my childhood."

"Oh. Oh, dear."

"My mother abandoned me."

He said this as if ticking a box. She was horrified.

"She...? How could she?"

"S'pose she had much better things to do with her life."

"God, has it made you bitter?"

"Yes."

His eyes were positively luminous, if a little troubled. She found herself staring at her own reflection in them. There she was in her linen dress, smiling stupidly. "You shouldn't be bitter, you know. It could give you an ulcer."

"At least bitterness is reliable. Hope always lets you down."

She noticed him stroking the smoked-glass panther-shaped armrest.

"I'd like..." There was a long pause which she didn't interrupt. "...One day, to become an absent-minded, benign judge."

"Ah, yes, good idea."

The lights seemed to dim all by themselves. Jazz piped up on the sound system. Strange, because she didn't remember turning anything on. Perhaps it was on a time switch on that sideboard. Or something attached to the kettle going off. It was trad jazz, the sort you hear in old-fashioned brasseries before the last orders.

She stole a look at her watch.

Miraculously, although she seemed to have broken rules one to five with the possible exception of rule number three, she was keeping rule number six, playing hard to get. Not for want of trying. He was staring amiably at the wall in front of him. The door to the bedroom was wide open. How could she direct him from the wall to the bedroom?

Something new punctuated the trad jazz. It sounded very like fingers drumming on a metal table, as if the very room was sharing her impatience. Then the lights on the walls began to emit coloured waves. Is this what the flat did? All by itself? She peered around the room for a clue as to how it could be happening.

There were tiny white metal punctuation marks all over the smoothly plastered walls.

Speakers? But where was the switch? She tapped the metal button closest to her. Nothing changed. Then she tried turning it. Something responded. The jazz segued into a piano sonata.

Jake shook himself free of his reverie and poured more wine into her glass, then into his own. "That's Schubert's Piano Sonata in C Minor."

"Gosh, is it?"

"I played the piano at secondary school."

The close-ups of wet sweet peas that were occupying the walls distracted her. From somewhere a spray was ejected, misting the air with something flowery. It was all very unsettling. She tried turning the button in the opposite direction. The Schubert swelled rather than died. Jake had moved closer and was gazing at her evenly while nodding his head. This also unnerved her. Perhaps he was wondering what they were both doing in a strange flat with a random occurrence of sweet peas, Schubert. She felt she had to say something personal too. "It's not that I feel insecure or ignored – well, not completely." She had to raise her voice above the music.

"It's not that we fight, or argue, or even mildly disagree about anything. He…" Oh, no, now there was no way round the 'H' word "…my husband – is not awful or even bad-tempered. He doesn't beat me or anything. This is my own… secret garden."

Jake was staring at the bottom of his glass with an intensity she didn't think the dregs deserved.

To hell with rules *and* vows. She moved closer and pointed at the inner sanctum.

He nodded.

She tapped her watch.

He glanced at his.

She began to unbutton her blouse, exposing her bra. It was the one she'd bought on a family holiday at Lake Garda. Her hands were shaking. God, this was hopeless. Wasn't he going to do anything to help?

After what felt like a whole Samuel Beckett play, he undid his tie.

Relieved, she kicked off her shoes.

He bent to undo his shoelaces. One snapped.

She launched herself onto his second shoe in what she hoped was a seductive way, tugging at its lace. The sonata crescendoed; the sweet peas gave way to something tougher – it looked like heather, she thought.

He abandoned his feet to her, and returned to his tie.

She liberated his nearest foot from its shoe and sock, began to tackle the other one. She tossed the broken lace across the room. It must have hit one of the sensor buttons, because the sonata died, and something else took its place. Men on horseback abruptly replaced the country garden. She didn't care. She had access to the soft long hair of this young man's legs. She uncovered his boxer shorts. They bore asymmetrical rows of frogs. She teased them with her fingers and sighed when a line of frogs rose to meet her hand. She thought she recognised the theme tune from *Ben Hur*. This was going to work! She wrenched herself free of her shirt, skirt and tights. He was pulling open a packet of condoms. She guided him to the bedroom, shirt tail flapping after him. The frogs soon adorned the light fitting; the shirt sagged along the skirting board, the background music intensified; a Biblical war scene played out in stripes on his hairless chest as he mounted her. For a moment she worried about finding the controls and changing the setting, but then her own long-lost settings took over. The chariots raced and she felt her own wheels going round of their own accord. She moved in ways that equalled the cinematography, and emitted shouts that drowned out all of *Ben Hur's* battle cries. Jake bucked and lunged like a thoroughbred.

Finally the sound stopped.

The chariot race was over. The room settled down to a low hum. Her last sighting of Jake before she closed her eyes, and gave herself up to nature, was of his amazed face. They lay beside each other, letting the sweat cool. Somewhere beyond a party wall she heard a voice say: "And here at four o'clock precisely, is the BBC news."

Jake opened one luminous eye. "Four o'clock? Shit!" He deposited a kiss on her lips. "Sorry, sorry, but I'm supposed to be at a court hearing."

She suspected this might not be true, but enjoyed every moment of watching him find his clothes. He returned to her, and smoothed her hair back. She liked that.

"Is tomorrow good for you?" he asked.

Her whole body blushed with pleasure.

"No, it would have to be next Thursday?"

"In the afternoon?"

"Yes."

"Here?"

"Of course."

He was gone, before her sleepy haze cleared and she remembered it wouldn't be her he would be seeing, if she played fair. She could imagine Fiona writing a new rule – play fair at all times; but would it work? She listened to the news bulletin – three armed pensioners had robbed the Halifax in Kilburn. Worrying about their future, she rose from the beautiful white linen, trailed over to the en-suite bathroom, stared at herself in several versions around the walls. Mascara was smeared over most of her face. She wondered how much was still blackening Jake's. In one mirror, her body undulated in waves of pink. In another image her backbone gathered muscles into a loose spiral. Apart from an appendix scar, she was a symphony of curves, Jake the conductor. They had become loved curves. She dripped bubble bath under the hot tap, letting the suds build as she tried to remember if she'd ever had memorable moments like this with Ted. Her mobile phone rang. The digits began with 0795… it must be Fiona. Angie was no good at deception. She pressed 'answer', and blurted:

"Look, candidate number six was late whereas candidate number three turned up on time. So I thought we should start with him. And he's glorious, gorgeous, extremely good in bed, and out of it. And I've broken rule numbers one to six. We've just had the best sex I can remember, ever. I know this suggests there's something a bit lacking in Ted. Perhaps there is."

There was silence at the other end.

Angie took a deep breath. "And the thing is, Fiona, candidate number three doesn't know yet, that it's you he'll be seeing next week." Her conscience was now clear.

"Well, well, well," said the voice. It was male, and low. "I hope you're going to get him to make a little room for me."

Her heart iced over.

"Cos I thought we had something special."

She'd made a terrible mistake.

"The zoo, darlin', remember?"

She couldn't reply. The soapsuds began to overflow. One took off and headed for the hall.

"*I* can be with you, same time next week."

There was no mistaking the scratchy, insinuating quality of his voice. In fright, she dropped the phone. It clicked off and rang a second time. She grabbed it, shouted into it:

"Leave me alone. Can you hear me?"

She shook. The reply was unexpected.

"Angie! Hello, is that you?" It was Fiona.

"Yes."

"I've got that nice student on the other line. Candidate number something or other at the tiger's. The one we agreed on. Anyway, his name is Frederick. He's very upset the porter didn't let him in. Told him there was something objectionable about his accent. Not a good way to treat our foreign students, don't you agree?"

There was a crackle. Angie felt the room sway.

"Well, don't you?"

Chapter 14

Fiona kept the phone to her ear as she watched Ray amble down the street, away from Crowning Glories, past the bagel-eaters, the loud-mouthed fruit-seller, gracefully dipping down under a ladder, where his back caught golden stripes of afternoon light for a moment.

"What?" The mobile reception was terrible; the line buzzed in her ear. "Speak up, Angie."

She watched Ray dodge a taxi and a cyclist and climb into his Saab convertible, parked in the Disabled bay. Bloody cheek.

Angie wasn't being at all coherent.

"Candidate number what? Rule number which? What are you on about?" Fiona couldn't remember Angie being this hysterical at school.

"I need to wear some fruit on my head," said a loud piercing voice from the rear of the shop.

"Hold on a moment..." Fiona said into the phone and walked over to her customer, who was now hopping up and down with excitement, a 'Strawberries and Cream' hat on her head, the giant red berries bobbing. "How do I look?"

"Er..." Angie was still bleating on the phone.

"Get a grip!" Fiona yelled down the line.

The woman flinched, but held out her debit card.

"Sorry, madam." Into the phone she whispered: "You've been absolutely hopeless with our first candidate. We need to talk about it…" She ignored the squawk, balanced the phone on the counter, and smiled sweetly at her customer. "You, madam, will be the belle of all belles, the queen of all queens. You look ravishing."

The woman looked unconvinced.

"Because 'Strawberries and Cream' is one of my very finest creations. It will outshine any hat in any room, hall or mountaintop. It is a live art performance, a walking seduction." Before the woman could change her mind, Fiona grabbed the debit card, peered at the name on it and plinked £275.00 into the card machine. "Pin number, please Mrs Endicott. Would you like one of my state-of-the-art boxes?"

"No." Mrs Endicott clutched onto her new hat, took back her card and a receipt. "I shall continue to wear it, thank you."

There was a melodic tinkle as the door opened, then quiet after it closed.

Fiona watched, satisfied, as her splendid hat entered the real world and hesitated on the street corner while the woman put out her arm to hail a cab. A taxi slowed, stopped. 'Strawberries and Cream' climbed in, and bobbed gently in the window, as the taxi accelerated away. She picked up the phone. "Now look, Angie…" The line was dead. "Silly cow." Fiona pressed 'Frederick' on the phone. It pipped once.

"Frederick, ya."

"I'm so sorry about today," she said. "I don't know what happened. But my friend is an awful panicker, and must have, well, you know… panicked."

"Panic? Why?"

"I don't have the faintest idea…"

"Fainting?"

"No, not fainting, Frederick. Faintest." It wasn't easy to

give the poor young man English lessons on the phone. "Look, why don't we – you and I – meet for a drink? You know – a gin and tonic? Or even a glass of lager? Say at 6.30?" She racked her brains for a location and one of her old haunts came to mind. "At the Blue Monarch in Rotherhithe."

"Does it have a room there?" he asked.

"No, it's a pub. An English pub."

"Oh."

He sounded disappointed.

She must be firm with this young man. He wasn't going to require some serious disciplining, was he? "Now, Frederick, you really must learn not to ask for what you want like that. You, we, I mean, must, er... skirt round it."

"Skirt?"

"Oh never mind."

She hung up. After what sounded like Angie's mumbled and miserable failure, she would have to make a supreme effort to satisfy Frederick's expectations.

She reached out, touched the nearest of her creations. A simple green felt hat with tiny silver stars embroidered around its brim. She held it to her cheek, enjoying its softness, then slipped it onto her head, smoothing her hair into its edges. She approved of what she saw in the mirror. Then she sprayed herself royally with *Amor*.

Jake tumbled into the court just as the first judge was summing up the preliminaries:

"…As to section 78, the issue is whether there was anything in the way the Applicant had conducted himself with regards to his issue, to his wife, now estranged, that in any manner suggested a renunciation of his rightful ownership in favour of…"

Jake slithered in next to Max, and kept his gaze on Carruthers' thick neck, praying he wouldn't turn round. Max smirked. Jake smarted under this knowingness, then realised that others were looking at him strangely. Even the expert witness, Dr Gold was frowning. Was he that late?

"Mascara," hissed Max, pointing.

Jake brushed his cheek with his sleeve. It was streaked black. He scrubbed his whole face, blushing. Max snorted. Carruthers turned, glared at both of them, reminding Jake of a bull about to charge. He was hugely relieved when the door opened at the back of the courtroom, with a clatter.

The judge stopped speaking. Everyone, including Carruthers, turned to stare. Jake also turned to see a small woman shaded almost entirely by an enormous hat. It was a hideous affair, a mass of blotchy chiffon and red baubles, all wobbling so violently that it looked as if it was about to speak or give birth or do something equally unpredictable. The hat-wearer was clearly the defendant, Ina Endicott. There was a collective gasp, then a stuttering round of applause.

The judge sighed heavily, gesturing for the court to be silent and the woman to take a seat. She did so. Everyone turned back to face the bench. The judge scowled around the courtroom, cleared his throat and continued.

"The Defendant's breach-of-promise counter-claim does…"

Jake put his head down, and wrote 'alleged breaches'.

"…Have some bearing on the aforementioned omissions…"

Jake heard Dr Gold tut. "Emissions?" Desperately trying to focus, Jake wrote down the word and stared at it. How was he going to survive until next Thursday?

Bursting with secrets, Angie skipped past the dozing porter, and out beyond the iron peacocks into the street alongside the zoo. The sky was indigo. Venus winked at her, as did a window-ledge, on which a row of pigeons were settling down for the night. She tried to shake off her memory of the man with the tattoos. He must have found her mobile number on that piece of paper she always kept in her purse in case she forgot it. Why on earth had she had allowed a man like that so close? She remembered his breath with repulsion, and his reptile-like speed. She must have been desperate. But that was before. And this was after. Something like a sea wind rose within her, and she couldn't help herself – she broke into a trot past an enclosure where long spotted necks towered above her. She looked up to see the gentle eyes of two pairs of giraffes. They must all be mating. Chuckling at the coincidence of this, she breathed in the sweet spring air, wondering at the chaos of apple blossom, and why traffic stopped in polite lines to let her cross.

She stopped at a small shop to buy three red mullet for supper, asparagus, and the first raspberries of the season. She would go back to observing rule number two –*keep everyone happy*. Ted would enjoy a nice supper. She was surprised to find the thought of him filled her with interest. Would he notice she had changed? She doubted it; and, even if he did, what would he put it down to?

Before reaching the cashier, she went back to pick up two chocolate pots for Alex and Dusty and, before handing over her credit card, added a few packets of condoms. Then realising she didn't have anywhere to hide them safely, she put all but one packet back on the shelf.

She worried about the man on the till noticing, but he was absorbed in watching the television on a high shelf. Football. She found herself nervously playing with her wedding ring, noticed how the engagement diamond sparkled.

She was wondering whether to hide them or take them off when, without warning, Arsenal scored a goal, and the shop-keeper cheered, waving a fist at the ceiling. Other members of his family, hidden until now behind boxes and a partition door joined him, shouting in unison. Quietly, she placed the condoms alongside all the other items, paid for them and left the shop.

She walked out into the heady evening, shopping bag banging against her thigh, lightheaded, dizzy, guilt beginning to take hold of her tummy. What on earth would her family think if they knew?

She would have to make it up to them somehow.

The kids could have some unhealthy snacks before supper. That would make them happy. Then she'd let them do their own thing and not fuss about it. If Ted came home early enough she'd make him a long martini cocktail in a special glass. She thought of his broad, handsome brow, the way he raised one eyebrow when he found her illogical. She'd have to make sure she didn't do anything too illogical, or logical for that matter; he might notice she was different.

While he was sipping his drink, she would ask him about work, and prepare the lemon and hot butter sauce for his asparagus spears, careful not to let them overcook. She never usually remembered anything he said when she was tired, or cooking. But tonight she would make a supreme effort to pay attention when he spoke so that she could repeat parts back to him when the kids were asleep.

And what about later?

Perhaps she could be naked in their bed for the first time this spring? That would please him. Assuming he wasn't asleep already.

But would it strike him as unusual and put him on alert?

She thought of his long brown back, the soft hair on his forearms, his rib cage curving like the eaves of a cathedral. He could do with a bit of pleasure too, poor man. Perhaps she could surprise him as much as she had just surprised herself. Now, there was a thought.

Chapter 15

A glow crowned the top shelf full of hats. It was warm for the first time in months. The night promised dew, parties. Fiona closed the shop early and hurried over Blackfriars Bridge. Small pink-tipped waves passed her, carrying papers, sticks, froth downstream towards the sea. A barge coursed by; laughing faces in the porthole windows reminded her of that evening when she'd met Angie again. She felt her steps double as she kept up with it and reached the Blue Monarch Arms breathless, but with half an hour to kill. She would call someone. She reached into her bag for her phone. Damn, she'd left it on the counter at work.

The area had certainly changed since she'd last been there. Down a small side street, she found herself in Rotherhithe Walk. God, it was unrecognisable.

There was no sign of the shambling old warehouse. Just a grey stucco office block. Except, in the fabric of the doorway was one of the old oak doorway pillars. Probably had a preservation order on it. She could just make out: Theatrical Costumiers. By appointment only, in faded letters.

Standing on tiptoe, she tried to see the roof of the building. A row of dishes perched along it now. Starlings used to live there, in the rafters. Or were they sparrows?

All the ferny pre-history jungles, Wild West saloon doors,

apes, robots, swords, discarded wigs that used to litter the roof tiles had gone. No sign of the nasturtiums and vegetables that used to grow on the window ledges. An air-conditioning unit stood, belching out stale air, where an avocado plant had sprouted from a pip she'd tossed into a discarded Roman helmet.

She peered through the grey metallic blinds; identical rows of computers faced her, all with rotating puce spirals on their screen-savers.

What was Stephanie doing now? She should have kept in touch.

That freezing cold day. She'd been on the hunt for a cappuccino and had stumbled into this street.

"Don't just stand there, come in, love," said someone in the gloom. A woman.

It had been difficult to see anyone in the dim light. And when Fiona did spot a large woman perched on top of a mountain of green fabric, her lips sprouting pins and needles like a spiky toad, Fiona thought she was hallucinating.

"If you can find the kettle, you can be a dear and make us all some tea."

Fiona could hear the others rather than see them, from a gentle whirring and clattering that seemed to emit from all the vast labyrinth of draperies. As she entered the room, she saw people hunched in front of busy sewing machines, wheels turning, gloriously coloured cloth bunched under them like clouds.

They were all so preoccupied, it seemed churlish to ask for the way to the nearest cafe. She poked about in the corner where she found the kettle. The plug fizzed and sparked. The tea caddy was fashioned out of rosewood and inset with mother of pearl; the teapot and cups looked like they'd survived two world wars. She threw in a handful of leaves, stirred. The seamstress left their machines and clustered, waiting for her to pour them each a cup. It was the first time she'd been 'mother'. In fact it was the first time she could remember anyone expecting her to do anything useful.

The tea smelt like linen and tasted dusty; but it was hot and she was made to feel at home. After that, it felt natural, somehow, to ask Stephanie for a job.

Half an hour later she was installed on a stool in the centre of the room. After a couple of days, Stephanie gave her a rickety table. By the end of the week, she'd acquired an old singer sewing machine with a foot pedal.

To her utter amazement, she found she could sew, cut, mould, create fantastical forms from any old thing.

Until Daddy found out, of course.

"What? A Gregoyan is working in a rag factory?!"

The streetlight came on behind her making it hard to carry on peering through the window. A jogger pounded past. Fiona took off her hat, shook out her hair, turned and headed back towards the pub.

The Blue Monarch Arms was the same old place. Well, it had done nothing to defy Daddy. The room glowed with gas fires, glittering eyes, reflections in beer mugs. The air boomed unevenly with conversations and laughter. Glancing at her watch, she realised she was still early. Now, where should she sit so as to use the dim lighting to her advantage? She was taking a seat by the nearest of the gas fires, when a hand tapped her on the shoulder.

"Good evening."

She turned. Frederick was so fresh-faced, ginger-browed and keen. It was awfully nice to see him again. She decided not to let him see she was pleased and scowled.

"Don't just stand there," she snapped, "go and get me a gin and tonic with plenty of ice."

Angie could hear Alex on his computer, playing a game that involved a lot of whizzing and Californian accents. Dusty was in her room on her phone, with the door open; she seemed to be agony aunt to half the school.

"But if Darren's being so difficult, why doesn't she just chuck him and choose Johnnie instead. I happen to know he proper fancies her..."

Ted wasn't noticing the jumper he'd given her for Christmas; he was trying to spear asparagus.

"Interesting business," he said.

Had she overdone the fake saffron? "What business, darling?"

"The question of ownership in general. In this case, sperm ownership."

"Sperm, sperm, sperm." She giggled. "Could we talk about something else?" She took his abandoned dish, dropped it into the washing-up bowl; a stray asparagus head peeped above the surface. She snorted.

"The business of who owns rights over what strand of genetic material in it."

"Sorry?" She tried to stop thinking of Jake bobbing above her. "Does someone have to? Does everything have to have an owner?"

"Of course everything has to be accounted for. This isn't the Middle Ages."

Deciding not to argue, she presented him with the next course – singed scallops which immediately reminded her of that glorious moment when Jake freed himself of his boxer shorts.

Ted poked at the scallops with his fork.

"I couldn't make a living as an IVF consultant if every man started asking for his seminal emissions back."

"No." Stifling a laughing fit, she plonked herself down opposite him, letting her breasts spill forward. "I suppose not." She thought of the moan Jake had let out at the summit of their lovemaking. Then she tried to think of something else. Jake searching for his pants. His legal collar. She wondered who starched it.

"Quite." Ted gazed at her, his eyes wandering downwards, frowning. "Are you alright?"

"Why?" Hope unfurled in her, like bracken. Perhaps he would fancy her again. But then, he might suspect someone else of bringing her back to her senses. And what senses! She couldn't remember when she'd felt so relaxed.

"You seem a bit tense. Are you okay? That Willoughby woman hasn't been goading you again, has she?"

"No, no, I'm fine." He didn't seem to notice that she wasn't herself, thankfully.

"It seems that the world's view on seminal issue ownership is changing; the substance now belongs, at all times, to the man, except when he has ceded his rights over it."

She imagined Jake screaming out: "I cede you my rights."

"Yes," she said, hoping that didn't commit her to an opinion.

Ted licked the fork clean, pushed away his empty plate, drained his wine glass, and pulled the paper towards him, scanning the headlines.

She found herself staring at the top of his head. She'd always liked its shape. It was the first thing that had attracted her about him at a Student's Union fund-raising evening. As the lights dimmed, and the others drank themselves into couples, someone handed her the calculator, and Ted the jam-jars of takings. He put his head down, just like this, and soberly separated the notes from the coins. And all she could think of was what a wonderful father he'd make. He was. Oh dear.

"You'll catch cold if you're not careful." He flicked past the small ads and over to the sports page. "You really should try wearing something warmer over your chest."

There was a time when her top deck would win Ted's attention back from anything. "I could drown here, and be happy," he used to say.

She packed the dishwasher and felt Jake's fingers on her collarbone, saw the dark hairs on his forearms, smelt his pungent sweat. From the next room was the sound of the newspaper pages turning. Ted was blissfully unaware. She felt like shouting out things had changed; she wasn't just a wife, mother and carer. Instead, she counted each drop of water dripping from her yellow gloves. One, two three...

It felt as if she was going to burst. She had to share her secret with someone. She threw the gloves across the draining board. They stuck there like jellyfish. She reached for her phone, dialled Fiona's number. It went straight to voicemail. Fiona must be home by now. Perhaps she switched off her phone in the evenings. Angie didn't know her home number.

"I'm just going out to get some air," she shouted.

"Hmmm, yes, take care," was his reply.

She found Dusty's helmet in the corridor, then reached up to unhook her bike from its attachment to the ceiling.

Chapter 16

The pub seemed too noisy to Fiona, other conversations drowning out her train of thought. She took her gin and tonic from Frederick.

"Thank you."

He sat down opposite her with his beer and grinned. His teeth were a little crooked.

"Cheers," he said and drained half of his beer. "To the manners of England."

She crunched an ice cube. "You might need to make a few notes."

"Ja." Out came his notepad computer. He looked at her expectantly.

It was rather gratifying having his unblinking gaze to herself. She folded her hands together on her lap as if posing for a portrait.

"If I say you mustn't do this, then you must. For instance if I tell you never to give me roses, then you must shower me with them at the first opportunity."

Frederick didn't look as if he was taking it in. Or was he struggling to translate her words into Russian? She spoke louder.

"But if I tell you I want us to be friends, friendship is the last thing I have on my mind. It means, either, we must be lovers or I never want to see you again. Okay?"

He nodded enthusiastically.

"You see the thing is, if I say 'take care', it means bugger off and die a slow death. If I say 'that was interesting', it means it bored me to death. 'You're looking wonderful' means you've got fat. Are you getting all this down?"

He didn't look up, just kept on tapping away.

The crescent moon was squeezed into a sky mostly taken up by roofs, aerials, neon and billboards. Angie leaned forward into the drizzle and pushed at the pedals. From somewhere behind Mornington Crescent a drain emptied. The bike was a bit stiff. Or was it that she was unfit? She crossed the road at the lights, swung left, coasting behind the Elizabeth Garrett Anderson Hospital, taking the back roads towards Kings Cross. She enjoyed the cool of the drizzle on her face as she got into her stride on a bike a little too small for her.

Frederick's knees were close to Fiona's; his breath was warm. She was running out of things to say; he hadn't said anything, he'd hardly looked up from his typing. She was getting so used to the sound of her own voice that she jumped when he finally spoke.

"You conjoin my seeming lack of understanding with first a place, then a map, then the lack of a map, all in one continuous argument. Not even Leibniz, in his theory of Monadology, attempted such sophistry."

"Ah. Absolutely."

Frederick's grateful smile seemed to wrap its way around her. No one usually paid this much attention to anything she said. She didn't know what he what he was on about, but his attention felt like a present from a distant relative – one that came in the post, popping with bubble-wrap, promise, foreign stamps and illegible handwriting, until you found out what it was: place-mats of horse fairs, or something feral in opaque glass. Frederick had such translucent ears, the red wallpaper seemed to glow through them. Of course she didn't know anything about his professor. Perhaps he had prominent ears too, ones that were long and twitching. It was all going to her head. Wait until she told Angie what a catch Frederick and his professor were.

She moved closer, took Frederick's hand, laid it on her lap, as high as her dress allowed without the crêpe crumpling.

"You can kiss me if you want, Frederick," she said.

He held back, scrolled down at his screen, frowning. "Does that mean that you are hungry, angry or that I should perhaps brush my teeth?"

"No, I mean, whatever you do, you must not kiss me here in this pub."

"Ah. Yes!" His eyes glowed. Closing his notepad, he moved closer and planted a wet beery kiss on her nose.

From Frederick Chizhevsky – fchiz@hotmail.com
To Hildegard Schnitzel –schnitzelhildegard@interbergen. fleishnet

Dear Hildegard,

I miss your Volkenbrood, your views on Spinoza, our walks by the sea in the autumn, when the sky grew black with migrating birds, when your husband, Herr Professor, was away in Munich, in Paris, in Cologne. Yes, the London theatre is expensive, but I have been invited to attend a free English Culture course by two English ladies who advertised in the newspaper, and who intend to teach me everything about life here. I would like you to stay with me when you come, but unlike the generosity of your mattress, I have only a single bed. Your Frederick

Angie chained the bike to the nearest air-conditioning outlet, towelled her face and her neck, and gazed at Chase Manning House. It was only vaguely familiar. The last time she'd been there, she'd been tipsy. She hunted for 'De Borzoi', then pressed the bell.

"Hello?" said a voice with a slight Midlands burr she thought she recognised.

"I'm looking for Fiona Gregoyan. I mean, De Borzoi."

"Third floor. Come right up."

A buzzer sounded; the entrance door opened. She entered the cage door opposite, tugged the two doors shut. The lift cranked into motion and flew up to the third floor. One bell was set in a gilt frame. She pressed it.

Lights made a trail through opaque glass to the door. When it opened, she heard Miles Davis playing somewhere, smelt fried fish and broccoli and found herself under the inquiring gaze of Fiona's husband. The hall was cluttered with shopping bags, the walls familiar now with their paintings of Saint Gregory.

"Hello," said Fiona's husband, wiping his hands on his apron.

"Who is it?" called a man's voice from deep inside the flat.

"Fiona isn't in," said the husband.

"Oh. Sorry to disturb you." She realised she still wore her cycle helmet. Flustered, she took it off.

"I'm Guy, by the way."

He too pronounced it *Ghee*. But with a tinge of a Birmingham accent.

"We've met," she blurted. "You probably don't remember but I've tasted your pigs in blankets, which were just as they should be." It was a lie; she hadn't managed to get anywhere near them.

"Glad you..." His eyes widened. "My God, aren't you Lady Beaverwood?"

Oh no, she'd forgotten all about her other persona. Not wanting to disabuse him, she put out her hand. He seized it, kissed it.

"Call me Angie," she said weakly.

"Oh! Enchanté!" His accent was suddenly from Paris. "Please do come in, your ladyship."

"It's sticking to the pan," shouted the voice from inside the apartment.

"Keep stirring, Ray," he shouted back. "I do apologise profusely, your ladyship, but my friend and I are attempting something a tad experimental. Please, please, do join us." He gave her a little bow, then stood back to let her through.

Not up to more experiments, certainly not in the guise of Lady Beaverwood, Angie shook her head vehemently.

"No, no. Perhaps you could just give Fiona a message."

"Of course, of course, your ladyship. What shall I tell her?"

Her cheeks began to burn. He continued to regard her with a deferential smile. He seemed oodles more cuddly than at the timeshare evening. In fact, she couldn't see why Fiona had any problems with him.

"Could I get you something? An Armagnac? Some *eau ordinaire?*"

She must look hot. "Oh, no, please don't worry. Could you just tell her that I called?"

"I most certainly will."

Clutching her helmet, she stumbled towards the lift. "Thank you so much, Ghee. Bye bye."

"Don't be a stranger," he called after her. "Come round any time."

She heard him shout, "Turn the heat down..." to his friend, before the lift clanked downwards. Feeling elevated in status, and rather unhinged, she unchained the bike, pedalled off along the road, her shadow dancing around her as she passed streetlights. Lady Beaverwood, of course. She should have used it with the snotty porter at the timeshare apartment. Perhaps he'd have been more cooperative? It would have been fun to pretend with Jake. The birds were keeping silent, the air smelled of honeysuckle not petroleum-drizzle; Mile End blinked, buzzed, hummed around her, like being inside the belly of an electric whale. A lorry overtook her, sharing its music with her for a moment – hip-hop, mixed with the driver's cursing as he swerved.

"Do you realise who you've nearly knocked over?" she shouted.

Clearly, he didn't.

She held her head high and kept on pedalling. It was a long way back to Mornington Crescent. She wished she could stop somewhere and tell someone everything that had happened that afternoon. She was composing a message for Fiona, when an unknown number blinked on her handset. She pressed 'answer'.

"Angie, are you there?"

Fiona sounded tipsy.

"Hi Fiona, I've been trying to reach you..."

"I'm with Frederick, using his phone."

"Just that I wanted you to know…"

"I know. You didn't keep your side of the bargain."

"No, I didn't think we had actually agreed on…"

"You bottled out – didn't she, Frederick?"

There was the sound of sniggering.

"I did not bottle out."

"Frederick is looking up 'bottle' on his thesaurus, but I'm certain he agrees with me."

He must be the student in the anorak. Angie hoped the porter had been courteous in sending him away. "Okay, I bottled out."

"So, if you remember, next Thursday it will be my turn. Rule number seven – alternate Thursday afternoons between us. And since you messed up today, next Thursday is mine."

"Of course, absolutely. Rule number seven."

There was a sound of muttering. The line was breaking up. The distance between her and Fiona seemed to be growing, rather than diminishing.

"I'm assuring him that I... will be there, ready and waiting, next week, aren't I Fred?"

There was a new sound, this time of something squelching. Angie assumed kisses were being showered on Frederick.

"Good luck," she said sweetly. "I hope you do better than I did, I really do."

"That won't be difficult."

There was a click.

Right – she would phone Jake, and move the location for next Thursday. She felt his surges all over again, heard his *Holy Mother* curse close to her ear lobe.

She swung back onto the bike and entered the stream of traffic in Old Street; lights in the old sweatshop windows streaked past her as she rode with a feeling of affection for Fiona, and a new loyalty towards their cause.

Fiona handed Frederick his phone back.

That Angie. She didn't seem to be up to timesharing anything, much less a lover. She just didn't seem to have the nerve for it. Frederick, for his part, seemed to have plenty of nerve. He'd pocketed his phone, downed the last of his third beer and abandoned his tablet.

"That's enough for now," she said, finishing off her most recent G and T and getting up a little unsteadily. "I'll see you next Thursday." Not able to prevent herself, she lunged over and buried a last peck in his ginger hair. "Don't be… er… do not, absolutely not, be on time."

He nodded, then shook his head, stood up and bowed.

"This is good, oh, no, really terrible," he said.

When Fiona reached home she located Guy in the kitchen where pyramids of fish- bones, crab-shells and vegetable peelings rose from all the work surfaces and where he was dashing between three spitting, fizzling frying pans.

"Hi, Guy," she said to his back.

"Hi, doll."

"What's for supper?"

"Nothing yet. But wait ten minutes and I want to try out three varieties of fish cake on you."

"Great." Obedient, she sat down at the kitchen table.

"One of your titled friends was looking for you," he said, his back to her while he continued frying something.

"Who?"

"In a cycle helmet too small for her. At first I thought she was from the Green Party, or one of those organic people with a vegetable box."

Fiona reached out for a knife and fork and held onto them. "Did she say what she wanted?"

"For you to return her call."

"Oh."

He placed a tiny, perfectly cylindrical fish cake carefully onto a plate and handed it to her.

"Seemed to think you would know her number. Don't you?"

Fiona was too hungry to go through a mental list of titled

women whose heads she'd adorned and couldn't think of a single cyclist. She tucked into the fishcake which tasted remarkably like a fish finger. "Hmmm," she said, her mouth full. "She rode here?"

"That's the sort of thing upper-class vegetarians do, get radical and hold up traffic."

The fish cake gone, she held her plate out for another. "Did she tell you her first name?"

"Yes, she insisted. Now what was it? Something surprising... beginning with an E... Edith, Edna, Eve... I'm sure she'll ring again if it's important. God, you're supposed to have sauce on the fish cake."

"Oh, sorry. Can I have another?"

He tutted, put another on her plate, dressing it with leaves of some description. "This one has another, secret ingredient."

Shoving aside the leaves, she chomped the second fish cake. It tasted exactly like the first. "I might need to taste another to be sure."

Sighing, he picked another fried ball from the third pan and placed that on a new plate. "You've also missed Ray," he said.

She attacked it with vigour. "You can tell him to bugger off." She wiped her mouth. "This is definitely the best one. It's bigger, for starters."

He had a ladle full of sauce ready for her fish cake; it was too late. He tasted it himself, frowned, and then let the sauce plop back into the pot. "He has an amusing, delicate dilemma to deal with in his apartment."

She scooped up the last crumbs. "Does he? What?"

"Seems he's lending his apartment to a lady friend for her, shall we say, extra-mural activities, and she's alarming the neighbour with her noisy cries of amorous pleasure."

"What?"

"It's not so much the exultations that seem to enrage his neighbour, but the fact that they are occurring at three in the afternoon. Very *de classe*."

Fiona let her fork drop with a clatter. "Sorry, could you repeat that."

"Oh, you know how these old queens feel about their peace."

"Who are you talking about?'

"Igor Gaunt, the actor. He's in number 42." Guy had his back to her while straining the sauce through muslin.

"Igor who?"

He added some Marsala to the liquid and stirred. "He's very funny. You've seen him on telly."

Fiona stood up, rocked a little, grabbed the Marsala from his hand and swigged some. It burnt her tongue. Three o'clock. Noisy. No one had been there. Ray, that bloody stirrer, was making this up. "I had no idea Ray's walls were so thin," she said, staring hard at Guy, looking for clues of what he'd been told or hadn't been told. The room was undulating.

Guy seemed intent on rinsing out the muslin.

"Now try it, fish cake or no fish cake…." He dipped a wooden spoon into the strained sauce, offered it to her.

She took a cautious lick. It tasted like pond water to her.

"Hmmm…" Her mind was reeling. Perhaps Ray was planning to blackmail her? "…Delicious," she said.

Guy took a mouthful himself. "Do you know, you're right, it will do. Thanks, doll." He turned his back to her as he stirred another pot of something greenish and fishy.

Or had Angie lied to her? This hit her in the stomach and made her feel sick.

Before she had to do any more tasting, she reversed out of the room and got upstairs somehow. In the bedroom, she kicked off her shoes, sat on the edge of the bed and gazed out of the window.

Angie said she'd bottled out of seeing Frederick. And Angie didn't lie. But someone had been making noisy love in Ray's flat. Unless he was lying.

At school, Angie's antics with Fiona's cast-off boyfriends had always been noisy. Embarrassingly so.

The building opposite leaked light in symmetrical holes, the nail clipping of a moon was snagged in an air-conditioning unit.

So, Angie had enjoyed her afternoon.

Wasn't Igor Grant in *The Spy's Code*? What a way to spend his afternoon – listening in to Angie's inner workings. She didn't like the sound of this one little bit.

And if Frederick wasn't the provider of Angie's squeals of delight, then who was? Funny, now that she thought about it, Angie hadn't sounded frustrated. She reached out for her phone, then remembered she'd left it at work. Damn! She caught herself scowling in the gilt mirror above the bed and tried smiling instead. This was supposed to be fun, wasn't it? Rule number one.

Jake drew his blinds, dislodging a cobweb, and opened his file on copyright law. He perched on the edge of his most uncomfortable plastic stool, hoping discomfort would keep him awake, took out a pencil, and began. Some hours later he awoke to the sound of dawn traffic, his drool on paragraph one, page one, awash with a dream of Angie, plump, gleaming and naked, holding up the Scales of Justice.

Chapter 17

"Two jacks and a king."

"Three twos and a… oh, dear, what did you say…?"

Angie pushed the door open with one arm and laid down the tea tray. Mrs J and Mrs E were facing each other, intent on their cards. She didn't want to interrupt them. The clock was ticking more loudly than usual. Cornflake was letting out loud cat-snores. Sid, the goldfish, was drifting upside down. The room was hot, airless. She went over to the window, opened the curtains wide, letting in a breeze. Sunlight spilled over the tops of dead red tulips. She tossed them into the bin.

"Did you say a two, dear?"

"Two what? – pm or am?"

The two old ladies were like synchronised swimmers; they sucked their teeth in unison, fanned their cards simultaneously, both holding them close to their hearts. They'd been friends longer than they'd been married. Funny how carefully they kept their cards hidden from each other, though. What if she managed to keep Jake hidden from Ted and Fiona all her life, but they all ended up in same old age home?

Angie stirred sugar into Mrs J's cup, milk into Mrs E's and kept the third cup black for Mr Aranovitch.

"Hearts, dear, two hearts."

Tick, tick tick.

If that happened, she'd have to keep the secret until death did them all part. She imagined Sid's demise – he would be first – his jam-jar coffin being lowered into a vole hole in the rose garden, the inmates singing 'All Things Bright and Beautiful' in their quavering voices. She saw the thread in the carpet at her feet wear down, felt her skin pucker, her joints stiffen, imagined the long day's sun dropping down to a low fizzle. Ted would die next, impatient with the limitations of old age. Fiona was certain to outlive all of them and get madder. And Angie would have to carry on keeping her secret.

"Mr Aranovitch, your tea." She walked over to the piano room, pushed open the door.

His chair was empty, a plastic mug of water, two capsules, a folded *Musical Times* on the table beside it.

She went back out into the hall. "Mr Aranovitch?"

No sign of him.

She checked the toilet. The tap was running, but no Mr Aranovitch. Her chest tightened. Relax, she told herself. The main door had a new eight-digit code he couldn't possibly master.

"Don't swear!" said Mrs E.

Angie went on into the television room, where other ladies were watching a young woman in high heels tug a carrot from the soil.

"Go on, love, get your hands dirty,"

No Mr Aranovitch.

This wasn't looking good.

Last time he'd gone all the way to Inverness on a haunted-castle coach tour. He might have stayed on, but the bed-and-breakfast's piano was out of tune, and he'd demanded a piano tuner be called.

Angie changed the channel to a neon-blinking quiz show, went back to shuffle the cards for Mrs J, dabbed at Mrs E's chin, plonked a fistful of fish food into Sid's tank, before heading upstairs to hunt for Mr Aranovitch. She paused. There was a kerfuffle downstairs.

"No, I won't!"

That sounded awfully like Fiona. Angie turned back.

"Oh, yes, you will."

"What if we have an emergency? Or a demise?"

Mrs Willoughby sounded very exercised.

"Then I'll move it."

Angie ran back downstairs to find Mrs Willoughby standing squarely on the Welcome mat, grim-faced, her arms folded.

"You'll remove it from the doctor's bay right now or..."

"There isn't anywhere else."

"...I shall call the police and have both it and you towed away. Just see if I don't."

"Er, Mrs Willoughby." Angie put her hand on the steel-like fold-up arm. "She won't be long. Will you, Fiona?"

Fiona wasn't complying with anyone. Her face was furrowed into a scowl.

"I don't know how long I will be. I've got scores to settle."

Mrs W lifted the phone from the hall desk, dialled. "Is that Highgate Police Station? This is Mrs Frances Willoughby. Yes, *again*."

"You'd better move it," said Angie.

"No wonder there are emergencies with her around," shouted Fiona. "And as for you, Angela bloody Riley, your antics in Ray's flat have the whole building talking."

"What? Outside! Now!" Angie grabbed Fiona by the arm, tugged at it.

"Okay, okay, don't tear my sleeve."

"There's a vehicle I want you to remove from the driveway

of Vetchling... V for viper, E for elephant, T for pterodactyl..."

Before Mrs Willoughby rounded up any more animals, Angie shoved Fiona towards the front door, down the steps and into the forecourt, where cherry blossom showered down on them and a robin sang. Angie glanced back at the building. The office window framed Mrs Willoughby's furious face.

"What are you talking about, Fiona?"

"The cries of rapture you were making on Thursday afternoon in Ray's flat couldn't have been achieved without some help."

Angie racked her brains. "Did the porter say something?"

"Just admit you've been lying to me."

Angie couldn't help herself; she grinned.

Fiona wasn't grinning; she was tearing apart a rhododendron flower.

"I did try to tell you, but you didn't want to listen."

Fiona plucked fresh blooms. "Well, I'm listening now, aren't I?"

Angie hesitated; her desire for Jake soared; her loyalty to Fiona gave her cramp. "Look, okay, I spent the afternoon with another candidate." She certainly wasn't going to say his name.

"Who? The candidate that didn't turn up?"

"He turned up."

"You didn't tell me he turned up."

"I didn't think he *would* turn up until later, at the apartment, when we..."

"I see." Fiona was scattering the blooms piecemeal. "So, this other candidate was a success?"

"Yes, yes, yes and yes. I mean no, he won't be suitable at all." To be shared, she thought.

"Not suitable?" Fiona reached for the rhododendron's last

shred of colour.

"I'm sure you'll have what I had too, with Frederick."

"But that's not who *you* had it with, is it, Angie?"

"Me? What does that matter?"

The branch was stripped bare.

Fiona was turning all her attention on her. "We have rules, don't we?"

"Sort of."

"Rule number three. Yes?"

"Choice of candidate..."

"To be strictly unanimous."

"Yes, well..."

"Not to mention rule number four."

"Equal portions of candidate to be equally shared..."

"We had a deal."

The windowpane was rattling. Miss W was mouthing something, the gold in her teeth flashing. She waved to Mrs Willoughby that she was coming. "Can we talk about this later?"

Fiona was now standing on a carpet of crushed petals, tears travelling down her cheeks. "Thing is..." she began. Rummaging in her bag, she came up with a spare pair of cami-knickers. She blew her nose loudly on those. "...I don't see how we can ever talk again."

"Oh..." Angie had no protection for this sort of thing; she felt the sort of despair that took her back to a damp brick wall at the edge of childhood where they'd opened their first cigarette packet together. Bert, Ben Rudy, Percy: they had all fancied Fiona first and her, Angie, last. She thought of Jake, savoured the way he seemed to want her – first, not last. Her heart boiled, fizzed, attempted to crack, slowly saturating her with the realisation that nothing had changed – she couldn't deny Fiona anything male. "I could introduce you to him."

"No. I want what you had. Nothing more, nothing less."

Fiona might get to meet Jake but he might not like meeting her. After a moment's thought, Angie gritted her teeth.

"Okay, when you go to meet him, wear your most outrageous outfit and be ready for anything."

Fiona plastered Angie's cheeks with tears and kisses. Angie knew they would now be streaked with magenta. She turned away, towards the front entrance, her legs heavy as marble fireplaces. She heard Fiona's ignition fire. Two things she was sure of – one, she hadn't given Fiona Jake's name. And, secondly, Fiona wasn't going to get her hands on him even if she did find out his name.

In the window, Mrs Willoughby was waving the desk phone at her. Trying to put a brave face on things, Angie tramped back up the steps and entered the office.

Mrs Willoughby was pale with fury and was holding the phone at right angles to her chin.

"I'll take over," said Angie, a little concerned that she was going to have to spend the rest of her day placating people. "Why don't you go and have your lunch."

"It's the German Embassy. There's someone in Baden-Baden calling himself Valentino Aranovitch of this address. I'm assuming you know where our Mr Aranovitch is at this moment. The other Mr Aranovitch has an engagement with the Westphalian Symphony Orchestra. I hope you speak German." She handed Angie the receiver.

Chapter 18

Fiona woke very early that Wednesday morning, with heartburn. She was about to blame last night's supper, but remembered she'd cooked it herself. She reached out for somebody to warm her feet on but remembered Guy was somewhere promoting his restaurants. What's the place that produces strong chilli? Sorrento or Marrakech? Was there a beach called Pimento?

She stretched, rolled over. It was so much easier getting up without him in the room; it was quiet. But it was also unnerving. She called it loneliness. It started in her belly and radiated to her fingertips.

She tried ringing Angie's mobile again, but the number was still engaged. She rang her home number, and reached Dusty, who said:

"Mummy's still in Germany, I think. Some old gaffer's done a runner."

Fiona's sense of disquiet increased. Had Angie now run off with one of the candidates without telling her? "Old? How old?"

"Ugh, you know, one of her wrinklies."

That could mean anything. The category could include her. Awful child. Could Angie have run off with the snake-fancier, the newly divorced man or someone else?

Perhaps she was emitting cries of rapture all over Europe. "He doesn't happen to be an opera singer called Rudolfo Miranda?"

Fiona heard the buzzer on a television quiz show, audience laughter and applause before Dusty said:

"Dunno."

"Do you know when your mother's coming back?"

"Nah, sorry. Yah leave a message?"

"Er, no. Thanks."

Click. The phone went dead, leaving Fiona more alone than ever.

Why hadn't she pumped Angie for more facts about the third candidate? 'Dress in your most outrageous outfit and be ready for anything.' That was the sum total of her advice. Fiona was thoroughly disconcerted.

Germany? She was sure she'd seen something in the paper about Rudolfo singing in Germany. They must be there together. Sneaky bitch. What was her new secret? She must have developed a new quality since school. All right, her breasts were more generous than Fiona's. Men like that. But so were her thighs. And men didn't like that. 'Be ready for anything.' What did that mean? Angie must have learnt some tricks, developed special bedroom skills. Fiona needed some professional help.

Herr Strimmel was small-boned and fine-featured and his dark suit contrasted beautifully with a halo of white locks. From the way minions tiptoed past him and acted on his every word, Angie assumed he carried a lot of weight at Baden-Baden's Troppen Institute.

"But Mr Aranovitch has retired from playing the violin," she repeated.

Herr Strimmel laughed. As did the ushers and house

manager hovering nearby. In fact they mirrored everything that Herr Strimmel did. The gilt-framed mirrors magnified every movement.

In case it was English that was the problem, Angie mimed an old man packing away a fiddle before putting his head down to rest.

The mirrors replicated her performance.

This set off soft new waves of laughter.

"Yes, yes, it is not until his last breath that the maestro can lay down his violin…" said Herr Strimmel.

"No, no, Mr Aranovitch's duties are…" What were his duties, exactly? To lie down and die without a fuss on a week-day seemed to be the sum total of them. "You see, Vetchling Grove takes his care very seriously and he isn't insured for world travel," she said, finally.

Herr Strimmel leaned forward to whisper: "We were a little shocked – no, alarmed – because Valentino really wasn't equipped for a journey. All he had was his velvet slippers – he didn't even bring a good suit. The Troppen Institute undertakes to meet all the needs of its artists. We have installed the maestro in our deluxe dressing room where he's attiring himself in new shoes and the suit we have procured for him. I think you will find him well cared for."

"But this wasn't a planned tour." There was no nice way of putting this. "Mr Aranovitch escaped from our custody."

Angie didn't know the German for 'aghast', but it would have described Herr Strimmel's expression perfectly.

"You don't mean prison?" He looked appalled.

"No, no, not prison. A home. He has escaped from his, er, home."

Herr Strimmel frowned. "An artist…" – he said this slowly as if she was stupid – "…is always engaged in escaping the ordinary world. And we have two choices – one is to attempt to limit his flight and the other is to also make the journey."

Angie could see the ushers and house manager all nodding as if this was a lecture they heard often, yet loved to hear. A queue of distinguished elderly ladies had gathered at the ticket office behind them.

"Do you have all of his recordings?" he asked.

"Er, no."

"We have signed copies of every one of Mr Aranovitch's live recordings, and a limited edition of his autobiography, also signed. We have been in communication for forty-seven years. I had lost hope we would meet, but now…" Herr Strimmel's eyes gleamed.

"Look, could I see him?"

"He cannot be disturbed before his rehearsal."

"Rehearsal?" Angie felt a little dizzy. It was eight hours since she'd eaten anything. Vetchling Grove's budget hadn't covered the cost of refreshments on her Easyjet flight, and she'd had no time at the airport.

"His audience are already here, forming."

Herr Strimmel waved at the line of ladies now stretching out of the entrance and into the street. "I have reserved for you a seat for the performance tomorrow night, and a room in our own hotel for tonight. Today, Valentino Aranovitch is in rehearsals and cannot be disturbed. So, if you will excuse me…"

He clicked his heels together, then bustled away, halo bobbing. His coterie minced after him.

Angie's phone rang. It was Mrs Willoughby. Pressing the 'busy' button, Angie walked out past the queue, down the steps and into the street. She wasn't prepared or dressed for this. She was in the same clothes she'd travelled in, had no plush dressing room and probably wasn't even insured. A wind was blowing, scatering petals from a basket of hanging tulips. The phone rang again. This time it was Elizabeth Bridstrop, a Camden Council social worker claiming she was Mr Sandovitch's care worker.

"Aranovitch," Angie barked. 'Valentino Aranovitch, and he doesn't need or want a care worker."

Fiona thumbed through the small-ad column of *The Lady* – counselling, hypnosis, karate. Under what category did the sort of reassurance she was seeking come? She tossed the book aside, paced about, had a coffee, and switched on Guy's computer. Could she Google 'being a sexually attractive woman'? She tried it. Several books on relationship problems surfaced as well as lunchtime classes in pole dancing. She downloaded the training video. The girl was nothing special, thought Fiona, shaking her own hips. And, anyway, getting a pole installed in Ray's flat might prove difficult. There must be other aids for the less agile woman. Who would have them? Sex shops? She typed that onto the screen. Shopping always boosted her confidence. At any rate they would have experts on the subject. Several shops advertised in lurid-coloured flashing logos. There was a smaller ad that promised discretion and good customer service. It was in Soho. She jotted down the address.

She stepped out of Piccadilly Circus tube station into the hatless throng of uncouth people who make London their business – paper-sellers, buskers, shoppers, beggars, women with pushchairs, men with briefcases and agendas, all getting in her way until she managed to find *Marquess Special Care Shop – all tastes individually and discreetly catered for –* in an alley off Windmill Street.

There was nothing discreet about the place apart from, possibly, the dim lighting. The door and window frames were glossy reds and black. The mannequins in the window were trying to appear dominant in tight leather. When she peered past them, she could make out rails of things that looked more like long rubber bands than clothes. The shelves looked a bit more promising. Apart from inflatable penises in various sizes, they had things in boxes. These might store something useful. She looked left and right to see if anyone was paying any attention to her. Apart from a man slumped on a step, they weren't. She took a deep breath, and entered.

The interior décor was garish Goth with chains hanging from the ceiling, and a surplus of leather.

"Can I help you?" asked someone with a Yorkshire accent.

"Possibly," answered Fiona, unsure as to what she was really looking for in the whip and handcuff section.

The assistant had perfect legs emerging from tiny leather shorts. She had knee-length blonde hair-extensions, and an architectured cleavage that Fiona wasn't sure was entirely female. Come to think of it, the voice was very gruff for a woman's. Well, if there was a man under that make-up, he could provide some expertise.

"Do you have anything other than sado-masochistic aids…?" Fiona asked.

"Whips, tongs and hanging hooks are our bread-and-butter."

"Oh, I see." Fiona was becoming mesmerised by the way the strange person's tonged eyelashes encircled a cold pair of snakelike eyes.

"Something to interest a younger man?"

This was a little too astute. Fiona looked around to see if anyone was listening. "Could be," she said.

"In that case," oozed the assistant, "you may need a little help."

If it weren't so urgent, Fiona would have slapped the woman's face.

"Don't worry, love, I'll take you in hand."

Alarmed, Fiona took a step back.

The assistant pulled scarlet leather thongs from the bottom shelf, gracefully allowing the street a view of metal-studded suspenders. 'She' held one, then another against Fiona's groin. They flapped there like doomed moths pinned to a corkboard. Fiona, who prided herself on a tall, slim figure, suddenly felt like a behemoth. The assistant shook her hair; it crackled with static. "No, a thong'd be wasted on you, love," 'she' said, herding the leather strips back into their burrow.

"It does say something for everyone in your advert, doesn't it?" Fiona was ready to storm out.

"With you, love, we'd be better off keeping it dead simple." 'She' climbed a stepladder, with full exposure of her own diamante thong, and come back down with a dusty box marked 'Lithuanian', which she tipped open. Frilly basques cascaded onto the counter. "I should start with some lingerie, ducky." 'She' teased the shape into something amorphous, "and leave the sex toys for when you run out of puff."

"We would like to film the maestro preparing for his inaugural performance in Baden-Baden. We're planning a camera crew for eleven hundred hours."

Angie pressed 'save' and listened to the next message.

"The British Council has arranged for a car to pick up Mr Aranovitch at five. Please tell us any of his dietary requirements."

Angie moved onto the next message.

"This is Frau Ilsa Streuenberger. I would like to invite Herr Valentino Aranovitch to the Hotel Bareiss in the Black Forest for a few days' rest after his performance. As my guest."

By late afternoon, Angie was no nearer to getting hold of

Mr Aranovitch, but her job description seemed to have changed from deputy matron at an old people's home to Valentino Aranovitch's full-time international publicity agent. Herr Strimmel must be very well connected.

She sighed. Vetchling Grove and Mornington Crescent seemed a long way away. And Ravensville Mansions even further.

After a frugal supper in a steamed-up restaurant overlooking a bus station, Angie booked into a student hostel and spent an uncomfortable night on a futon which folded down off the wall.

In the morning, brilliant light awoke her from an unpleasant dream in which she was being asked to sing to an audience of thousands. Groggy, in search of fresh air, she stepped out onto the tiny balcony. It was perched over a pretty old square, where couples were already enjoying the early spring sunshine on the benches. A street vendor was selling narcissi to one such couple. On the balcony across the square, a woman was hanging rows of twinned socks to dry. A pair of wood pigeons cooed together on the balcony below. And an old couple held hands as they strolled below her past the market stalls, one choosing, the other paying. Two men snogged under a statue of a Prussian general. Two women shared water cupped from a fountain. A pair of young roller skaters glided together, in graceful communication, like swans. She was the only lone figure in the whole landscape. She turned to go back into the room.

She sat down on the edge of the futon, and pressed *home* on her mobile.

"Ted?" she breathed.

"Yes." He sounded relaxed.

"How's everything?" she asked.

"Oh, fine," he replied. "Where are you?"

"I'm still in Germany trying to regain one of Vetchling's

runaways."

"Uh huh."

She could hear Dusty shouting something about a missing tennis racket against the noise of a plane overhead.

"It's at Evan's, being restrung," Angie said.

"She's not going to like that." He sighed. Angie wanted him to say he missed her. "I think I'll write her a note," was what he said.

"Mr Aranovitch's become a celebrity," said Angie. "I have no idea how I'm going to persuade him to come back to Vetchling Grove."

"Lucky old bastard." He laughed.

She didn't want Ted to be amused; she wanted him not to be coping.

"My lasagne needs eating," she suggested.

"We made pancakes, don't worry."

"Love you," she said, quietly.

There was a long-distance crackle.

"What?"

"Love you."

"Oh. Ditto," was his response, too brisk to be any solace.

She closed her phone, lay back onto the bed, stared at the gold-leaf mouldings on the ceiling, and thought of Jake. Breaking another rule, she couldn't remember which one, she rang Jake's phone. His voice mail came on; she decided to send a text.

'Meet me at the zoo cafe, A.'

Fiona was so burdened with her new purchases that she took a cab back to Crowning Glories. There were three women waiting on the doorstep, anxious to go inside.

"Terribly sorry, but I've been waylaid," she said and began to unlock the door.

The nearest lady told her that they all had so admired Mrs Birchington-Smith's prize-winning 'Strawberries and Cream' creation at Ascot that they wanted her to make hats suitable for each of them.

The door was a bit stiff, so Fiona had to turn round, kick her parcels out of the way and lean her back against it. The furthest woman – a razor-thin lady with protruding teeth – was giving Fiona's shopping bags a very stern look. It was too late to hide the *Marquess Special Care Shop – all tastes catered for* logo – a stilettoed woman leading a man-on-a-leash.

"For a friend in need," Fiona said. With a heave, the door opened, she knocked over the bags, scattering their contents all over the pavement. Quickly, she gathered the objects, but one of the boxes flew open and released one of the mechanised toys. Why hadn't that shop assistant wrapped things better? Fiona was helpless as the human-sized gloss-lip-sticked lips snapped into a furtive kind of life on the street. Suspecting the transvestite of sabotage, Fiona tried to usher her ladies inside. "Come along now…"

"Look at it move," said the first woman.

"I want one of those," said the second.

"I blame the internet," said the third.

The mechanism was now moving along towards the taxi rank, its tongue writhing.

Fiona positively manhandled all three women into the shop, abandoning the lips to a rhythmic dance that propelled it past an astonished taxi driver. Fiona banged the door shut. But they had all gathered at the window to watch the lips cross the road where Fiona prayed they would be flattened by a delivery van.

"Right, let's start with measuring your heads," she said briskly to the three ladies' backs, trying to behave as if this was a normal working day.

Chapter 19

Desperate not to be late for his date with Angie, Jake felt in his pocket for his phone. Where was it? God, he'd changed jackets, but not moved his phone. Well, not to worry. He sneaked a glance at his watch. One twenty five. Half an hour to get to Regents Park. He could just about make it. Better had; he'd been obsessing about her all week. Her great milky-white tits were threatening his ability to finish sentences; her majestic undulations intruded every time he turned a page; her short shallow breaths, her giggles, could startle him at any point in a slippery legal phrase.

He glanced across his desk at Dr Gold, who was taking up the only unbroken chair in the cupboard Jake and Max called their office. The doctor was wittering on about some document he hadn't received.

"I thought I'd sent *you* the original," Jake lied, grateful he'd learnt the art in Barnados.

"Well, it hasn't arrived." The doctor began to riffle through some papers in the mess of reference books, notes, old sandwich wrappers that occupied the desk.

Jake gestured him aside and began to rummage furiously. "I'll find it." Where was the bloody thing?

The bloody doctor wasn't to be put off; he was shaking out *The Human Fertilisation and Embryology Act* document.

It disgorged stray crisps, a Post-it and a document.

Jake's heart missed a beat. Didn't the Post-it have the details of his afternoon date? He lunged for it, seized it, screwed it up and pocketed it, apologising vehemently. Luckily, the doctor was too busy reading the document to notice. He was settling onto his chair, unscrewing his fountain pen.

"Where shall we start?"

Jake couldn't be delayed any longer. "If anything needs clarifying, I think you'd better check with Max," he said. "He's my senior." That should do it.

The doctor scowled. It was clear that he didn't trust Max.

Jake didn't trust Max either. But Angie was Max's gift to him.

"Where will you be?" persisted the doctor.

"Me?" Jake felt trapped. "I have a, er, business lunch."

Jake caught the doctor glancing at his frayed shirt cuffs; he tried to draw them back under his jacket.

"How many businesses do you have?"

Jake got the point – he should have fewer lunches and spend his bank loan on a new shirt. He wriggled with discomfort.

"When will you be back?"

"Around about four, I hope."

"Where are you going for this business lunch? Paris?"

Jake felt dissected by the doctor's clear, surgical gaze. "I'll try really hard to be back by three-thirty."

"If you're in some sort of trouble…"

"Trouble? No, of course not. Now then..."

"If you ever need my help, you only have to ask."

Jake shook his head, touched by the man's concern; it reminded him of one of his long-lost, well-meaning foster dads. "Thanks, though. See you later."

With a gesture that stalled somewhere between a salute

and a wave, he got himself out of the door, taking the stairs three at a time. He sprinted past the security guard, was through the wrought-iron gates and along half the length of Strand in less time than it took a squirrel to bury a peanut.

The flat seemed much too quiet and dimly lit for an afternoon of excitement. Arthur, the art installation must be off. Fiona poked at an exclamation button. Triangular patterns covered the walls, xylophone jazz streamed into the room. Good, that would do. She put some coffee into the percolator, and opened one of the bedroom windows – just enough to make the blinds flutter suggestively. She loosened her frilly peach basque so that she could breathe a little, pulled her silicon garters as high as she could, although there did seem to be some incompatibility between her thighs and their elasticity. She gazed in the mirror, putting on her specs to see more clearly, and adjusted the cloth flowers in her hair so that the kirby grips were pointing inwards rather than outwards. She found the Seven Deadly Sins perfume bottle, tossed plenty of it over her neck, cleavage, insides of her wrists; she sprayed her mouth with breath freshener, and tried to keep a fresh coat of scarlet lipstick away from her teeth. The entry-phone buzzed. She slipped her feet into high fluffy black-and-scarlet stiletto slippers, and tiptoed towards it. Then she threw the door open, smiling, blowing a kiss like a bubble. It burst. She froze.

Standing there in his duffel coat, with a bunch of red roses in his hand, was Frederick. He looked her up and down, wolf-whistled.

She'd completely forgotten to cancel him.

"Oh, no, oh, dear." She scrabbled for an excuse. "I forgot, no, I was too poorly to call you. You see, I have a horrible, infectious... the doctor's checking for Dengue fever."

Frederick didn't seem put off. He winked at her, stepping forward, pushing the roses into her arms. "That's a fever of the tropics. That means you are hot, and waiting for me."

The installation contributed the biting strains of a tango to the proceedings. Damn the bloody thing.

"No, no," she said, trying to keep the thorns at a distance. "You might catch it."

"Ha, that means you want me to take hold of you. Da dum." He chimed in time to the music, kicking the door shut, stuffing one rose in his teeth, tossing the others to the ground, taking her in his arms, and dancing her backwards.

To her amazement, he was rather good at it.

"I learnt to do this at home. In Greifswald it is very popular."

This wasn't going anywhere close to plan; it wasn't even logical. He'd taken her accursed English lessons too much to heart. And he had rhythm. There was a rattling on the landing outside which meant that someone on the ground floor was summoning the lift. That could be Number Three.

Frederick twirled her round and round on her high fluffy stilts, then propelled her sideways.

Freed from his grasp, she lost control, spinning towards the bedroom, her basque unravelling, which made it difficult to plan strategically. She landed on her back on the cushions, dizzy, undressed, and out of breath. He was poised on the edge of the bed, beaming, about to throw himself at her.

She racked her brains for an honourable retreat. Why had she ever taught him to read things as their opposite? She only had herself to blame.

"You remember your lessons, don't you, Frederick?"
"Yes."

His eyes glittered with expectation.

"I want you to fuck me," she said.

He chewed at the inside of his lip, computing this.

"Do you mean it?"

"Er, no, er, yes!" Even she was getting confused. "That's what I mean!"

Nature seemed to waging a war with Frederick's new understanding of her lessons. He wasn't leaving, but on the other hand, he'd paused. She decided to build on this. How could she combine his worst fears with this new language?

"I love you," she cooed.

He shook his head, frowning; his knees remaining on the edge of the bed.

She needed something with more threat, or perhaps more promise. She remembered how she'd lost her most full-blooded, rampant boyfriends: "I want you to marry me, Frederick."

That drove him onto his feet. He backed away, and stood, arms folded, his back to the wall.

"Really?" He was backing off now.

"Er, yes, I hope so." She was trying to reassemble her basque ribbons.

"You want to undo me? Break my heart into pieces?"

"What? Yes. Not exactly." She could hear the lift stopping on their floor. Things were urgent. Deciding to go for broke, she flung herself at him, pawing at his toggles: "I want to have your dear, perfect little babies."

Jake was too busy getting back his breath as he stepped out of the penthouse lift to pay attention to the pale, freckly man who pushed past him into it. It was only later he remembered the man's words as the doors closed:

"She's completely crazy."

Chapter 20

Fiona thought she heard the lift descend. Then the door-bell chimed. The art installation's tango added a lurch of violins. For a second time she threw open the door, not blowing a kiss until she was sure where it was heading.

A young man was standing on the doormat. He had dark curls, green eyes, and a smile that faded when he saw her.

So, this was the real Number Three.

He was rather a dish.

"I do hope you like to tango," she said, a little breathless.

He stepped backwards, not forwards.

Was she too exposed? She hoped that in her haste to be rid of Frederick she had knotted her basque's laces coherently.

"Come in, and make yourself at, er, home..." What name did he go under? She stuffed the laces behind her back. "I'm Fiona."

He was hesitating.

"Fiona," she repeated.

He was peering beyond her, into the apartment where lights were swirling and the crackly recording of 'Adios Muchachos' was persisting. Angie had forgotten to give her his name. Or was it intentional?

"My close friends call me Fidzi."

Fiona tugged at his arm to draw him in, nameless or not;

the muscles were tense.

"Gorgeous. I mean the flat. I hope Angie gave you time to enjoy it." At the mention of Angie he softened and Fiona managed to coax him inside. There was a silence when they entered the room. An uncomfortable one. She waved at the stark furnishings and pointed directly at the red-resined art-work. They didn't seem to be getting anywhere. She had to make a huge effort to propel him towards the sofa under the bay window. "Intimate, yet exclusive," she said. "Sophisti-cated, but tender. Don't you agree?"

He came to an unsteady halt with his back to the sofa, hands pressed together in an attitude of supplication, some-how, glancing around as if he was expecting someone else to be there. Ridiculous – what did he think this was?

"And I would love to know more about you…" She gave him an artful shove that made his knees give way and had him perching on the edge of the sofa. "I'm afraid I don't speak any other language but English. Do you?"

He was shaking his head.

Had Angie's afternoon passed without words being exchanged? Perhaps she didn't know his name either. Could this candidate really have given Angie so much pleasure without saying anything? Was it possible? Ray must be lying about the noisy orgasms. "You can speak, you know."

The young man opened his mouth, but nothing came out. Perhaps he was in awe of her. Yes, that was it. After homely Angie, she must seem exotic. In a show of grace and generosity, she extended him her hand.

He examined it as if he expected mushrooms to sprout.

"I am Angie's better half," she said, putting her hand back at her side. Oh no! Did it sound as if they were lesbians, or offering a ménage a trois? For goodness sake. He had answered the ad. He must know the deal. "But of course, don't feel you have to speak, if you don't want to." She waited for him to make up his mind. If that's what he was doing, he wasn't sharing his thoughts.

"I've heard so much about you from her, I feel I know you already." At least it pointed out that she knew that he knew what he was here for.

He was smiling now, but without mirth. What did he remind her of? A dog. Yes. No, not any old dog – Tiger, her Jack Russell. In a flash of inspiration she remembered his dog-training lessons. Well, all men were animals at heart.

She kicked off her mules, so as to reduce her height a little – breathed in, let her arms hang loose. Then she fixed his gaze with hers, and in a low, calm voice, uttered the simple command:

"Relax!"

He sat his ground rather as Tiger had. She half expected a growl.

She became aware of a length of hose passing the window. What a time for the gardener to be watering the terrace pots! Perhaps that was what was bothering the young man.

She leaned over him and closed the blind behind the sofa.

In the twilight, the sound of spray on leaves was strangely loud. The art installation lent the beat of a drum to the atmosphere. This wasn't helpful. The dog-trainer said that if you didn't have a tail, you had to invent one; that locating it in yourself and others was a basic negotiating procedure. Directing a smile down into the gloom, she smoothed down her outfit, waggled her bottom slightly, then placed herself quickly, and seductively, beside him. Then she tried another simple command:

"Lie down!"

By way of encouragement she lay right back against the cushions, to find them wet. Water was hissing through a crack between window and ceiling, releasing a fine, cool mist. She turned, lifted the blind, tapped at the windowpane, making an urgent 'move along now' gesture to her hidden antagonist somewhere outside.

Still no response from the young man beside her. She was considering putting her feet in the air to show that submission was something they could do together – when he spoke.

"Where's Angie?" he said, making her start. He had a soft voice she hadn't been told about.

"What?"

"I was expecting her to…"

"Oh, Angie's gone. Pfff! She had to go away suddenly."

"But she *is* coming back?"

Stay positive, she told herself. At least he was communicating. "I expect so. But it's not as if we need any lessons from her, do we?"

Angie settled down into her plush front-row seat. Attending the performance was the only way Herr Strimmel was going to allow her to see Mr Aranovitch. The theatre was exquisite – miniature baroque in style, with ornate boxes reaching up in bulging chocolate-cake-tiers each side of her, venerable white heads dotting the balconies, nodding benignly at each other, filling the air with erudite chatter. The tiny stage was fringed with layers of thick burgundy velvet, embroidered with musicians in golden thread. An open, ancient Steinway piano graced one corner. The light dimmed, the audience letting off scurries of restiveness as they rummaged or plumped down into their seats. The hall grew silent.

A single spot lit the stage. A figure with a violin tottered into its radius. He bowed stiffly, acknowledging his audience with a smile, and the instrument. It was Mr Aranovitch. Very slowly, he straightened, and poised over his own shadow.

Jake kept his voice measured and his reactions slow. Clearly, he was in the presence of a madwoman. She was not only dressed in some kind of low-cut straitjacket, but she also made jerky, unnatural gestures and seemed to be having a bizarre, shouty relationship with a water pipe on the other side of the window. She was soaking wet and coming on to him with the most obvious moves in the history of seduction – if that was what she was doing. He tried to move backwards so that she couldn't reach him until he was clear what she was up to.

Why wasn't Angie here?

Had something happened to her?

He wished he hadn't left his phone behind. She might have tried to call him.

On the other hand, she could, perhaps, be hiding somewhere, as a joke. He swivelled round to look into the bedroom. There was no sign of her.

It was hard for Fiona to stay assertive, what with this candidate's truculence, the water cascading against the glass, and the weird creaking noises 'Aspirations' was making. She preferred it when it played the tango. She pressed her face against the window. The nozzle of the hose was pointed straight at her, flooding her vision of a ferret-shaped face, which seemed to be leering at her.

"Switch that off," she yelled at him.

The man outside snarled compliance, before giving her a view of his spectacularly tattooed shoulders as he withdrew the hose She imagined she saw a flash as he turned. Surely it wasn't from a camera? Times might be hard, but gardeners don't generally double as photographers. She returned to the matter in hand.

The candidate was now peering into the bedroom as if he

expected Angie to be hidden there somewhere. The art installation was now adding some piano chords to its score and was projecting arrows onto the walls, pointing in contradictory directions.

"She didn't tell me she'd be away," he said.

"She'll be back for *next* Thursday."

His shoulders drooped.

Fiona felt infuriated that he was more interested in who wasn't there than in who was. "But I'm here – me – Fiona Seta Elena Gregoyan, daughter of a shipping magnate, and granddaughter of a princess – here as planned. Me. I."

Things weren't going well. This wasn't going to relax him. She had to stop waving her arms around and bring her voice down. In her defence, she wasn't used to this sort of carry-on; men normally took more interest in her than this – there was a time when she had to fight them off.

"Now, what would you like?" she asked, more softly. "Coffee? Wine? Something stronger?"

"Planned?"

"Yes! We're all in this together."

She felt overdressed, brittle, hay-feverish. How had Angie netted this, this Adonis? Because, inexplicably, that was what she had done. "Don't worry. Come here." She patted the cushion beside her. It was wet.

"I'd better go," he said.

"No, no. Absolutely not." This was humiliating. If this youth thought he was going to turn up next Thursday and monopolise Angie, he was bloody well mistaken. Fiona tightened her laces, straightened her back. "Because if you leave now, you will never see either of us again."

She was gratified to see that this stopped him in his tracks.

"The deal, you see, would be off."

"Deal?

The art installation's creaking was joined by a groaning,

the piano chords with something that sounded like an iceberg cracking. She would attend to it later.

"When I say we're in this together, we are. One Thursday it's Angie, the next, it's me. That's it. That's what we swore on. We go back a very long time and we never renege on a pact."

This worked. The young man moved towards her. Even 'Aspirations' was rendered silent.

"Was there something about the advert offering two women that you didn't understand?" She was trying to deepen her voice, make it sexier, she hoped. "You know – the ad?"

"Two women?"

The piano was back on the sound system. This time in the form of a badly played duet, or so she decided.

"Yes." Was he simply thick? At least, Frederick could comprehend written English.

The young man was staring at the pyramid of wet cherries she'd placed on the coffee table, as if seeing them for the first time. "Advert? It was my friend who found that."

She was puzzled now.

"He put me up to this." He was muttering now. "His idea of a joke."

Jake was beginning to feel dizzy. How could this woman and Angie possibly be friends? He recalled Angie's great green eyes that showed such interest in his ambition to be a judge, the way she was accident-prone, and giggly. She was delightful, shy, bounteous. She couldn't have anything in common with this unstable harridan. Or could she? Now the woman was even offering a twosome. Deluded or what? Was she on drugs? Were her pupils dilated? It was hard to tell. Her eyes were caked with eye shadow or some such stuff.

Jake wished to hell he'd read Max's advert.

Could Max have misunderstood what was expected here? Now that he thought about it, Max had recently muddled the case notes between Court Four and Court Six resulting in a schoolgirl being accused of armed robbery and a hardened criminal of graffiti in the tube. Could the same have happened here? But even Max would know the difference between one and two women. Could this one possibly be Max's girlfriend? No – Max would have to be on medication to get into a situation with this creature. But, then, he was strapped for cash. Was this a business transaction? Could this dreadful person be paying Max for his services? Was there that much of a shortage of available men? Or was she a sex-starved maniac ready to risk all for a shag? He'd heard it was a diagnosable condition. He was paralysed with indecision. One way or the other, Angie needed his help.

For all his good looks, Fiona didn't like this candidate, desire him or approve of him. He was slow-witted and certainly did not know how to make a woman feel wanted. In fact, he had all the charm of a paperclip. But she had to prove to Angie, herself, and the world that she could have him, in spite of everything, damn him. She changed tack.

"Angie told me she had a wonderful time with you."

He looked even more suspicious. "Did she tell you that?"

She decided to embroider the truth a little: "She says she's longing to see you again, that she's counting the days, hours, minutes and the seconds 'til then."

Aha! This tactic was working where dog training had failed.

She continued this new approach. "But, because we are such bosom chums, she'd *want* you to enjoy yourself..." She pushed him back onto the cushions, turned to the table, tossed a clutch of cherries into the air, opening her lips to catch one as it fell. The others plopped onto the rug around them like goose droppings. Letting her captured fruit dangle from her teeth by its stalk, she leaned over him, savouring the cherry pip with little dabs of her tongue. Keeping her gaze on his, she took her time, withdrawing it into her mouth to do her pièce de résistance – a stone-removing trick she'd learnt on a summer holiday in Georgia. Dispensing with the pip, she discharged the perfectly cored ball onto her finger where it quivered, intact. This she waved under his nose, intending it to promise future delights.

"Et, voila!"

He merely blinked at her gift. "What have you done with her?"

The monster was now doing something with a cherry while fixing him with a funny look. She didn't even notice that cherry juice was oozing down her strait-jacket and onto the carpet, leaving red splodges – or were those marks there before? Had the creature tricked Angie into divulging the liaison and taken her place? How had she disposed of Angie?

Something dropped from the woman's tongue with a ping. It landed on the glass table and stayed there. Could it be the cherry stone, or something more sinister? As he stared at it, his blood curdled; it felt as if it had trouble getting round his body. This person had assassinated Angie. It would explain the strange get-up (she had escaped from a locked ward) and agitated behaviour (she was high from a kill). He'd been on a Criminal Law case recently where the murderer grew excited, licking his lips and enthusing wildly about television cookery programmes when asked about his victims.

Sweat burnt his armpits; his voice stuck in his throat like a cat down a mouse-hole; his heart pounded on his ribs in protest. How far was it to the door?

Now that he thought about it, having a man watering plants right outside the window was strange. It wasn't hot. The gardener could be her accomplice.

No, he couldn't leave. For Angie's sake, he had to be brave. "I want Angie's phone number," he said as firmly as he could.

Angie held her breath as she gazed down at the small figure on the stage. This was no longer the forgetful, doddery, stubborn resident of Vetchling Grove with an anti-social need to hum and wander. Here, inhabiting every inch of his perfectly ironed suit, was a master musician, with long fingers, a ramrod-back, bearing a wise, thoughtful, urbane expression, which seemed to flicker with an awareness of each individual person watching him. But could he really remember how to play? Angie could hardly bear to watch. She narrowed her eyes, when for a second, she thought she caught him winking at her. She forced herself to grin back, her discomfort building. She felt the anticipation tighten around her, as if they were all peering over a precipice.

Then, with the skill, passion and dexterity of a teenager, he plunged his bow into the heart of his violin to summon the first potent notes of Bach's Partita in B minor, hurling them over the cliff edge. The notes tugged, tore at the tight hold she had upon her feelings, until she could keep back tears no longer. She cried because this frail old man in his pool of light had such courage and dignity. She felt consumed with the certainty of her own life ending one day, with no such swansong, the point of her entire existence sinking without trace into a washing-up-bowl of meaningless daily events. She could feel herself sinking into a chasm of depression. An image of Jake swooning in Fiona's expert arms surfaced, provoking her to small sobbing gasps of fury and despair. "Never," she said aloud.

Chapter 21

"Angie's number?" Fiona repeated. Now they were getting somewhere. The candidate might have a scared-rabbit sort of expression, but at least he was asking for something. The only problem was – Angie's phone number was the one thing Fiona couldn't give him. *Do not give the candidates our phone numbers* – rule number nine. If she started breaking one rule, well, the whole lot could go down the pan.

"I suggest we start again, with some alcohol, and see where that gets us."

She had to report some success to Angie. At the very least he wasn't going to go before the time was up. Leaving him perched on the edge of the sofa, she headed for the bedroom and her stock of outfits. She pulled a black cocktail dress with a high collar from her bag. That, and a single string of pearls – sombre, sedate. He seemed to startle easily. Then she scraped back her hair into a white ostrich-feather hair-band, toned her lipstick down to a soft magenta and headed for the kitchen. There, she could have done with Guy's expertise. He could mix a killer cocktail, two sips of which made anyone as legless as a tadpole.

Ray's vintage wine collection was in a chilled, locked cupboard.

Her own champagne, brought along for what she thought

would be a frothy occasion, seemed unequal to the challenge of seducing this candidate. She needed something just short of dynamite. The fridge was bare of anything alcoholic. Where was the bottle Angie should have left for them? *Leave a bottle for next week* – rule number eight.

She climbed onto a bar stool, searched the tins for something to mix into the cocktail. There was cooking sherry, Tabasco sauce, a Drambuie miniature, and something cloudy in a Pimms bottle. She sniffed at it – it seemed all right. The fridge yielded some olives, lemonade, ice. She retrieved two long glasses from the dishwasher. They were frosted with tiny, cavorting, long stick figures, and were grimy, so she ran them under the tap before sloshing a liberal mixture of all the available substances into them. The liquid went a livid green, which she adjusted with a few squeezes of tomato paste. She topped the concoctions with ice, olives, a toothpick and a dusting of Herbes de Provence.

When she returned, the candidate was on his hands and knees peering under the sofa.

"What exactly have you lost?" she asked.

He was red in the face when he straightened up. "Nothing."

She walked over, handed him a glass; the other she downed in one. It tasted like a cheap chilled wine with a fiery grass-clipping sauce that someone had sweated into.

"Wow," she said.

He held his glass at a distance and blinked at it.

"It won't hurt you. Come on, try it."

He took a tiny sip.

She settled back into the sofa and, since he was hardly forthcoming, chose a subject at random.

"I've had husbands who loved me for what I was, or so they claimed, lovers who loved me for what I wasn't, or so they claimed, and a life I've devoted escaping my father and making bespoke hats global. I adore hats."

He was nodding. At least he was listening.

She noticed he was approaching the windowsill with his drink. Perhaps he needed air.

"Of course, Mummy was beautiful; everyone said I looked like her when I was born, which is lucky, since Daddy resembles a bloodhound."

He seemed to wince at the word blood. Probably a vegetarian. Never mind, she told herself.

"Don't imagine for a second that I want you to make love to me. But if you want Angie's number," – that caught his interest – "... you're going to have to work for it."

She rose, and headed for the bedroom, feeling a tad unsteady. The cocktail certainly had a punch to it. She didn't bother to look back to see if he was following.

He was. He came into the room and stood behind her. There was the air of the student about him – a fearful mustiness. What on earth was she going to do with him now?

With a grand gesture, she lifted the bed cover.

"See what I've bought for all of us." She stopped caring that her voice was beginning to slur.

A selection of whips, adjustable handcuffs, wrist-holds, penis-holders, oiled dildos, white-chocolate condoms, electrical ticklers, comic-character vibrators were laid out in decorative rows.

"Toys." She found herself stumbling backwards in her effort to give him time to appreciate the range.

His breathing seemed to accelerate. That must be a good sign.

"Sss's amazing what you can buy over the counter." She couldn't have him thinking they were on prescription, or had come from the Internet.

He bent over the collection for what seemed like ages. Was he adding up carbon emissions? People were obsessed with them. Then he chose one of the boxes, examining it in great detail and read the instructions.

She held her breath. Perhaps he really was interested in the game? This must count as a breakthrough. Perhaps he could think himself into a state of compliance. She stumbled past him, pulling the box free from his grip.

"Yes, yes, and yessss…" She leapt onto the bed, kicked the other aids to the floor and tipped open the box. "Strip-Sssscrabble." Fixing him with as much of a steady gaze as she could muster, she added: "If you win, you get Angie's mobile number."

With a grim determination, he was shaking the bag containing letters.

"But if I win, you –" she added, throwing decorum to the wind, "– will… hic… tell me your bloody name."

Backstage at the Troppen Institute was brimful of music lovers of all ages, clinking glasses and tucking into sausages of one sort or another. Angie had to stand in a long queue to reach Mr Aranovitch who was holding court among a bevy of beautifully dressed mature ladies, one of whose hands he was covering with kisses. There was no sign of his former frailty; he was gleaming with vitality. She could hear snatches of conversations around her in which 'maestro' and 'virtuoso' featured. The queue stretched behind her round the auditorium and out of the street door. More people must have heard of his arrival and come along to the party. She had received her instructions from Mrs Willoughby to bring him home by air, keeping the receipts, but how was she going to entice him out of the building, never mind into a taxi?

"Mr Aranovitch…" She was rehearsing this. "It's time for you to come home. Your daughter will be very worried." If only this were true. There was a daughter in Hove, who had power of attorney and was to be informed in emergencies, but since the day she'd driven him to the Home, tight-lipped, she'd never returned.

"Remember that Thursday night's supper is your favourite fish pie."

A catering minion in a frilly cap and pinny was distracting him with a caviar pastry. Angie sighed defeat, and took one herself.

"There's the summer outing to Kenwood, Mr Aranovitch. You have to tell us if you're coming now, or Edith Tunderwell Walsh wants your ticket." She gazed across the room at him among his coterie of admirers. How could a deckchair under an umbrella on a rainy evening in Hampstead, listening to Tchaikovsky being dampened down, compare with all that he was being offered here?

He was being addressed by a dark-suited young man thrusting an open diary under his nose. She imagined that he would have engagements and events booked up to his funeral by the time she reached him. Was that such a bad thing? She could hear Mrs Willoughby: "This is all very well and good, but what would these foreigners feel if his medically-diagnosed dementia kicked in, and he swore at them with fried egg in his sideburns, while forgetting to go to the toilet?" Mrs Willoughby got most of her ideas from reading awful detective novels.

But Mr Aranovitch seemed perfectly urbane and at his ease.

"Don't be irresponsible, Angela, Doctor Lewis is very worried about him."

Now that she thought about it, Doctor Lewis had diagnosed all the inmates of Vetchling Grove as suffering from Alzheimer's. Could he have other motives than the health of his elderly patients? Mr Aranovitch was as fit as a flea here, now. Could Dr Lewis have medicated him with drugs that made him seem doddery? Was he paid by the drug companies? Or give golf holidays? Or did he simply enjoy a feeling of power?

The crowd around Mr Aranovitch was increasing, the level of debate animated rather than patronising, which was all the Vetchling staff could offer.

"You have to bring him home quickly and discreetly, before he causes any more trouble. Beware of gentlemen of the press. I had to dispose of one only yesterday."

It was too late now; the room was popping with champagne corks and camera flashes.

"Vetchling…"

But if his family had been refugees from the Second World War, surely Germany owed him something? Why couldn't he be given refuge here, in Baden-Baden, if that's what he wanted?

If only he had someone or something he cared about back home, she might be able to reason with him. There was Sid. She imagined taking the goldfish hostage, sending demand notes in his name: 'Come home or Sid gets it!'

Angie found herself with teeth and fists clenched as if doing battle. Was it possible that her afternoon of passion with Jake had completely unhinged her? That it was she, not Mr Aranovitch, who was losing her marbles?

Far away she heard:

"Angela! How are you?"

From a wavy spot in a misty crowd of gabbling, jewel-encrusted ladies, Mr Aranovitch was beaming at her, and was beckoning her over.

Chapter 22

Fiona balanced the Scrabble board on the pillow nearest her, the score pad at his side of the bed, the pencil at hers. In Strip Scrabble you have to get thirty points to claim an item of clothing from the other player.

"You can have the first choice of letters," she said, handing him the bag of tiles.

He grabbed it, shook it very energetically, dug into it, then sighed at his i.

She fished out an x. "Now, we're cooking," she said.

Tossing her pearls behind her, she took out more letters and laid down 'expert' with a flourish.

"Aha," he said, extending it to 'expertise', swinging into the lead.

"No, you don't!" She edged 'slow' into a double word score.

"Damn," he said, missing a turn so as to change all his letters.

She added 'hat' to the w and gained twenty points.

He grimaced, put aside his second i, and added 'ut' to the t, scoring twelve.

Her addition of 'ly' to 'slow' gave a heady 33 points.

"That earns one item of your clothing," she said, triumphant now.

"If that's what it takes..." He handed her one grey sock.

She was on a roll. She won his other sock with 'snog', and his tie with the double letter score the 'g' awarded her. He didn't score very highly with 'love'. Silly man wasting his v on that. By adding a d to his word, she nabbed a triple letter score, winning both his jacket and trousers. She tucked all his clothing under her. With each win she rose higher, feeling more and more comfortable and secure. Okay, she lost her pearls to his 'runaway'. She was a little miffed that he didn't argue, letting her count them as an item of clothing. However, if he scarpered before his time was up, he would have to do so in his boxers.

In a lull, she caught him peering at her phone as if he wanted to read the numbers. Oh, no, he wasn't going to have Angie's number that way. She tucked the mobile well down into her basque lacings and edged closer, wiggling her bottom a bit for effect. He didn't seem to notice, so while he wasn't paying attention she cheated, giving herself nineteen points for sheer perseverance. "I'll have your boxers, thank you," she cooed, holding out her hand in what she thought was an inviting way.

Rather dispassionately, he removed them and handed them to her.

He was naked now, apart from his wrist watch.

In her basque, skirt, stockings and mules, she felt rather overdressed.

"Tum tee tum," she hummed, taking time to fold away his green frog-decorated underwear into her pile of plunder, in what felt like a reversal of a striptease act.

"Try not to crease them," he said. "I was planning to go back to work in them."

"Oh."

Naked or not, he was as romantic as a filing cabinet. Exasperated, she turned he back on him, plumped all his clothes into a cushion, taking care to crease them as much as possible, before sitting on them to gaze pointedly out of the window. She could hear him mutter something to himself as he took a new crop of Scrabble tiles from the bag.

The plants were dripping wet, the air a steaming haze. The gardener was sunning himself on the roof. He was looking at her with interest. At least someone was.

She loosened her laces, pushed one shoulder forward, tossed her head back and peeked at him through half-closed eyelashes.

Behind her, she could hear more muttering as tiles were plonked onto the board. He really was an appalling young man.

The gardener winked at her.

"Nice get up," he said. "Suits you."

He had rather splendid gold fillings and a wicked grin.

"Is it at all possible that you play Scrabble?" she asked, sweetly.

"I could have a go."

With the speed of a reptile, he slid over to the ledge closest to her. He smelt of foliage and tobacco; his arm was rippling with dark hair and muscles, and covered in the most intricate tattoo, of something worm-like. He stuck his head through the window, and whistled.

"Quite a little get-up we have here."

Then, before she could reply, he climbed in, and settled down beside her.

She was gratified that the candidate looked exceedingly put out.

"Don't I know you?" he said very sharply to the gardener.

"Maybe, maybe not. Maybe you know my twin brother. I have a few of them."

"Never mind all that. Since you're here..." Fiona showed the gardener her remaining two o tiles. "Where can I put them?"

The gardener considered this.

"The zoo," shouted the candidate.

Did the man have no manners?

"I don't have a z," she tried to point out.

"You! You were the thief who picked my pocket."

Before she had time to protest, the candidate leapt to his feet, and launched himself at the gardener. She thought she heard a thud of a fist on bone and screamed. The candidate went flying. The gardener let out a low laugh. She tumbled over as they both shoved past her. Clothes and Scrabble letters flew in all directions; the Scrabble board clattered to the floor.

"Come back, you bastard."

The candidate grabbed his boxer shorts before she could stop him.

That wasn't on.

"You can't wear your things back unless you win them."

He wasn't listening.

"You're in this together, aren't you?" he said. "Thieving and hostage-taking."

"Excuse me?"

There was a crash as the gardener hurtled out of the window onto the roof; another as the candidate dived after him, disappearing down a drainpipe.

Thief and hostage-taker? The room went quiet. A breeze from the open window chilled her. So much for plans, rules, games and dog training! The bed looked as if it had been savaged by a pack of hounds. There were fragments of words, stray sexual appliances, batteries, parts of Number Three's suit, a scuffed shoe, feathers, a watch and footprints besmirching Ray's lovely Egyptian cotton. A rout. And, worst of all – she might have to admit defeat to Angie.

She picked up the watch. It was a scratched imitation Rolex

bristling with gadgets. He'd come back for that, surely. Or perhaps this would be something she could salvage from the disaster. She could perhaps say that he'd given it to her as a keepsake. Yes, she liked that idea. He hadn't won Angie's number, so he couldn't contradict her. She fiddled with the dials. The barometer promised rain, it was sixteen degrees, and the time was fifteen thirty-six. She could stop it right there and swear that it had stopped at the climax of their lovemaking. Hmmm, how long had Angie spent with him? She moved on the time to four o'clock, and then threw the watch against the wall. The Perspex cracked, but the watch ticked on.

Chapter 23

Angie regretted not having learnt languages at school. She couldn't seem to make Dr Henkelschneiffer of the Baden-Baden Sanatorium understand that it was Mr Aranovitch who needed help, not her. The psychiatrist was a crisp, self-assured, grey-haired, headmistressy woman, whose English was perfect. However, Angie felt there must be some nuance missing in the doctor's grasp of the situation. For his part, Mr Aranovitch had spoken to the doctor in fluent German, beamed at Angie – "so good of you to come" – and had been allowed to swan off to another musical engagement. And Angie was now trapped in this airless room.

"In this city, we are great admirers of Mr Aranovitch's work," said Dr H.

"He's a marvel," Angie agreed, "but Alzheimer's, or senile dementia, is what our National Health Mental Diseases doctor has diagnosed." She felt she needed as many words as she could summon to keep this woman's penetrating gaze at bay. She wished she had some more to hand. "Is that the same in German? Confusion of mind and incontinence of body." She tried making some whirling motions with both arms.

Dr Henkelschneiffer showed no clarity deficit. "I have observed no signs of confusion in the behavior of Mr

Aranovitch." Her blue eyes glittered behind tinted lenses as she followed Angie's movements. "However, there are disturbing signs of mental fragmentation in one or two of his associates."

"I'm sorry, I may not seem to be making much sense, but I haven't had much sleep," Angie tried explaining.

"I see." The doctor took a pad from the desk. "How long have you had trouble sleeping?" Her pen was poised.

"I haven't been in my own bed recently and…" Angie became unnerved by Doctor's H's note taking. "I'm just a little disorientated, tired, in need of a bath and some home cooking. I'm sure Dusty's missed her trombone lesson and the gerbils haven't been fed. There's some lasagne at home I know will go to waste unless I…" She grew conscious of the damp patches under her armpits. "I apologise if I'm a bit whiffy."

The doctor peered at her, hmmmed, the ballpoint moving continuously. "What medication are you using at the moment?"

"Er, none, I mean…" Under this scrutiny, Angie found she couldn't stop talking. "I'm terribly sorry if you feel I have in any way insulted Mr Aranovitch, or the city's admiration of him." Angie tried shrugging with what she hoped was nonchalance.

The doctor was still writing, occasionally raising her eyes to look at Angie as if she was developing a rash.

Angie wished she would stop. "I'm sure I've…" She was waving her arms again. They were hard to reclaim. "…Totally failed in my duties here, so perhaps we can forget all about him, and…" She made a supreme effort to stop gabbling, took a breath, sat on her hands, and tried to stick to the point. "Look, I can phone the Home and leave the matter between you and them." She fancied she could hear the blood coursing in the doctor's veins like ice clinking into a glass. A bird chirruped just out of view and somewhere someone coughed.

"What exactly is your role in what you call this 'home'?" asked the doctor, finally.

This was terrible. Angie could tell by her emphasis that she thought it was Angie who was the inmate of an institution, not the old man. She tried clawing her nails into the steel of her chair to prove she wasn't dreaming.

This was noted down.

"Look, I love Mr Aranovitch too." A vision of Jake intruded into her thoughts. She pushed him away, forcefully. "Deeply, truly, fully and completely."

The doctor frowned, hummed a slight tune, then enunciated her words carefully. "In my professional opinion, you appear to be suffering from Wernicke's Aphasia. Is that the same in English?"

"Sorry?"

"This particular aphasia is named after Dr Wernicke."

Was this a German bedtime drink?

"The condition is caused by pressure on the temporal lobes of the brain. It gives the compulsion to utter random word sequences." The doctor put down her pen. "And, what is worse, an unreasonable belief that they make sense. You may find this difficult to follow?"

Angie nodded her head furiously, then decided that was the wrong response, so she shook it just as energetically.

"I think we need to run some tests."

"I'm perfectly alright, it's Mr Aranovitch who…" Angie gave up fighting for her ward. "Call my husband, he's a doctor. Please." She rummaged for her phone, found it and threw it onto the table. "He's under T."

The psychiatrist moved the phone across her desk with her fingertip as if it was a murder weapon and placed it in a plastic bag from the drawer in her desk. Then she smoothed a fresh piece of paper onto her clipboard, snapping down the metal clip with a firmness that rattled the windowpanes, and said:

"Just answer one or two simple questions. Which continent is the Sahara Desert in?"

Really, Angie thought. This is getting ridiculous.

Doctor Henkelschneiffer's gaze was unrelenting.

"Africa."

"Tell me the name of the late Princess Diana's mother."

"What?" Was the doctor mad?

"Do you or do you not know the name of the late Princess Diana's mother?"

"You mean the stepmother?"

"Answer the question please."

Angie felt all her resistance drain out of her. "Er, no, not offhand."

"Offhand." The doctor noted this down. "Tell me the name of the President of the European Commission."

Angie racked her brains. Nothing happened. "Oh, dear. Does it begin with a P? No? M? No, no an S. Yes, that must be it." She could see this dithering proved her horribly in line with the diabolical diagnosis the doctor was pursuing.

"You say you have a husband?"

"'I'm not just saying I have one. I have one."

"And what is his middle name?"

"Er…" Ted's middle name was Wally after his grandfather. Angie stared back at the doctor, and kept her mouth shut. There was no way she was going to give Dr Henkelschneiffer that piece of ammunition.

"He hasn't got one."

Dr H pursed her lips, then examined the fingertips of her left hand.

Just as Fiona was giving up on him, the candidate re-appeared at the window. He vaulted back into the room, gathering his shirt, suit and tie together before she could argue. His eyelid was swollen, his right knuckles looked bloody, and he was angry.

"If you don't let me speak to Angie in person, I'm calling the police," he said, tying up his shoelaces with a grim air.

"How dare you threaten me." She put her pearl necklace back around her neck.

He picked up what looked like a telephone, and tried dialling nine nine nine. This merely restimulated the art installation. Its projectors introduced rolling dunes into the debate; a camel strode across the bedroom wall in the direction of the bathroom, and a lady sang something soulful in an unrecognisable language. He scowled at the receiver, determined to turn it into an ordinary phone by sheer indignation, undeterred by the desert caravan passing over his ruffled shirt.

She couldn't help herself. She relented.

She pressed *Angie* on her options button, and handed it to him.

Dr Henkelschneiffer reached for her office telephone.

"With your permission, we shall ring this person you call your husband," she said.

At that moment Angie's mobile tinkled.

The doctor unzipped the plastic bag, opened up the phone.

"Doctor Henkelschneiffer, hello?" She puckered her lips into a disapproving o as she listened to the other voice.

Angie tried to protest. Wasn't this a breach of some vital human right? It was her phone call, wasn't it? But then she had doubts and closed her mouth. She was having doubts about everything. That wasn't good in these circumstances.

"She is here, of course." The Doctor was speaking slowly. "No. We are investigating her state of mind, so I will not comment. Are you her husband? No? Who are you?"

Angie found herself having trouble breathing as the psychiatrist wrote a name onto her questionnaire.

"Is that spelt with a D or a J?"

"Can I take my own call, please?" It was extremely humiliating to have to beg for something you thought you owned.

Doctor H behaved as if Angie no longer existed, and continued speaking into the mouthpiece: "I see, Herr Bollard. But, as you are not a member of her family, I…"

Angie could bear it no longer. She lunged at the doctor, knocking her sideways to wrench the mobile from her grasp. It didn't seem to surprise the doctor; she merely brushed herself down.

"Jake, Jake…"

"Angie, is that you?"

"Yes, yes."

"Are you okay?"

She took a quick peek at the doctor who was seating herself back behind her desk. "I'm fine. Absolutely fine."

"Thank God."

"I just have some questions to answer before I can get away."

"Get away from what?"

She couldn't go into it. "Don't worry. How are you?" she asked.

Her heart was beating too loudly to hear his reply. Conscious of the doctor rapping her fingers on her desk, she pressed the phone to her ear. "Is Fiona there with you?"

"Yes, she's here," he said.

This was very awkward. She took a couple of deep breaths. "Did you find the bottle of wine I left for you? It was recommended in the *Observer.* I hope you're having a lovely time..."

Not wanting to say anything more revealing in front of Dr Henkelschneiffer, she cradled the phone at her ear and returned to her seat.

The doctor seemed to lose patience finally.

"Who won last year's Eurovision song contest?" she barked.

Fiona was beginning to feel a little more at ease. She'd managed to win the Scrabble game, close the window and discover the candidate's name. He'd shouted it down the phone.

Jake.

This was a huge step forward, but now he was yelling into the receiver as if his life depended on it.

"Austria," he was shouting.

It didn't make much sense to Fiona. Or was that where he and Angie were planning to meet?

"Rise like a Phoenix."

Was he speaking in code? Had he and Angie made up a language of their own?

"When can I see you again?"

He was staring down at the phone with a very worried expression. Angie must have rung off. Fiona grabbed her phone back from this Jake before he could memorise the number. She decided to give up trying to understand him. Simply getting him to understand her was challenging enough.

"Do you believe me now?" she said. "She's perfectly alive and well."

What on earth was the matter now? He was staring at her in a new catlike way.

"Where is she?"

"How should I know?"

"Aren't you close?"

"Thick as thieves."

"She sounds as if she's in trouble."

"Nonsense." Angie always took precautions. "She's too old for that sort of thing."

Pipes whistled while he made a mess of his tie. He seemed to shudder. "Will you let me see her?"

"Yes. Next Thursday."

He brightened.

"But only if…"

"Only if what?…"

"…you promise me you'll tell her we got on."

"Got on. Us? But…"

She stared at him long and hard and let time pass.

"When I see her…?"

"Hand on heart."

"Here?"

"Where else?"

He struggled into his coat.

"You're sure? Next Thursday?"

"Only if you promise."

He sighed. "If you insist."

"I insist."

He nodded, then turned and ran out, his coat flapping.

She listened to the lift announce its arrival on the landing, humming as it took Jake down to street level. He would be back for Angie, all right, but she feared the only way he would come back for her was if someone drugged or dragged him.

Usually, Jake loved the spring. It reminded him of his first foster home, a city farm with ducks and baby chicks and an old dog that snored on the tiles outside his window. He always thought of it when the sun shone. Damn! Nearly four thirty. Felt like he'd been in there for a century. He had to get his skates on. He had to hope, no, believe he would see Angie again.

But what about after that? Supposing this madwoman was a close friend of hers? How could he disentangle the one from the other? Did they go together like paper and glue?

The solution came to him as he helped a blind man onto the C11 bus.

He was going to have to find a replacement for himself on his next afternoon with Fiona.

The bus drove off. Did the blind man say Hackney? The bus was going to Hendon. Jake watched it disappear around a bend in the road. Oh well! There must be old folks in Hendon as well.

But who could he palm Fiona off onto? He couldn't imagine Max coping with hearing about her, never mind the real thing. Who else? Who could be persuaded that a staring-eyed, domineering woman with strange equipment and a frightening taste in underwear was a catch?

He reached the Law Courts just as the gates were closing behind the figures of the expert witness, who was struggling to carry all the books and files, and Max. Max, though empty-handed, still seemed to have trouble managing his own coat and umbrella.

"Bollard," called the doctor. "What took you so long? How was Paris?"

Chapter 24

Rain was falling; it was a long queue for taxis. Angie was feeling cold, damp and defeated. Mr Aranovitch was still in Baden-Baden. She had failed.

Still, at least she had managed to get back to Heathrow with her marbles intact. No mean feat. It was so lucky that Jake had called. And it was nothing short of miraculous that he knew the winner of the Eurovision song contest! How did he do that? Is that what law students did in their bed-sits – watch song contests?

She shuffled forward in line, behind a group of women in burkas, who were enjoying a private joke.

What if Ted had called instead? He wouldn't have known the answers to Doctor Henkelschneiffer's questions. He could have spoken medicalese to her, of course. They could have blinded each other with science. But then, he special-ised in analysing FSH levels and DNA abnormalities, and Dr H in defining Wernicke's Aphasia, whatever that was. They would have been at cross-purposes. And Angie would now be a small barred room, heavily sedated, no question.

Jake was heaven-sent. The one thing she wanted more than anything else – well, after a hot bath, clean clothes, kisses from her kids and a gesture of recognition from Ted – was to see him again.

She watched the darkly clad ladies squeeze into two taxis, only their eyes showing. They were still laughing. It might be at her.

Fiona could hear Ray and Guy still downstairs. Their voices drifted up to her with the smell of caramelising sugar. It sounded like they were arguing. Probably about money. Let them. She wiped mist from her study window and looked out over the wires and roofs. The sun had very little day left in it. The river was down to its muddy greys; clouds promised nothing but drizzle. She felt terrible. Had that Jake candidate unnerved her? Or was Angie not the same sweet friend she once tormented? They didn't seem to be friends now; they were rivals. Seagulls wheeled past, calling.

There was always Frederick.

But she'd tossed all the other candidates' details in the bin, so how would she contact him?

He came from Greifswald, he said.

She scanned the top shelf for the big Atlas, took it down, shook it free of crumbs and nail files and found the Baltic. Greifswald was a small city on the very edge of page 52. Where did that get her? Should she fly there and ask for him? That was ridiculous. She might know his first name, but not his surname. From now on she was going to demand everyone's full names and write them down. You never knew when you would need them.

She caught herself in her mirror looking pale, strained. And that wrinkle on the side of her nose? Was it new? She needed something to lift her face and her spirits. A new hat. Yes! A Frederick-memorial hat!

She tipped open her home remnants box onto the work-table and picked some out some possible fabrics. Then she unrolled her tools from their canvas holder and laid them out in order. Scissors, staple gun, box cutter, darning needle, glue.

Now, what did she know about him? Was he Russian? Or German? She tried to remember her one and only trip to Germany. It was to Munich for a strange tie-cutting festival. She chose green felt, shaped it into a peak. She remembered a lot of beer being drunk and every meal was accompanied by cabbage. She gathered lime green taffeta around the olive green peak, and tacked it into place. It looked a little barren. She added a pheasant feather.

A memorial to dear Frederick. A sweet-natured, rather direct man. He still could be. But what was memorable about him? She fished in her tall sweet jar and pulled out five wooden toggles of varying shapes and colours.

She attached them loosely along the brim where they could dangle.

Apart from his toggles, did he have any defining feature?

His astonishing sense of rhythm, of course. And his philosophical mind.

She searched the top bookshelf for something suitable and found Great Minds of the Ages – the Reader's Digest edition. Leather-bound. Daddy had given her the series for her last birthday – along with a DVD of the trooping of the colour. Some business associate must have given both to him. Right! She needed something savvy. With a distinguished title. Aha! Thus Spake Zarathustra. Using her box cutter she cut out the pages. Then she stuck strips of cardboard to the remaining frayed edges so that the book was now a hollowed out, leather-bound container. Reaching up, she took down her miniature musical box decorated with trees She glued it down into the hollow, and wound it up, attaching the winding key to the book cover with a thread so that when you opened the book, the music played. She stitched the whole edifice onto the crown of the felt hat and admired her creation

– a green felt hat adorned with green cabbage-like taffeta, toggles, and feather upon which a leather-bound copy of Thus Spake Zarathustra stood. And when you tried to read the work, you heard, instead, 'The Teddy Bears' Picnic'.

The Cock and Bull was its usual, end-of-day scrum; clerks of the court, judges, barristers, legal secretaries elbowed each other for a place at the bar; the bar staff were a blur of swinging arms and hands. The till jangled, money changed hands; cases were won and lost, pleas bargained, mitigations negotiated, all by faces glowing above foaming beer, white wine or the deeper tones of blood-red claret. Jake handed the doctor his pint, and squeezed in beside him.

Max was hovering nearby, slurping at his lager, pausing only to bellow at a near miss in the football match on the TV.

"Max," shouted Jake above the noise, "be great if you could go and get some dry-roasted peanuts…" He pulled out the twenty-pound note that he'd earned at the off-licence.

"Right." Max banged down his glass, spraying both of them, seized the note and began shoving his way towards the bar.

"How did you do?" asked the doctor.

Jake tried to remember what his excuse for the lost hours had been. He could summon nothing but a vision of that mad woman's crazed laugh and the array of threatening equipment she'd laid out on the bed.

"Time-consuming?" persisted the doctor.

"Er, yes, quite."

"The things you have to do to get ahead."

Jake was touched that the doctor seemed to know what he was going through. He must be used to dealing with women; he was an expert on sperm. and married. Jake took a deep breath. "Look…" he began, then his nerve faltered.

"Yes?"

"Thing is…" Jake sensed there'd be no going back after this.

"What's the matter?"

"I've got this situation…" Jake stared ahead at Max who was now behind the bar pointing at the highest nut packets. The barmaid was unfolding some steps.

"A woman?"

"Two."

"Two women?" The doctor looked genuinely concerned.

"A blind-date-twosome." This was awkward.

The doctor toasted the air as if they were member of the same conspiracy. "Here's to the free and single life."

"I, er, thought since you…" Jake realised he was whispering, "…are happily married, you could give me some advice."

The doctor laughed. "I know less about my wife now than I did twenty years ago."

"The threesome's their idea."

"No wonder you're off in the afternoons."

"You see, I fancy one of the women, but not the other." His thoughts were snarling up into a rush hour; none of them getting anywhere. "And I don't know how to…"

Max was now climbing the stepladder. The barmaid had her back to him, while attending to the other customers.

"What are they like, these women?"

"Oh, one's really kinky…"

"Kinky?" The doctor's eyes were gleaming strangely. "A mature woman? Well-endowed?"

To Jake, Fiona was a heady whirl of threatening actions. "I reckon."

The doctor leaned in close.

"You want me to distract the other one, keep her occupied?"

"The other one's normal."

"Normal? Boring! We've all had too much of that."

Jake remembered the pets at Barnardos – all normal, supposedly, the rescue-hedgehog and a three-legged kitten. "No, well, I haven't."

"You want me to take care of the normal one?" The doctor looked suspicious.

"No, no, it's the kinky one I want to sort-of sublet."

"How much is all this? Fifty quid? A hundred?"

"What? No, no, nothing like that."

The crowd was parting. Max was weaving back towards them.

"It's just that she may be unpredictable, erratic, deranged even." It was a relief to get that off his chest. "I thought you could, maybe, talk to her?"

Max arrived with a heave-ho, throwing assorted packets of nuts onto the table. He swooped to grab a stool, ignored the protests of its former occupant, shoved it between Jake and the doctor and sat on it. "Useless fucking barmaid "

Jake yearned to thump him.

The coat hooks were empty of hats and scarves; the boot rail was boot-free; Einstein bolted away out of the cat flap as if she was a stranger.

"Yoo hoo! I'm home," Angie shouted.

There was no reply.

In the kitchen she was amazed to find the surfaces gleaming. Even the dishwasher was clear, and smelt of the sea. A vase of white roses sat in the middle of the breakfast table, their petals tightly closed. She raced up the stairs, still calling: "Ted!… Alex!… Dusty!"

Both kids' beds were tightly made; their rooms arranged

as if for a photo-shoot. She stopped at her bedroom door listened, before entering.

The only disturbance to the clear lines of a professionally cleaned hotel room was the document title – *Property Disputes of the Twenty-First Century* – which lay on Ted's bedside table, along with his reading glasses. The books and magazines that usually lay scattered at her side of the bed were gone.

Was Dr Henkelschneiffer right?

Was she imagining she lived here?

Could there be pressure on the temporal lobes of her brain after all? She grabbed the phone, dialled Ted's mobile. It told her he was unavailable and gave his office number. She scanned the room for anything she could call her own. The only thing th at lay untouched and unwashed was her hairbrush, choked with strands of her hair. She disentangled them from the brush, wound them around her little finger.

This was real. Jake had touched her hair. Jake was the last real person to come close to her. Could she allow herself one short call to find out…? Find out what exactly? That she needed him?

By now, Fiona probably had his number.

"Fiona?"

"Where the hell are you?"

"Home."

"And how is Rudolfo?"

"Who?"

"Your daughter said you were in Germany with some old guy. You can't fool me. I know who it was."

Rudolfo, the enormous opera singer. How ridiculous! Just like Fiona to think this. "It was work."

"Hmmm."

Where did this new clipped tone come from? "Sorry, can't you talk?"

"I can talk."

Angie took a huge breath. It did nothing to calm her nerves. Her throat was dry. "How did your afternoon with Jake go?"

There was silence at the other end.

"You did have your afternoon with him, didn't you?"

"Yes, it lasted exactly two hours and thirty-five minutes," said the unfamiliar peeved voice.

"And?" This was like drawing squeals from a pork chop. Something in the vicinity of her heart was hurting. "How did the two hours and thirty-five minutes go?"

"Very nicely, thank you."

"That's grand."

Angie didn't register putting the phone down. The conversation must have ended somehow; otherwise she wouldn't be standing in front of her chest of drawers wondering if her clothes were still where she'd left them.

Ted found himself smiling on the tube home from the Cock and Bull; he hadn't felt this chipper since taking over the captaincy of the Medical Stumps cricket team, and winning against a team of surgeons, the Nips and Tucks. He should do a bit of work on assessing the relevance of dehydroepiandrosterone in IVF success levels; the file was in the top of his briefcase; he kept it closed and looked around.

The carriage was very crowded. He moved sideways a little to allow the young woman next to him more room. She had the big eyes, full bust and air of helplessness he always looked for in a woman. But she was rummaging in her huge bag for something. And rummaging infuriated him. Angie did it all the time. She was always losing things. The woman finally came up with a broken box of perfume samples, oozing smells.

Ted knew she was going to have to look all over again for a tissue, so he handed her his packet. She took it, nodding as if she had a right to it, without thanking him.

With Angie away, there been none of this gritted-teeth waiting while she hunted for keys, an address, money. He'd had rather a good time at court, and in the pub, and at home doing a spot of tidying up. He thought of the young barrister – Bollard – polite, gentle, and clueless. He reminded him of himself, a few years back. The rummaging woman was looking at him strangely. He realised he was grinning. Was that woman Bollard mentioned really kinky? And voracious? Hard to believe. The poor female was probably merely insecure, needing to feel better about herself.

Of course, he'd do what he could to help. He'd be more than happy to. After all, he'd always tried to support Angie – colour-coordinating her clothes, giving her driving lessons, dropping her off at keep-fit classes, teaching her bridge, checking her blood pressure after every spat with Mrs Willoughby. Though, somehow, she never seemed to notice his efforts.

Angie was supposed to be back today. He sighed. He hoped she'd notice all the pains he'd taken to get the house back into order? A new leaf. There was a new outbreak of rummaging next to him; he almost missed his stop.

Fiona tacked the last toggle into place on the Frederick hat. It looked great.

"See you later."

From downstairs.

"Bye, doll."

The door slammed downstairs. Had Guy and Ray both gone?

Never mind. She checked the hat for loose pins and stray threads before putting it on her head. The green clashed with her pale skin; the shredded taffeta looking as if sauerkraut had been tossed liberally over her head; *Thus Spake Zarathustra* opened out heavenwards, and 'Teddy Bears Picnic' tinkled, the toggles moving in a sequence, as she shook her head. Splendid. *Frederick* suited her.

Chapter 25

Derek checked the address on the card, then looked up at the gilded number 9 welded into the closed golden gates. They were crafted in the shape of waves, with great shipping liners cresting them. On each side of them was a bronze dolphin with a golden bell in its mouth.

"Must be worth a bob or two."

He glanced up, counted four surveillance cameras and doffed his cap at the nearest. The paved road led through a yawning avenue of yew trees to a gabled mansion. He gauged the height of the railings protecting it – six feet, each ending in a razor-sharp spear pointing at the leaden sky.

"Probably poison-tipped. There are other ways in but over the top of the gate, Derek, old man."

Donning his leather gloves, he pressed the bell, which chimed.

He didn't have to say anything. The gates unfolded, then closed soundlessly behind him. Checking that the file of photos were nice and secure in his jacket pocket, he strode up the drive. And kept on walking. The mansion just didn't get any closer. It was weird. After what seemed like weeks, he found himself in a maze of hedges. He was dusty, sore, thirsty, but he kept on going. There was no sign of the mansion now; there was a bench. He sat on it, breathless, rattled and rested his head in his hands. He heard a swish, looked up and found himself blinking at the shrill nose, hooded eyes, tracing-paper skin of Elijah bloody Gregoyan.

The daffodils on the mantelpiece had long since shrivelled to yellow paper exclamation marks. And rain smeared any vision of the outside world behind Mrs Willoughby's tight curls.

"But he's happier in Baden-Baden," insisted Angie, shivering. They'd switched off the heating as they did every May, never mind the temperature. She suspected this was a policy designed to kill off the older inhabitants, the administration's equivalent of a clearance sale.

Mrs Willoughby didn't appear to be chilled; she was pink with irritation, Mr Aranovitch's file in front of her. She was silent while wiping her brow with a lace hanky.

"I couldn't exactly bag him and throw him into the hold of a budget airline." Angie had only been given the money for a cheap ticket after all.

"Hrumph."

Angie sneezed, rummaged in her pockets for a tissue, and came up with Mr Aranovitch's unused air ticket. Not quite knowing what to do with it, she placed it on top of the file. "Perhaps we should accept that he isn't coming back to Vetchling."

Mrs Willoughby glared at the curled airline ticket as if touching it would make her complicit in Mr Aranovitch's continuing absence. "We will be doing nothing of the sort. We have a duty of care. A duty entrusted to us by his daughter, who I may remind you, holds enduring power of attorney."

"But he's happier..."

Mrs Willoughby silenced her with a look.

Why couldn't they both simply accept the wishes of Mr. Aranovitch? After all, they had both been sent on several weeklong training programmes, which drummed into them that their custodianship of these frail people at the end of their lives was only temporary, and they had to learn to let go. Anyway, if she was to see Jake at two, she had to get going. "Then, maybe his daughter could visit him in Baden-Baden."

"She will be doing no such thing. We cannot alert her to his disappearance until we establish Mr Aranovitch's status and permanent residence. We have a waiting list this high," she tapped a dusty box file, "waiting for his room. I had hoped you would have the training and wit to realise that the ravings of a man with senile dementia are not to be taken as the truth."

Angie edged towards the door while Mrs Willoughby extended her monologue to include the German nation in general, the errors of psychoanalysis in particular and the effects of dehydration on the mentally infirm. She'd just finished a murder mystery where the crimes were the result of the perpetrator's inattention to a plentiful daily intake of water. She concluded with the observation that although most of the faces on the group photograph above the mantelpiece were now sadly no longer a living part of the group, they, at least, were properly accounted for. She preferred her wards to be released from her care feet first – that paperwork was already prepared.

Angie squinted at Mrs Willoughby's desk clock – nearly one-thirty. She felt feverish. Her heart began to flutter. Would Jake turn up? Fiona might have devoured him, frayed cuffs and all. Angie chewed at her index finger nail, and then moved onto her middle finger, savaging it. After her time with Dr Henkelschneiffer, uncertainty about everything was consuming her. Even Ted was unpredictable; he'd taken to dry-cleaning the oven-gloves. "Why don't you fly over and talk to the psychiatrist? You'd be so much better at it than me."

"I may very well have to." Mrs W's drone slowed down to Sunday Service.

"Some of the residents are demanding I arrange a coach party to Baden-Baden. They've written to Head Office. Mr Aranovitch has been ringing his old bridge companions, telling them stories, inflaming their passions. I am now, of course, screening his calls, but…"

Angie decided it was now or never. She clutched at her stomach. "Oh dear," she said. "I've got a…" With her other hand she pointed at her lower belly in a way that she hoped covered all her female organs. That way, she wasn't lying, altogether.

Mrs Willoughby gave a look, which froze Sid in his turn around the tank.

Angie moved to the door. "It can't wait. Sorry." She grabbed her coat and ran.

Fiona was in her shop with her phone off and the blinds down. Angie was due back according to Mrs Wrinkleberger or something and she might arrive any moment demanding a heart-to-heart before meeting Jake. The doorbell chimed. Damn, was that her? Rain and misted up windows blurred her view of the street. She crouched down behind the counter. It chimed again. And again. It wasn't like Angie to be so insistent. She wiped a corner of window. The torso of a large man protruded from a dripping umbrella. There was something about his tummy that looked familiar. He rang again and knocked on the glass, bellowing, "Fiona," in a baritone she recognised.

She let him in.

"At last, the right..." He sent a spray of water into the room as he stamped and pumped his umbrella. "...Hat shop."

"Rudolfo."

"My dear..." He levered himself down onto her chair and beamed at her, a beatific, wet, round face. "Our adventure with the fishes was so exquisite, you disappeared so dramatically, leaving your sweet, lost perfume simmering so eternally in my heart, that I swore to the gods, my mother, and my personal assistant, Brian, that I would not rest until I could find you again to conclude my song."

She remembered the endless warbling in the aquarium. "Could the singing possibly wait?"

"Certainly. What would you like Rudolfo Miranda to wait for?"

Angie sneezed all the way to Ray's apartment block in the seeping rain, barked hoarsely at the porter, then coughed all the way up in the lift. She heard the BBC announce the two o' clock news from the neighbour's flat before she turned the bend on the seventh floor and found Jake standing on Ray's ethnic doormat; he was also blowing his nose.

"Are you alright?"

"I was going to ask you same thing."

Flustered, she fumbled with the key.

Jake took charge of the lock.

"After you," she said.

She was glad he went on ahead of her, into the flat; the blood behind her cheeks bubbled like lava. He waited for her to sit down. She couldn't bear to repeat anything that he could have done with Fiona, so she kept on standing. And so did he. The lights dimmed; birdsong played on the speakers.

"I've brought you a present." He took a CD from his

inside pocket. "This is what won the Eurovision."

She took it, touched.

"I thought, maybe, we could listen to it together." Was it her imagination or was he shy?

There was the face of the bearded lady.

"You shouldn't have."

He looked around for a way to play it.

She went over to the art installation, searching for a CD player in the confusion of controls. Aha, there was one. She switched a knob from Auto to CD and inserted the disc. The electric lights went off. Only daylight lit the room.

"*Go about your business. Act as if you're free…*"

Tentatively, she perched on the edge of the sofa. He placed himself next to her and looked at her expectantly. She didn't want to bring up the thorny matter of Fiona, so she didn't. He looked as pale as she felt. The miracle was that they were here together. They both sneezed. She felt a flood of warmth towards him.

"Do you need anything?"

He began to cough. It was a tired dry bark that spoke of late nights and pot noodles. "Maybe a hot drink?"

"I'll see if there are any lemons."

She made for the kitchen; he followed. She opened the spice rack, he the fridge, colliding as they bent. They apologised simultaneously, then separated again. She found three lemons; he found a honey pot. Her spoon met his knife. Both of them were sweating. She had never heard of lovers sharing viruses, wasn't sure what to do – should they head for the bedroom or stay at arm's length?

The art installation projected slow-moving molecular globules onto the walls; she thought she recognised the smell of eucalyptus in the air-conditioning. It soothed her throat. Even the animals in the zoo below were coughing.

She led the way back to the sofa, both of them carrying

hot toddies.

"What about going to bed?" he said.

She nodded. They went into the bedroom and lay down, side-by-side, quiet and companionable, sniffing and sipping in turns. A train whistled from the direction of Paddington, a steamy damp sort of a whistle, and in the kitchen something clicked.

"What did you do today?"

"Oh, help my team. We're defending a plaintiff's property rights."

She searched for his foot with hers. Both of them were wearing socks. "Where's the property?"

"It's everywhere and nowhere. That's what makes its rights so difficult to apportion."

"Sounds like a game," she said, plumping up the pillow.

"A game?" He disengaged his feet, sat up, looked alarmed. "What sort of a game?"

Chapter 26

Fiona arranged the full coffee pot, milk jug, sugar, spoons and cups on a tray in front of Rudolfo.

He took her hand and squeezed it in a rather old-fashioned way. "I have brought us little somethings." He let go of her hand to dig deep into his raincoat. "From Demels in Vienna. *Et voila.*" Producing a cardboard box, he opened it to reveal two miniature worlds nestling in tissue paper.

"*Sachertort,*" he said.

One of the cakes had a tiny fairy tale castle on its top, with small faces at the chocolate windows. The other was a miniature orange grove built on chocolate earth complete with tiny marzipan gardeners. They were exquisite.

"Choose one."

She hoped he would give her both and pointed at the orange grove.

Rudolfo beamed his approval, and poured out coffee. Then he lifted the castle and bit into it, tiny faces disappearing in one fell swoop. "A rhapsody."

A tiny bit dismayed, she held tightly onto the orange grove.

He lifted the remains of his castle, and swallowed it whole, washing it down with his coffee. "To enjoy things deeply and fully, you should never hold back."

The orange grove was so pretty, she didn't want to bite into it.

Rudolfo gazed at her for a moment.

"Close your eyes," he suggested.

She kept them wide open.

"Come come, don't be afraid."

How could he possibly know about her fearfulness? Did it show?

He was wiping his full lips with a voluminous piece of silk cloth. "You know much more about everything when you relax. The fount of all knowledge is here…" He pounded his chest with his fist. "In your heart."

"More coffee?"

"No, no. Listen to me. You can't keep the world away by staring at it. Close your eyes. Listen instead. With this." He put his right fingertips against the beating of her heart. "That knows everything. Life. Music."

She peeked at him through half-closed eyes.

"I'll prove it to you by singing one single note, and, because you have music in your heart, you will tell me the key."

Her piano lessons at school had ended with Daddy's suspension of the music teacher. "I'd rather listen to the cries of a butchered goat than you playing that instrument." She told herself to relax; this time she closed her eyes fully.

There was a deep resonant warble that warmed her left ear for a few moments, tickling it with countless vibrations, before disappearing somewhere in the direction of a pile of folded headscarves.

"Well?"

She guessed wildly. "What about B flat?"

"No."

"F, then, er, minor?"

"Listen again."

All this attention was very gratifying. She screwed up her nose.

His warbling vibrated inside her head.

"D sharp?"

"Perfectissimo."

"Goodness."

"You were born to enjoy life."

He was so gloriously pompous. She giggled, keeping her eyes firmly shut, when a tinny, jangling intruded into the room. It was coming from the direction of her coat, which was slumped over the back of her chair. Damn – she thought she'd switched it off. She opened her eyes, reached over, rummaged, snapped open her phone.

"I'll talk to you later," she said into the phone.

"Elena!"

"Daddy?"

"I am outside," he barked. "Let me in."

She looked up at the window. He was there under the awning.

Rudolfo gently took the mobile from her, dropped it back into her coat pocket.

"What's the matter?" he asked.

She rushed around, wildly pulling berets from shelves until finding one to fit him. It was pink. She drew it down hard over his tight curls. "Pretend to be buying this." Without waiting for a reply, she raced to the door, snapped open the lock.

"Closed for business at two-forty-five? Is there a curfew?" Daddy handed her his open umbrella, passing into the shop without a word. She tugged at the dripping spokes and swore, staring at the bus stop, and realised from the digital information board that it was a quarter to three. Angie would be enjoying Jake's attentions by now. She could just see them, beautifully lit and sculpturally conjoined, chiming together, Ray's tamed finches flocking to their window to peck at his croissant crumbs and trill. Damn them. She sighed and followed Daddy who was heading towards Rudolfo without appearing to see him.

"Oh, Daddy, this is Rudolfo Miranda. You must have heard him sing *La Traviata*, or *Don Giovanni*, or Pinkerton in..."

Daddy didn't seem to hear her.

"And he's buying a beret, woven from merino wool. It's winter in Argentina right now, you know."

She pulled out a chair. Her father had already found her wrought-iron one, and was wiping it with a handkerchief so white it dulled all the hats in the room. All her school shirts had stood out like that, making it so difficult to mingle. Then he sat down, and folded his handkerchief back along its fault lines.

"I wondered if we would ever meet again," said Rudolfo, quietly.

Daddy turned to regard him, without appearing to recognise him.

"Moscow. I was Bluebeard in the Bartok."

Fiona hoped against hope that he wasn't going to sing it.

"Gregoyan Shipping sponsored a staging of the opera in aid of the World's Orphans. We drank, you and I, quite heavily, toasting those poor parentless children. You must, surely, remember…"

"The Gregoyans succour all and sundry. We are as beneficent as cows."

"Daddy..."

Rudolfo winked at her and carried on. "It was a glorious spring… what year was it?... a night in bloom, the evening was graced by… what was her name? So exquisite, so delicate. I had met her earlier that season in Kiev..."

Fiona noticed that Daddy seemed to find his seat unsatisfactory; he shifted his weight backwards and forwards.

"…Her father was the Minister of Bread, I believe…"

"No." Daddy waved a fist in the air as if to silence him. Unfortunately it dislodged a pile of straw boaters she'd been meaning to dust.

"…Varushka – Varushka of the beautiful-shaped loaves."

"Enough!"

Rudolfo wasn't in the least bit intimidated. "She had a voice. I had such plans for her."

This seemed to make Daddy sweat. He used his folded handkerchief to dab at his forehead, streaking the brilliant white dark.

"You bought her," Rudolfo said, his shoulders slumping.

Daddy had never loved anyone but her mother. Or so he kept saying. What was Rudolfo talking about? Daddy was muttering under his breath.

"I will have your voice blacklisted," he said.

"Varushka? When did you meet this woman?" she asked.

"It was 1999 – yes, spring 1999…" Rudolfo mused.

"But…" She thought of her mother slipping away quietly in her private hospital ward that year, candles flickering around her. Health and Safety had had to be bribed to allow those tiny flames. But money hadn't kept her breathing. "…That was the April that Mummy died."

"Nonsense!" With a wave of his arm Daddy flattened her tiny orange grove.

"She did…"

"Would you like me to absent myself?" Rudolfo asked her.

She didn't want him to leave her alone with Daddy, but what exactly happened in the spring of '99 had now become a family affair. She nodded. And, now that she thought about it, why was Daddy here? He never usually deigned to visit Crowning Glories' head office.

"Do you have any other colour but this?" asked Rudolfo, pointing up at his hat. "I cut a better figure in rust, or maroon."

Ignoring Daddy's angry snort, she picked out an aubergine beret, handed it to Rudolfo.

He reached over, seized her hand and kissed it. "It was meant that I found you in your enchanting shop of hats." He covered his curls with the beret. "Tomorrow I shall be in Buenos Aires where I shall introduce them to aubergine. Goodbye."

Daddy drummed his fingers on the wrought-iron table-top, while Rudolfo wrote a cheque for the beret, taking his time, adding verse to a tune:

"Varushka! You once knew a girl called Varushka!..."

The light bulbs nearest to Rudolfo swung wildly; the light dimmed.

"That's enough," boomed Daddy.

"So lustrous was her hair, inviting was her stare..."

Purple in the face, Daddy rose to his feet.

"You did nothing but declare…"

Daddy raised his fist and would have hit Rudolfo had he not skipped sideways with surprising agility. "All others as… Babushkaaaas."

Rudolfo dodged another flying fist while rattling all the metal objects in the room with his 'aaah's.

Fiona raced over to open the door and closed it quickly while Rudolfo shook the last drops from his small umbrella on the doorstep. Turning her back on him to face a furious Daddy, she tried to ignore Rudolfo's full-throated, "Babush-kaaaassss," moving down the street past the taxi rank and around the corner.

She composed herself before saying – "Well, Father?"

Chapter 27

"We don't have to do games, if you don't want to." Angie noticed Jake was trembling. What on earth had Fiona been up to last Thursday? Of course, she would have dazzled him with her seduction tricks in this very bed.

Jake coughed weakly.

Fiona must have exhausted him.

"This must be very sedate compared to last week," she said, then regretted saying it.

"You're telling me."

Perhaps it was worse than she feared. "Oh." She stared at the lines of what looked like multi-coloured dragonflies streaming across the wall beside her. "I'm not like her," she said.

"No, you're not."

He put a feverish hand on her tummy.

She didn't know whether to move it or take hold of it, so she pretended it wasn't there.

"She's mad," he said.

"Yes, so inventive and creative."

He coughed again. "I thought she'd done you in."

"Done me in? How hilarious."

"It wasn't funny. I kept looking for a body. Under the bed."

This was baffling. "Was looking for bodies a part of the game?"

"Who knows with her? I reckon I was lucky to escape with my goolies intact."

"Don't be silly, she's harmless." She thought of Dr Henkelschneiffer's icy stare. "As harmless as I am."

"You're not..." He whispered this, pulling her close, kissing her on the lips, before delicately placing kisses in a moist line down her nose, chin, and between her breasts. "...Not at all harmless." Throwing back the covers, he continued his journey downwards.

She tugged at the covers, trying to reclaim them and her dignity. "Hold on a minute, last week you were doing this with *her*."

He stopped dead.

"I most certainly wasn't."

"Oh? Weren't you?"

"No I was not!"

"Why not?"

"Because it's you I thought I'd be seeing. And it's you I wanted to see."

"Really?"

"Really."

She could hardly believe that Jake actually seemed to prefer her to Fiona.

"And she's a nightmare."

"Gosh, no, she's... Well..."

"Happy?"

"Sort of..."

She marvelled how her body opened up to his warmth, all that was alive in her surging towards him. She pulled him closer and sighed just as he sighed.

Then something strange began to happen: she became aware of another presence in the room. On the ceiling, to be exact. That was where the face of Fiona came into focus, wearing an unhappy, wounded expression, her cleavage revealed by a basque top.

Angie blinked. The nightmarish image persisted. Stop feeling guilty, she told herself, and closed her eyes while Jake's ministrations grew more and more inventive.

As they rolled around in synchrony, her eyes opened and were surprised all over again by the persistent face hovering over her.

"Go away," she hissed.

"What?" whispered Jake.

"No, no, do carry on please…"

She tried outstaring the strange Fiona on the ceiling. The eyes stared back at her. It was weird. Dr Henkelschneiffer's words circled round in Angie's head, too, along with a shopping list and an attempt to remember when she'd last felt anything as wonderful between her legs.

"Jake, oh, oh, oh," she said.

"Angie, oh…" he gasped from below the covers.

"Yes, yes, yes," she found herself shouting.

"Oh," returned the voice from under the covers.

Her heart felt as if it would burst with joy and scatter something like petals all over the room. She stroked Jake's wonderful thick hair.

"Thank you, thank you, thanks…"

He surfaced, tugged at her to mount him. She was happy to oblige. He rocked and muttered and came to a crescendo, gasping her name. She let herself roll off him, enjoyed watching his chest heave. He had wide, flared nostrils she hadn't noticed before, and he wheezed slightly, his chest rising and falling. She combed his chest hairs with her fingers; they were wiry and bounced back at her.

He wriggled. "Ssss, it's ticklish." He had such a lovely strong teeth when he laughed.

She lay back, covered in sweat, deliciously exhausted, gazing upwards. There was no face on the ceiling now, or voice of Dr Henkelschneiffer in her head. Jake was still laughing softly. Or was he coughing?

She wished she didn't have to wait two weeks to see him again. If she broke all the rules, they could meet on Tuesdays or Wednesdays or even Saturdays. All she needed was an excuse for Ted; the kids wouldn't notice. Then there would be nothing stopping them from seeing each other any hour of the day, any day of the week, in every kind of weather, over all the seasons. She saw herself nipping out to the park to see him on Christmas Day, between putting the spuds in to roast and burning them. Her head spun.

Jake's breathing slowed. He sounded as if he was falling asleep.

A window must have opened in an adjoining flat. She could hear the four o'clock news. A footballer had strained a tendon, an MP had resigned, and a gas pipeline had been blown up somewhere foreign, bringing a whole city to a standstill. Angie's arm was getting heavy and her eyes were closing as she listened to something about a groundbreaking ownership trial. A woman was claiming possession of her ex-husband's sperm. It sounded awfully familiar.

"I've heard about this case," she said.

Jake tensed, then sat bolt upright. "Oh, fuck!"

"It was fine…" she said, wondering whether they were talking about the same thing.

"Sperm," he said.

"We did use protection." This was getting embarrassing.

He groped under the covers. "My boxers..."

She dived under the sheet to retrieve one of his socks with her teeth, growled as she tantalised him with it, sure this would amuse him.

It didn't. He seemed preoccupied. He reached out for the

sock without smiling and put it on briskly, muttering. She caught 'property disputes', 'freezers', and 'rights-of-way'.

"What's the matter?"

He had his pants on now, and both socks, and was facing away from her, pulling on his trousers.

"I've just remembered something important."

"More important than…" Oh, God, she was sounding needy.

"No, no, sorry, more urgent. I'm supposed to hand-deliver an amendment to the court. I mean, I was – I'd completely…"

He seemed to be having trouble with his buttons.

She couldn't help herself; she stood up too, teased his fingers free of them, and undid each, so he could redo them in the right order. "There."

"Angie, I'm so sorry, but I have to go!"

"Oh, no…" She watched him move towards the door and couldn't bear the uncertainty of it all. She lined up all her joys – her nearly grown-up children, the cats, Sunday mornings, Naxos harbour at dusk, her recipe for chocolate brownies – oh, and Ted, well, ten years ago. Actually her heart emptied at the thought of Ted. God, Jake had got under her skin. "Jake, what are we going to do about this?"

He turned to look back at her, with a quiet, thoughtful, tender regard.

"I could come back later," he said.

Her heart tightened and hurt. She found she could hardly breathe.

"Later? Er…" How would she get away? Ted would make a mess of the chicken salad; Dusty needed to be told off about her trombone practice, or lack of it. Alex needed a bit of TLC after football. And then there was explaining all this to Fiona – and what if Mrs Willoughby phoned Ted and he knew that she wasn't at work?

"Oh, no, not later," she said and watched his shoulders slump.

"When then?"

"Next week."

"Okay." He was half out of the door.

"Next week is Fiona's."

He stopped, turned to stare at her. "What?"

"Every other week. We had a deal." She hoped she sounded brighter than she felt.

"You want me to humour your friend every other week? Are you serious?"

She didn't want him to do anything of the sort. The idea made her feel sick. Her whole body was clenching against it, but her feelings towards him were so overwhelming she felt as if she was being swept out to sea on a very small canoe with no paddle. "In all the years at school and after, well, I've never reneged on a deal."

"Please tell me you're joking," he pleaded, coming back towards her.

She stood up, letting the covers fall away, reached over, drew him down and kissed him hard on his lips so that they parted.

"No," she said. "I can't."

Chapter 28

Rudolfo's 'Varushka's finally faded out of earshot, the burst light bulbs swinging wildly, his heavy scent lingering in the air. Fiona supposed it was an aftershave from Buenos Aires, where men were still shaved by barbers. She found the silence in the room oppressive. It seemed to be originating from Daddy, who was bowed over her wrought-iron table in the dim light, his bald pate glinting while he reached for his briefcase. He was refusing to look at her or answer her question; his forehead seemed to bob about in the air, its surface as smooth as an eggshell, his brow too stubborn for wrinkles as his fingers cracked open the lock of the briefcase.

"Did you hear me, Daddy?"

Still ignoring her question, he drew an envelope from the case, short exasperated breaths escaping from him as if they couldn't wait to get away. What was the matter with him?

"Daddy?"

He slapped a brown envelope onto the table, then extracted photographs from it, laying each down in front of her. Then he leant back on his rickety seat, and stared at her with pursed lips.

The pictures were blurry, and upside down. But the image was unmistakable.

"Oh."

There she was, in her basque and pearls, laces dangling, looking as if she'd just landed on a museum collection of erotica by parachute, and was about to catalogue it. The awful Jake looked, if anything, even sillier, his naked parts dangling limply, his brow pinched together in a frown.

"What did you think you were doing?" Daddy shouted, making her jump.

"It's called Scrabble, Daddy."

"Like this?" Daddy was pointing furiously at what she assumed was her state of undress.

This was ridiculous. She wasn't a child any longer. "Have you hired one of your lackeys to spy on me?"

"Hrummph!" He jumped up, the coffee pot tipping onto the floor. "Lackeys? This is blackmail."

"Don't be silly. Who...?"

"This petty blackmailer..."

"...Would bother to....?"

"...Has threatened to have these pictures plastered all over the papers, naming you, my daughter as this... this... low- class, backstreet slut!"

How dare he take the moral high ground with her!

"Excuse me..." Fiona scooped up the pictures and waved them at him. "While Mummy wasted away you were cavorting with that Ministry-of-Bread woman ... that Varushka who didn't even have the wits to play Scrabble."

"Scrabble has nothing to do with it." He grabbed the pictures back. "Your husband needs money. Is that it?"

"Don't involve Guy in this."

"Is a corruption of your own flesh the way you ensnare that maggot? Trying to blackmail your own father?"

She took a deep breath, her thoughts reeling. Could this have something to do with Guy? No, surely he wouldn't do anything like blackmail. But Ray? He knew that she was in his flat that afternoon.

How else did the blackmailer know enough about her assignation to take these shots?

Daddy layered the pictures back in the envelope with steely care. "Fiona Elena, you have never shown any talent for business before."

This was going too far. Crowning Glories was a going concern, thank you.

"First you accuse me of being a slut, then of being a black-mailer and now, as if that's not enough, of being too stupid to be either. Really, Daddy." She burst into tears.

He waved an arm as if to silence her. Well, he bloody well wasn't going to. She sobbed more loudly.

"We must remember who we are," he said.

"We? What are you talking about?"

"The last of the Gregoyans." He shook his head sadly. "Strangers from a vanished world."

"Oh, for goodness sake!" She wished Rudolfo would reappear and sing a whole opera to drown all this out.

"It is a name that survived annihilation to be feared in all the ports of the world. It is born of blood. And it will be both of our heads that sink in shame when this noble name becomes the laughing stock of the world."

He was moving towards the door with a finality that didn't bode well.

"What are you going to do about it?" She dabbed at her eyes with her sleeve.

"Are you going to…" he jerked his chin contemptuously at the envelope, "…do this 'Scrabble' again?"

She hesitated.

He gazed at her. "Answer me, Elena."

Loyalty to him was as old as anything she could remember.

He turned to face the street in his embattled way, as if expecting the street to deliver more enemies. She hadn't noticed his stoop before. His shoulders sagged, his coat buckling in folds downwards, with a weariness, like a skin that was too big for him. Suddenly, he seemed old. All his terrorising hadn't stopped time. With a pang, she found herself worrying about his mortality. This frightened her.

"Of course not."

Chapter 29

Jake raced up the steps from the Underground station and found himself faced by a mob. They were shouting and waving banners.

"Excuse me," he said. No one could hear him. Damn. He took a step onto the road and was jammed tight in a jumble of thick wet coats and bad breath. It took him all his strength to stay there before he was squeezed like pus out of a pimple, back onto the pavement. How was he to get across to the Courts?

"I need to get to work," he shouted to a stately woman in a nurse's uniform. "It's urgent."

"Not as urgent as this, love."

The only bare space was under a banner a few steps ahead. The logo featured a Renaissance Madonna and child, over which 'LIFE' was scrawled in red paint. By falling to his knees, and crawling, he reached it, then stood up. The banner's pole was held high by a fiercely bearded man in thick glasses, shouting – "Life! Life! Death to the abortionists."

"I'll take that." Jake grabbed hold of the pole.

The man resisted, suspicious.

"Don't worry, I can manage." Jake tugged more forcefully.

The man glared. "You a member?"

"A founder."

The man's grip slackened. Jake seized the pole, and side-stepped with it, nodding enthusiastically.

Miraculously, the path in front of the banner cleared; Jake made progress inside what felt like the peristalsis of a wet human caterpillar. He found himself warming to the workings of democracy, as the crowd carried him forward, placing him a few steps parallel to the courts, where camera flash bulbs were sparking. He tried to plough past a microphone labelled 'Euro News'. But the young man wearing a cap and a sneer blocked his path.

"Are you supporting the rights of the unborn child?" asked the capped man, shoving the microphone under Jake's nose.

"Er, what? No of course not." Jake tried passing his banner back to his nearest neighbours, but they had a grinning skull-and-crossbones with God loves babies imprinted on theirs, and didn't want his.

"You mean you're on the other side?"

Jake nodded, hoping that would cover it.

The reporter wasn't satisfied.

"Exactly what are your views on abortion? Tell me!"

Jake let the banner go. Instead of sinking to the ground, it stayed where it was, attached to him, kept aloft by a body of shoulders, a breeze stretching it open.

"Bloody disgrace," muttered Jake in an effort to blend into the crowd. Then, ignoring the reporter, he reached up, retrieved his banner, and rolled it up. Pointing the tip of the pole at the Law Courts, he used it like a lance to charge past everyone, into the gate. There, with a shout of triumph, he planted the banner upright in a flower pot, flashed his card at Security, and hared on, unchallenged, into the courtyard, and on into the main hall.

The hall was thick with flustered lawyers sneezing, with paroxysms that rattled the light-fittings, sending papers and toupees flying. Was this due to the sudden appearance of spring? Or some change in all of their circumstances? Jake looked about but couldn't locate Max; he caught sight of Dr Gold on the other side of the hall, just as he disappeared into a corridor. Jake ran after him. When he reached the doorway, there was no more sign of him. Jake raced on to Court Twelve. Dr Gold was standing just inside the door.

"Which of your businesses was it this time?" he asked, curtly.

Jake could see he had every right to be annoyed. "I've got the notes." He produced *Embryonic Cell Division and the Law* from his coat pocket.

"Fat lot of use that is now."

Jake was about to reply but realised it was no use. The doctor marched on, down to the front pew where Max sat. Still clutching his research, Jake followed. The pews were full, heads turned as they made for the front. Jake slid in beside Max.

"You're in big doo-doos," Max hissed.

The judge sighed theatrically, as he waited for them to settle.

"Court may rise."

They all rose.

"The civil case of Endicott versus Endicott is dismissed."

There was a gasp in the room. Jake was dumbfounded. What had he missed? He nudged Max who ignored him.

"All costs are awarded to Kenneth Endicott."

There was a scream behind Jake. "You bastard!"

"Order!" The judge glowered at the back of the courtroom and waited for quiet. "The Crown Prosecution Service will be bringing new charges against Ina Endicott for criminal theft of Kenneth Endicott's seminal property. Court dismissed."

What was he talking about? "What is going on?" Jake

whispered.

The judge swished out, followed by the clerk of the court.

Pews creaked as people gathered their belongings; voices broke out into disputes. In the back, the woman's voice began shouting again.

"It's my baby, you fucking bastard."

The doctor passed Jake without comment. He turned to Max.

"Come on, man, tell me."

"She broke into the freezer, nicked the sperm, and got herself pregnant. Game, set and…" Max was staring at the front of Jake's shirt.

Jake looked down. His tie sported a *Kill lawyers, not babies* sticker. "Now look, I can explain…" He ripped the sticker off; it stuck to his finger. He picked at it, glowered at it, stamped on it like an errant bluebottle.

"You're a complete wanker!" said Max.

"No, no, you don't understand…" As if to illustrate a point, Jake tore off his tie, jabbing frantically at it to remove any remnants of the sticker.

"Wait 'til Carruthers gets hold of you."

"Whose side are you on, Max?" Jake feared he knew the answer.

Fiona gazed out of the window at a crowd. It was noisy, growing and seemed exercised about something. There were banners and a great deal of shouting. They might break her shop windows if they got any more agitated. Should she call the police? What would she say? "Prospective hat-pillagers on the loose – come quickly!" She doubted they would come at all. This is what husbands were for. She located her phone in the feathers drawer and dialled.

"*Casier aux Homards, bon jour.*"

"Guy? Is that you?"

There was a clatter of dishes and something that sounded like steam.

"Fiona?"

Guy sounded surprised to hear from her.

"Apart from the fact that the world seems to have gone mad, I'm absolutely bloody marvellous. How are things with you?"

"No, no, non..."

Who was he talking to? His voice was tremulous, as if he was facing sudden death.

"What's going on? Have you got a crowd outside your restaurant too?"

"Put it down!"

"Put what down?"

"It's the pastry chef... he's... Not there! Oh God!"

"Guy?" There was the sound of pots banging and a flash of something that could have been thunder. She knew so little about his day-to-day world. "What's going on?"

"Blighter's knocked out the sous chef. The scallops are all over the floor... Table twelve is still waiting for their..."

The phone went dead. This was the drawback of having a cook for a husband – culinary curtailments to most conversations, mostly in the form of steam, smoke, or Health and Safety officials. He was never there when she needed him. The windows were rattling with the pressure of the crowd outside. There was nothing she could do about calming them down. She should try calming herself down.

She picked up her Frederick-memorial hat, and dropped velveteen cherries randomly onto the crown, resolving to glue them down wherever they fell. The shouting outside became a chant. There was drumming. She forced herself to focus. Poor lost Frederick. Could she track him down and meet him, perhaps, on a Tuesday? She turned the hat around, threaded a wave of unbleached silk around each of the cherries, drawing both ends up onto the crown where she tied it into a soft creamy bow. She was so absorbed she was hardly aware of the bell tinkling as a customer did enter the shop. She jumped when the woman said:

"I want a hat."

The woman was short, flushed and strong, with a large head. She was familiar but Fiona couldn't place her. Aristocracy – or a labour MP?

"Of course, have a look around."

"No, a bespoke hat."

"For a wedding?"

"Yes, my husband's re-marrying his secretary."

"What? You mean he's married her before?"

The woman smiled with no warmth, then patted her belly; she looked pregnant which didn't make much sense to Fiona.

"In that case, you're better off without him," she said.

"Could you make me an angry hat?"

"I can make any hat you want."

"Good." The woman's lips tightened into a grimace.

"Within reason," Fiona added.

"Well, then," said the woman.

"Do you have a design in mind?"

"As a matter of fact, I was thinking of something steely with horns that rattle when I move."

Fiona nodded in what she hoped was a noncommittal way. "Do you have a colour in mind?"

"Blood red."

"Hmm, well, red."

The woman advanced towards Fiona, with her hand outstretched and a grim look of determination.

Fiona stepped backwards.

"My name's Endicott. I'm on your system somewhere."

"System or not, you need to give me a deposit, Mrs End-icott."

"Fine. I'll pay in cash."

Chapter 30

Angie could smell Jake in the air, on her skin; her lips were rough from his ravaging.

Did he really prefer her to Fiona?

Nothing like this had ever happened before.

She made the bed, tidied the bathroom, looked up and saw Fiona's glum face hover over the side table in the hall. "Go away, damn you." Angie stormed over to the apparition. It disappeared. She backed away; it reappeared. Then disappeared again as she crept forwards.

Was she delusional? Unnerved, she began to doubt everything. Perhaps Dr Henkelschneiffer was right?

She turned away slowly, then back quickly to see if the ghost was there when she wasn't looking. This was difficult to verify.

She held her fingers up to Fiona's face. They were shaking. But, more importantly – they were also bathed in a flickering light. It was gloomy outside the window. The lighting in the room was subdued. Where did the stream of light come from?

She peered into the stream. It seemed to be emerging from a tiny hole on the opposite wall. She went up to the hole, put her hand over it. The light went. As did Fiona's face. When she took her hand away the phantom reappeared.

Okay then, it was a projection.

From the art installation Fiona called Arthur.

In that case, it must be possible to switch the thing off. It couldn't be too difficult; she always dealt with glitches on the ancient computer at Vetchling. It was one of the few perks of the job. Right. She scanned the room to see if there were any obvious switches. Was the installation connected to the mains? Or to a battery? The furnishings were too sparse to conceal any wires; the walls were smoothly plastered. She was about to go to the other room, when she noticed a single clean crack from ceiling to skirting board. She ran her fingers along it, found an indentation, and pulled. A panel lifted away from the wall revealing a hidden cupboard. Aha – a control panel. That must be it. It was too strange looking to be regulating the central heating.

There was screen showing a baffling array of coloured arrows, dots, dashes and zigzags. There must be some sort of index, or manual on what they all meant. She walked over to the only shelf in the room and found: A Pictorial History of Flea Circuses, One Thousand Sandwich Recipes, and The World's Most Remote Post Boxes. She took down One Thousand Sandwich Recipes and stood on it to give her some height. From her new vantage point she noticed a sim card stuck to the wall behind the machine. She removed it, took it over to the tiny slot. There was a whirr. This was promising.

A photo of Fiona unfurled – coquettishly posing on her back and wriggling slightly with her legs in the air, look-ing remarkably like a Jack Russell demanding tickling. This image multiplied, and was projected onto the skirting board.

This didn't improve matters. How could she get the instal-lation to stop reproducing Fiona in this way?

There were two buttons, red and green. The red must be the off-switch. She pressed it once, twice.

Multi-coloured bubbles bearing Fiona's disgruntled face bounced across the living room wall, disappearing into the miniature topiary beyond the window ledge. Then there was nothing. So far, so good.

What about the green button?

The wall divided into a myriad of split-screen images of unclad Fionas scowling into leafy glades, accompanied by Vivaldi. An electric violin replaced the piano; the split screens showed close-ups. Was there a list of files somewhere? Was that a mole? God, this was hopeless!

She peered down a line of incomprehensible icons.

And went back to the mole-like thing. She pressed it with the tip of her finger and a list of letters appeared. Progress! She scrolled down to F. There was a 'Frumph', a 'Freak', but no 'Fiona'. She went up to D and found 'De Borzoi.' Aha! She poked at this. There was a whirr. Identical black and white photos multiplied over the walls. None of them looked like Fiona, no, the image quivering over the lampshade was of a naked man lounging in the crook of the other's arm. Ray! This was his flat, and this must be his personal home-movie, which she really shouldn't be watching, but couldn't help herself. He drew long and hard on what looked like a joint before handing it over to his partner with a lingering kiss. In desperation Angie swiped the nearest arrow.

The face of Ray's lover loomed huge. The balding head looked awfully familiar. So did the smile that looked as if it was being squeezed out of a toothpaste tube. Fiona's husband!

Fiona hadn't said anything about her husband having relationships with anything other than his griddle. But there was no doubt about it.

Why hadn't she said anything? Or even hinted? They'd always shared their secrets in the past.

The realisation came slowly. Her friend couldn't possibly

know anything about this relationship.

Turning her back on the ghostly Ray-and-Guy wallpaper, phantoms now laughing at some private joke, she found her bag, opened her phone, stared at Fiona's name and forced herself to dial.

Fiona's, "Hello," sounded relaxed and happy.

"Hello Fiona, um…" Her nerve failed.

"Never mind that. How did it go with Jake?"

"Ah, him."

"As far as I'm concerned, he's a dead loss."

In these circumstances Angie felt it was important not to gloat. "He does manage to cheer me up a little," she said.

"You don't sound very cheerful. What happened?"

"I… look, could I come over?"

"Yes, sure, come to the shop and I'll cheer you up," Fiona said. "I can't leave; I'm making an angry-hat to a tight deadline. Bring a bottle."

Angie felt dizzy at the thought of alcohol. "Good idea."

She rang off, and then noticed the last of the buttons. It was a slate grey. She pressed it. The room went dark, quiet. Birdsong from a bush outside punctuated the silence. What should she say to Fiona? Ted would know how to broach a difficult subject with tact and ease. All those disappointed couples he dealt with professionally. How was she going to do it?

"How do you feel about Ray's relationship with Guy?" An answer to that wouldn't clarify anything.

"How well did you know Guy before you married him?" was going to sound like she was prying. Anyway, how well did a woman know any man, before, during, or after marriage?

Angie hated scenes. She liked the flat landscapes, long twilights, and slow seeping skies of her native Norfolk, where winter gave way to spring without very much fuss. Perhaps she should keep her own counsel, supporting Fiona in a sisterly way, boosting her self-esteem, instead of initiating an embarrassing naming-and-shaming ceremony. Coward, she told herself.

She would have to steel herself for one of Fiona's awful emotional tornadoes. The first time she'd thrown one, Angie had had to part with the last of her precious, saved, sixteenth-birthday cake to get her to go home. Then there was that prize ticket to a Rolling Stones concert that she had had to offer her when Fiona failed a biology exam. And on the ice-skating competition outing, her own beautiful skates.

Fiona would expect compensation for the news.

Sooner, or later.

Oh, God. Angie looked around the room's clean white lines and chrome fixtures, sterile now with the art installation silent. The sun wobbled beyond the wall of the roof terrace, plucking gold from the wildlife sculpture before sinking without trace. She stared at her hands. They'd smoothed Jake's thick dark hair. They'd stroked his sweat-gleaming arms. She turned them over and peered at the back of them as if they were stray animals.

She'd only just discovered Jake. She'd only just met him.

But could she keep him?

She saw Ted tidying away her kitchen spices, packing away her share of their wedding presents into boxes, and checking her car's engine-oil for the last time before she became Jake's what? – Partner? She tried to place him next to her at a dinner party with Gregory and Sandra, twenty years his senior. Goulash and Cote du Rhone, with glasses and spectacles glinting in the candlelight. They would be arguing over stamp duty and the merits of atheism in tight, clipped voices accompanied by silencing looks. She shook her hands, reclaimed them, sighed, reaching for her bag, rumaged, found the scrap of paper on which Jake's mobile number was scrawled, and got his voice mail.

"Jake." She did it crisply. "This is Angie. I want you to be nice to Fiona next Thursday. Very nice. For me. Please."

Jake saw that his discarded banner was now bent double in the flowerpot, furling and unfurling in a breeze. Someone had given the baby a moustache and the Madonna a boob enhancement. Jake decided one artist was responsible – it was the same crazed purple ink. A few cardboard vuvuzelas lay, trampled and forgotten, on the pavement. Dusk was descending. The street was quiet. He wondered if he would be appearing later on the ten o' clock news. What if counsel saw it? He shuddered at the effect this would have on Carruthers.

In great trepidation, he listened to his voice mail, then replayed the message.

It didn't make sense. How could Angie ask that of him?

Fiona must have some hold on her. There was no other explanation.

He crossed the road on the zebra crossing, not bothering to look left or right.

A deal, she'd said. Spending another afternoon in the company of mad Fiona would kill him. It was out of the question. End of story.

He pushed his way through a group of northerners getting off a coach. It had begun to rain again.

She was clearly embroiled in some deadly bond.

Pulling his jacket over his phone to keep it dry, he played the message again. 'Be nice' were her words. The Cock and Bull! Of course, that's where he was supposed to be. He broke into a run. A shout behind him, then irregular running footfalls meant Max was on his heels. Damn! Max was like a homing pigeon. How to shake him off? Jake slowed to a snail's pace.

"Coming for a drink?" asked Max.

"No, thanks, I'm in a hurry."

Max didn't seem to hear. "Bloody case. Sperm seems a tricky thing to bank on. Counts and all that, you know."

"Yes, yes."

"But, as males, it's all we've got to bring to the great biological feast."

Jake wondered how Max could wax so lyrical about something he knew nothing about.

"Could we discuss the case tomorrow, Max?"

"You'll be ringing me the minute your mug is splayed on the telly. That cameraman seemed to like your face, mate." Max looked at his watch. "About two minutes past ten, I reckon."

"What? Seriously?"

"And if you want me to hide you in a cupboard, you'll have to spill it out."

"Spill what out?"

"Which one is better...?"

"What?"

"In the sack...?"

Jake turned to stare at Max.

"How did you know there were two of them?"

"There have always been two. Remember the Post-it note?"

"It didn't say two women."

"You really are such a twit, Jake. You're not fit to be let out."

"It said two?"

"It said ladies. Are there more?" He began to walk on, very slowly.

"You know, Max, you should get out more."

Max made a face.

"No, you should. Look, you may not be good-looking, but …" Jake racked his brains for something Max could offer a woman. "Max, you've got the gift of the gab. Jokes make them laugh. They like that. Tell them a few of your stories. You've got a ton of those."

Max was sticking to his side like a stray dog that wasn't going anywhere 'til he got fed the titbit he wanted.

"And Max, I know I've got you to thank."

Max's breath was tickling Jake's earlobe.

"Get off. Fuck's sake, if I tell you about them, will you help me out?"

"Maybe."

"One could just possibly be your perfect cuppa rosy."

"Which one?"

Jake had a bad feeling about divulging anything more to Max. But he was desperate. "Okay, so there's a quiet, homely one and a kinky one."

Max was staring at him, nodding.

"You can have the kinky one."

"Why? Is she crazy or something?"

"Did I say crazy? No, no, I said kinky. Look, I'll make do with the homely one and you could go to Las Vegas or somewhere with the other one..."

"I could?"

"Yep."

"What do you mean 'kinky'?"

"She's just a little jumpy, that's all."

Max was staring into the crowded pub, shaking his head. God, the man was hopeless.

Jake pushed the pub door open wide, and peered in at the heaving crowd trying to see who Max was fixated by. There at a far table, unruffled, a pint and a newspaper in front of him, was the good doctor.

"So Max, what's it going to be?"

Max appeared to be trembling.

"Want a drink, old boy?"

Max had a strange glint in his eyes.

"Look, if you can't make up your mind..."

Max was nodding his head like a buoy on a rough sea. "Some other time mate."

"...I think I can see someone who can..."

Jake pushed his way towards the doctor's table, forcing wine glasses to lift and chatting pairs to part.

"Would you like some company?" he asked the doctor when he got there.

The doctor put down his glasses, folded his paper and smiled. "Sure."

Jake placed himself onto the seat opposite him, leaving a space for Max. But when he looked up, Max wasn't there anymore.

"How are things?" asked the doctor.

He seemed genuinely interested.

"Can I get you another?" asked Jake.

"Thank you."

Jake made up his mind while counting out his change at the bar. The doctor was an adult and could always say no. In fact, he might be doing the doctor and the mad woman a service by putting them together. The doctor was a professional, after all. And if there was one thing she was in need of, it was professional help. Jake carried the beer and a pint of Guinness back to the doctor's table. The doctor looked up at him with a quizzical half smile.

"How are your various businesses?" he asked.

Jake sat back down, took a slug of his own drink, before trying out his vocal cords.

"Thing is..."

Chapter 31

It was drizzling. A cool mist drooped over the Regents Park Canal, oozing drops into the sludgy brown water. Angie was wet, flurried, her legs aching from pedalling at speed along the towpath, when a horrible realisation came to her.

With a spray of water, she skidded, braked.

What if Arthur recorded *everything* that happened in that flat?

She saw Jake rising and falling over her – lips, torso, erection, smile – randomly flashing before her, frozen, distorted. Was that all now included in the installation's picture library? And she, having the time of her life, would that be aired on the walls whenever the damned thing felt like it?

She felt the whole world was tilting, as if it had lost its moorings. Leaning the bike against a wet bush, she took a few deep breaths.

How did the bloody contraption work? It must be like a computer. Files? Was there an index? F for flesh? S for sweat? O for orgasms? How would it know the names of anything? Blood pounded back into her head; sweat made concentric circles under her armpits.

She had to get back into that flat and find 'select all' and the 'delete' buttons.

She turned round and cycled back onto the road and over the zebra crossing, not waiting for traffic to stop.

There was a volley of furious hooting. A moped swerved, a torrent of abuse escaping from its rider. The deep growly East End voice sounded vaguely familiar.

She shook her fist at the rider, not waiting for his reply, instead driving the pedals, faster and faster, not stopping until she entered the gates, threw her bike into the azaleas and pressed her index finger onto the entrance-monitor.

The mechanism buzzed; the door didn't open. She banged frantically at the glass. The porter rose from the distant gloom and ambled towards her.

"It's not letting me in," she yelled into the intercom.

"Your clearance is timed," he replied into the speaker-phone, his voice tinged with his usual contempt.

"Timed?"

"It says so clearly above your head."

Her fingerprint was enlarged onto a screen; under it read: Entry Thursdays 1400 – 1800.

"But I've only just left."

He pointed at the digital clock – 18.45.

"Can't you just let me in? I have keys to the upstairs flat."

"Would you like me to phone the owner?"

He picked up the receiver, waited for her reply, his eyes twinkling with something she didn't like.

"No, no. Wait!"

Was Ray up there, right now, reviewing the afternoon's action like instant replay at the World Cup? And laughing his head off?

None of this was a good idea. Angie developed very cold feet.

"I'll, er, come back another, er, time."

The porter gave her a doubtful look, replaced the phone, shrugged, and shuffled away back to his dark, hidden corner.

She stared up at the elegant, unyielding portico with its discreetly placed cameras. Was she being recorded at this very moment? Apart from hurling her bike at the shatter-proof glass there was nothing else for her to do but go, desperately hoping that 'Angie in flagrante delicto' wasn't filed in the installation's range of mood-enhancing options.

The angry-hat was turning out a bit of a mess. Fiona had covered its cone shape with stretched black-and-red-striped organza to which she'd attached aluminium arrows, pointing at each other.

The idea was… evoking conflict. She held it up.

Not totally convincing. Did it just look like a confusing roadwork? Oh dear. She laid it down carefully and stared out at the street.

Angie hadn't sounded quite as exuberant as before. Good. Maybe they could ditch Jake now and go for Frederick, or Rudolfo, or both – a sort of Fredolfo. But, did Fiona want to share them with her? What sort of timeshare was this to be? Angie's monopoly of Jake had hardly been shared.

Fiona had to admit it: she was angry, hurt even. He was supposed to be their lover. Thursday was their shared afternoon. Fiona was going to bloody well insist they keep sharing Jake and Thursdays, and extract him bit by bit from Angie, damn it. She could arrange afternoons with Fredolfo on Wednesdays or Tuesdays and keep that all to herself.

Outside Crowning Glories, Angie dismounted and peeked into the fluffy oval-shaped interior. Fiona was sitting at her work table, absorbed in her sewing, a mass of dark hair pulled back under a ruby red scarf, her pale face quite serene. Angie remembered the girl whose father dictated every subject and bribed every exam result. And here she was now – an ordinary milliner – an upmarket one perhaps, but a hat-maker all the same. Nothing to launch ships about.

"Hi!" Angie struggled to get the bike into the shop without scratching the paintwork or dripping onto the carpet.

"You look terrible," Fiona said evenly. "Did Jake beat you at Scrabble?"

"You're the one who beats me at Scrabble."

"Me? Really? When?"

Angie could see the high-ceilinged common room, rain leaking into a bucket, and feel how cold their fingers were when they rummaged for letters. Fiona couldn't possibly remember how hopeless she was. She had to boost Fiona's confidence with anything she could. "At school. You were an absolute whiz."

"Must have been cheating," said Fiona.

"Cheating?" This was her chance. She took a deep breath. "I'm worrying about our husbands."

"Our what?"

"My Ted. Your Guy."

"Oh." Fiona frowned as if someone had brought up politics. "Was Jake that much of a disappointment?"

Angie was determined to persevere. "What would Guy do if he found out?"

Fiona broke off a thread with her teeth. "I'd like to think he'd kill Jake, and make passionate love to me. Why?"

Angie tried to replace the lounge lizard she'd seen floating on Ray's apartment wall with a swashbuckling version.

"No, seriously."

"Yes, seriously."

Angie watched Fiona stab a freshly threaded needle into a line of thick white stitches.

"And, anyway, what would your doctor do?" Fiona tugged the thread tight.

Angie wasn't going to think about that now.

"What would you do if you found out Guy was cheating

on you?"

Fiona looked at her from under her long lashes.

If Angie didn't know better, she'd say it was a sly look.

"Guy cheating on *me*?"

"Yes."

"For goodness sake, his whole life is a cheat. He's only a trumped-up dishwasher from Birmingham. Everything else about him I invented."

Angie looked at Fiona's dark moist inquiring eyes, her smile of ownership. Angie couldn't do it. Revealing the truth would give her some sort of superiority and Fiona would never tolerate that. Their friendship wouldn't survive. Angie could hear Fiona's shrieks, tears, subterfuge and revenge plots, all involving her.

"Do you know how to work the art installation you call Arthur?" Angie asked, instead.

"Oh, yes." Fiona bent back down over her work. "But it's safer if you just leave it alone."

Fiona obviously knew even less about the bloody thing than she did.

Angie searched for some way out of the tangle they were in.

"Let's replace Jake with someone else," she said.

Fiona stopped stitching and blinked, suspicious. "But I *like* Jake."

"Wouldn't you prefer the huge opera singer, or the student from Belgrade or wherever?"

"You want Jake all to yourself."

"That's not it at all. I just want you to be happy." For one glorious moment, she genuinely meant it.

"I am happy. You can replace him with someone else if you want, but I'm going on as planned." Fiona's lips tightened in a way Angie knew too well.

"In the same flat?"

"Of course."

Angie sat down. With a supreme act of will she forced herself to smile. "We started this together and we'll carry on together."

Fiona stopped stitching to look at her.

"Jake…" Angie felt nauseous. "Asked if…"

"Your nose is twitching," said Fiona, and laughed.

"…You could switch it off, Arthur, I mean. Jake says it puts him off his stroke."

Fiona brightened. "Was *that* his problem?"

Angie nodded. "Yes, he has a horror of technology – says it doesn't do to let technology to get mixed up with emotion." She peeked at Fiona to see if she was convinced. It was hard to tell. "The very idea brings him out in awful spots, terrible sweats, uncontrollable shakes. And that's just the idea."

Fiona put down the hat she was working on. Its spikes looked like metallic deer horns in the rutting season. "He should have simply said something."

"So, Fiona, next time you're there, you should switch off Arthur."

"You really think it will make a difference to his, er, performance?"

"Yes."

"Oh, good. Let's open that bottle of wine, then. There are some of Guy's handmade poppy-seed crackers under the Pinocchio hat."

Angie found the packet under a cushion.

Fiona clinked Angie's glass with hers. "To us," she said.

Chapter 32

Derek was chuffed with his most recent acquisition – a gleaming new blue moped. He'd only nicked it a week ago and was growing rather attached to it. On these two wheels he could dive in to see Trixiebell with a quick-getaway insurance plan. Pulling his cap right down, he entered the neighbourhood he called his own. Near Sharpneedle Street he opened the throttle and did a fancy skid close to the kerb.

Murphy's Off Licence was closed. The dry cleaner's shutters were down too. Diddy's pet shop, at least, would be open. Slowing down, he craned to see through the blinds. The only light left shining in the shop was the neon tube in the tropical fish tank. It was awfully dead for a Thursday. Where was everyone? Was there a funeral?

He puttered on, past the oozing rubbish, into the backstreet parking lot, where he got off the bike. He steered it over to a dark corner under the fire escape and switched off the ignition.

The row of windows across the parking lot was dark. No glint of light. No sign of anyone around. Can't be too careful though, he thought. Rummaging in the pile of tins and cartons, he found a cardboard box. He ripped that into strips and covered most of the chrome so it wouldn't catch anyone's eye. That should work. He was heading for the stairs when he saw something that made the hairs rise over his tattoos.

A silver Rolls Royce stretch-limo was nosing silently into the street. And instead of doing a U-turn as such a vehicle should do when finding itself in his neighbourhood, it stopped right in front of the main entrance to the building.

There was only one person he knew that owned such a beast.

Fuck. How had the bugger followed him here? And, now what? Brick walls on all sides. If Derek managed to get past the limo, he could, maybe, be up those stairs and into Trixiebell's before he was recognised.

Whistling 'The Hills Are Alive', he tried trotting briskly past the endless white wings of the limo. Hope was looking like a possible option, when the nearest opaque window peeled downwards to reveal the very thing he'd most dreaded seeing again – the stony mug of Elijah Gregoyan. The eyes seemed to fix onto his like magnets. To make things very much worse, a finger belonging to the dreaded blighter was beckoning, while the back door of the limo clicked open with horrible synchrony.

Derek's legs came over a bit unnecessary. Even if he bullied them into compliance, they had four floors to cover to bear him to safety. And, if they failed him? It didn't bear thinking about. Gregoyan wasn't the sort of man who liked his invitations rebuked.

Derek wobbled the few steps towards the limo, looked up at a row of squat pigeons taking up firing positions on the ledges above, shrugged, spat, climbed in. The door closed quietly after him just as finally as the inner door of Pentonville Block E had once done.

It was dark inside the car. Unreal. Some sort of pillow slid into place behind his neck; armrests rose up beside him. A seat belt whipped across his lap and pinioned him.

After a minute, he tried to speak. "How the fuck did you know you'd find me here?" That hadn't come out quite right. It must have been Trixiebell. She was the world's biggest gossip. Wait 'til he got hold of her!

Something that felt like a warm human hand began to knead his shoulders; he hoped that was what it was doing.

"Steady on," he told it.

It carried on regardless.

His eyes adjusted to the gloom enough to see Gregoyan's beaky profile in the forward compartment. Derek waved weakly. "Didn't think we'd be hooking up again quite so soon," he said.

With a jerk, Gregoyan barked a command at the driver. All Derek could see of that individual was the gold-crested top of his cap.

The car started to move.

"Where are we going?" His voice was wavering.

No answer from the glassed-in compartment in front.

The motor glided off so slowly he could see the neon-lit fancy goldfish through the pet-shop blinds.

It was a shame there was no one to see him being borne away in a limo.

Could be even more of a shame if there was no one to notice him not returning.

Had Gregoyan insisted on an early night for the entire neighbourhood? Derek felt sweat trail down his spine. Was he being kidnapped? He tried to imagine Trixiebell or Da Derek doling out some ransom money. What was he worth to them? A big zero floated into his mind and stayed there, attached to all the reasons he tried to give them to miss him. The horrible truth was they'd be more likely to pay for him not to be rescued.

Get a grip, he told himself. This Gregoyan's a foreigner; he's not going to want ay doings with the law. On the other hand, he's a rich foreigner – he probably was the law.

They were now passing effortlessly along Commercial Road, the very spot Great Da Derek had taught him his art – "Knock 'em one way, cause a bit of a distraction. Apologise like. Then, fingers in and out like silk." Dead, of course. Old bastard. Must have speeded up a bit, though you couldn't feel it, 'cos they'd reached Blackfriars Underpass.

"I've read your police file," said the voice.

Derek jumped; he couldn't help it. Calm down, deny everything, he told himself. "Police file? You'd be mistaking me for somebody else."

"Dated February the ninth."

Which episode did this refer to? Handling stolen goods? Assault? Currency? Theft of a motor launch? Arson? He really should take Trixiebell's advice and keep a diary. "February? Wasn't in the country."

"I have a job for you."

"A what?"

"A job, work, legitimate employment, a way to keep you off the streets. And in anticipation of your services, I have already paid three thousand pounds into the account of Miss Trixiebell Fullop."

"Three thousand snicker? I wouldn't trust her with three quid."

The red light changed. The great beaut accelerated soundlessly. Derek could hear his heart thump against his ribcage like rain pounding on beer cans.

"What sort of services?"

"You will be paid in cash when you've completed the project."

Had he heard right? "Cash?"

"That's what I said."

"How much?"

"That depends."

Derek didn't like uncertainties where money was concerned. He liked to know exactly what he was getting his hands on. They were alongside the river now. "On what?"

"Your performance."

"I can't sing or dance. And I only ever work alone."

"Three thousand pounds is what I'm offering."

"Three what….?" Derek now felt his heart soar.

"Of course, if you refuse my generous offer, everything I have on you would provide very interesting reading for Tower Hamlets police."

Derek knew that particular outfit very intimately. Down to the chief inspector's gold front tooth. The river flashed grey and silver.

They veered right past the Parliament building, then swung left into a side road, and weaved a path through a series of side streets Derek had never seen before. When they came to a stop, he felt queasy. The door opened silently, letting in a cold draft. He peered out at the wide pavement under a green and white awning. There were trimmed trees in pots leading up to some posh entrance and a man in livery at the door. Derek put one foot onto the pavement to test whether he could leg it if he wanted to.

"Just out of curiosity," he said, "what job were you offering?"

"Waiter," came the answer down the intercom.

"Waiter?" He stared at the well-groomed diners in the window opposite. They were the sort of victims he only ever read about. "Waiter! But that's no sweat."

"And, as a waiter, you are to investigate the affairs of this restaurant."

Derek took a fresh look at the awning. 'Casier aux Homards' looped across it in gold paint. Beneath it was the name 'Guy de Borzoi, award-winning chef'. "Is that it?"

"They've got a uniform for you. They're expecting you.

Cover up those tattoos."

Derek wiped his damp hands on his trousers, eased himself out of the limo. He turned back to give his agreement to Gregoyan, but the windows of the limo were shut fast and the wheels were turning.

"...With the sound of music..." he whistled as he sauntered past the man in livery.

The doorbell chimed. Fiona took another peek at herself in the hall mirror. Twin-set, pearls, a demure hat. Prim, restrained and intellectual was the way she was going to present herself to the awful Jake. Let him work his way around that! She threw open the door, pursed her lips.

A stranger stood on the threshold. He was middle-aged, in a glistening white Paul Smith shirt and a dark woollen suit which must have been cut in Milan. His smile was engaging, yet something around his left eye twitched. Fiona was aware of a musky smell she couldn't place. Who was this? A doorbell confusion? He doesn't look like a salesman or a creditor. Perhaps he was one of Ray's friends. "Hello?"

"Are you Fiona?"

This was awkward. "I could be," she said.

"My name is Ed. Ed."

He looked left and right, which she thought unnecessary; the corridor was empty.

"Bollard sent me."

"Bollard?"

"Jake."

"Oh, him."

"May I come in?" he asked.

"Yes, but where is he?"

"That's why I'm here."

"Oh?"

Without waiting for a reply, he walked on ahead of her into the sitting room.

She left the door to bang shut, and followed.

He was standing in the middle of the room.

God, was this man here to deliver grim news? "Has he had an accident?" She had a vision of the awful Jake in some NHS hospital, with drips connected to his arms, his legs suspended and in plaster.

"Who?"

"Jake."

"Oh, no, he's fine. But he told me you need some help."

"I do?"

Could this be Jake's father? He could just about be an older, more urbane version. There was something similar about the brown eyes and the way they both seemed to confuse her with an unexploded bomb. That could be genetic. Only, this man was showing more interest in her than Jake had during a whole afternoon with her in very expensive lingerie.

"He said you were..."

"Did he?" It was hard to imagine Jake noticing anything about her.

"Very interested in games."

Oh God, this man wasn't some sort of Scrabble fanatic, was he? "Well, I did bring some Scrabble and we did, er, play, but he was hopeless and lost."

"Let's have a..."

"Yes?"

"... Pot of tea, perhaps. Get to know the root of the problem."

The stranger was leaning forward.

"If playing games was such a problem, we'd all be in the lunatic asylum."

"Indeed? Tell me more." He looked genuinely concerned.

She would put the kettle on. On her way to the kitchen, Fiona touched up her lipstick, then banged about in cupboards, her hat getting somewhat in the way of her vision. Her search yielded an array of packets she would need specs to identify.

Behind her, he entered the room silently, and picked out 'First Flush Darjeeling'.

"Milk?" he said.

She led the way back to the sitting room where they sat down on the sofa like bookends. He poured, holding the pot high over her cup. Steam rose.

"Jake told me about your little experiment."

"I don't know what you're talking about."

"He's a hopeless romantic, the young man."

"Him? I'm the romantic."

Ed was sipping his first flush Darjeeling while regarding her with calm brown eyes.

"What he didn't tell me, though, was... how beautiful you are."

It was a long time since anyone had called her beautiful. "Oh?"

"But then, he's young and inexperienced."

This couldn't really be Jake's father, could it? He was liberal, possibly too liberal. "Are you related to Jake?"

"Good God, no. We've been thrown together quite by chance."

"Yes, we have," she said.

"No, he and I have. I wasn't referring to us."

"Us? Oh you mean us?"

He held out his hand. "I was wondering..."

She found herself staring at his smooth long fingers.

"...If you would accept me as Jake's replacement?"

She seized hold of his hand and shook it. Then feeling insecure, she let it go just as suddenly.

"Temporarily, at least?"

"Is this Jake's idea?"

He paused too long for her liking.

"Why don't we forget about him? And concentrate on you."

She nodded a little too enthusiastically, and pretended she had an itch at the back of her neck.

He reached over, removed her hat. Her hair tumbled down.

"I think... that you are even more beautiful without your hat. You have such wonderful hair, it needs showing off, not hiding."

She found herself gawping at him.

"It's as if you've been forgotten under a Christmas tree, all beautifully gift-wrapped, the party crackers going off in the next room."

He moved closer.

All this attention was making her cheeks hot.

"What do you say to us playing a few of your games?"

This man was beyond her wildest dreams. She felt an absurd desire to introduce him to everyone she knew.

Chapter 33

The Spring Celebrity Concert was one of the high points – in fact, the only high point – of the Vetchling Grove year. Angie was trying to concentrate on arranging twelve ancient chairs in two neat rows. But an image of Fiona and Jake with their arms and legs entwined kept popping into her mind. Stop it, she told herself. It was time she stopped this ridiculous game, this absurd idea of time-sharing a lover. It could never work.

Her spirits sank.

One day at a time.

Starting with today. Her wards were the lucky ones. They, at least, had none of her insecurities. They knew where they were heading and simply wanted to put it off. Oh dear, what a terrible thing to think.

Of course, after the brouhaha of last year, Mrs Willoughby hadn't allowed Angie to organise this year's concert.

Which was a bit galling since the ukulele orchestra had been a huge success two years ago and the World War Two tank-battle quiz an even greater one the year before that.

Last year's event had promised another memorable evening. Angie couldn't be held entirely responsible for the magician's nervous breakdown. After all, Marcos Svendini had got rave reviews on the Internet.

How was she to know that he'd a pathological phobia about old age? She was sure she'd told him it was a Golden Age facility.

It all seemed okay. Marcos was a whirl of silk scarves and rabbits. The inmates clapping, interrupted, laughed. It was only somewhere in the middle of an act that involved two rabbits and a lot of raw eggs, he started to shake. Then he began to cry. The raw eggs cracked, the dove flew, the rabbits hopped off into the hall and Marcos sank to the ground, sobbing. Doctor Singleton had to have him carted off in an ambulance. And he was never seen again.

As for the rabbits, they set up home in the rhododendrons, then began to make ghostly appearances. Diddy saw one of them through the basement window and thought it was a visitation from her late husband calling her home. She died later that same evening. Then Flora saw the two of them at the bathroom window and promptly fell down the stairs. They began to be seen as bad omens. 'I saw a bunny' was now shorthand for 'call the undertaker'.

Angie heaved the last of the ancient chairs into its place and placed a footstool under Sid's fish tank to provide a resting place for Mrs Samuelson's prosthetic leg. Then she heaved the grandfather clock to the left a few inches so as to squeeze in a thirteenth chair, scraping the skirting board.

Mrs Endemion and Mrs Jarelewsky arrived simultaneously.

Mrs J was tapping Mrs E's arm. "Haven't we met somewhere before?" Angie sighed. They never remembered that they knew each other.

"Ermintrude Endemion. Pleased to make your acquaintance." She proffered Mrs J a hand.

"Thank you."

Angie rummaged in the hall cupboard for the cards they would need. "Here you are," she said, handed them the pack, and led them back into the hall.

"Do you play rummy?" asked Mrs J.

"Oh, no, dear," said Mrs E. "I wouldn't know how to begin."

"Ah, but I will teach you."

Angie settled them down in opposite wheelchairs with a table between them.

Metal clanked against the banisters. Mrs Samuelson was reaching the stair-lift on her Zimmer frame, and was banging for attention.

"Stay there," Angie shouted.

She couldn't attend to everyone at once. Where was Mrs Willoughby? Angie managed to help Mrs Samuelson, her Zimmer frame, and her unstable prosthesis onto the stair-lift. Other buzzers began cawing like crows in a cornfield.

"I'm coming. I'm coming."

As she raced back up the stairs she heard the front door burst open. It let in a blast of wet wind and the horn of a distant lorry.

Peering back through the banister she saw a small figure standing in a puddle, a red-and-white-spotted umbrella in one hand and a violin case in the other.

"Mr Aranovitch!"

He had returned. She froze. This was awful. What if Dr Henkelschneiffer was with him? She shivered. He appeared to be alone – thank God. He also looked frail and vulnerable. This was urgent. She must help him to flee before Mrs Willoughby saw him and trapped him back into the routine of the Home.

"Go – quick... escape..."

"Escape?" Mrs S was attempting to dismount the stair-lift by herself. "I hardly think Lily would approve of that."

"No, not you, Mrs S."

Mr Aranovitch peered blankly up the stairwell.

"Mein Gott, Angela. This hole of old hell still smells. Last year's cabbage. This day's vee vee." He held his nose. "Open ze vindows or I can't perform."

"Perform?"

"But of course."

He wasn't coming to be the 'star performer', was he? Surely not.

This was cunning of Mrs Willoughby. "Don't drink or eat anything until I come down," Angie called.

It took Angie ages to gather together all the old ladies and get them downstairs with dignity. Edwina tried to hide in the broom cupboard, and Maggie had managed to down half a bottle of cooking sherry, but by 3 o'clock sharp Angie had all thirteen, including Mrs E and J, sedated, in chairs, gazing out in various directions. Four young rabbits could be seen playing on the lawn, but Mrs Willoughby had still not appeared. And where had Mr Aranovitch gone? Angie felt she should go round with a brush and shovel like Mrs Tittlemouse.

"Mein darling Angela, you are too beautiful and young to live here," he whispered suddenly in her ear.

She realised he'd been crouched on the footstool, under the fish tank, like a smiling toad, communing with his old friend Sid.

"Please, please, go back to the open road," he said.

"No, it's you who must leave," she whispered back. "Before Mrs Villowbottom, sorry, Willoughby arrives."

He shook his head, stood, turned his back on her and walked to the front of the room.

"Dear friends, I have come to thank you for your company over many years. And to bid you a proper farewell. I would like to play you a Paganini Capriccio."

He raised his bow, and began to play immediately. Mr Aranovitch sawed, plucked, tormented the wild notes into a long feverish vision – there it was, dancing in front of her – herself and Jake together writhing, cavorting, making love on crumbling balconies, on polished, empty dance-floors, ice-rinks that sparkled with cold and the skates of other lovers rushing past, sandy beaches quivering in some foreign heat, entwined, in and out of bed, in and out of tune as time flew over them. Dusty, Alex and Ted fell away from her in sad, darkening spirals.

"I'll have your queen, dear," said Mrs E, shrill and clear, startling Angie out of her reverie. Jake disengaged his arms and legs to glide on past her, mouthing something she couldn't make out over Mr Aranovitch's violin. And standing clearly in front of her like a persistent ghost was Fiona. With that sly, complicit smile on her face.

At that moment Angie knew. That even if she found the courage to divide her home and possessions in half, leave Ted, and alienate her children, she wouldn't have the wherewithal to claim Jake from Fiona. She always lost to Fiona in the end.

She wiped tears away with her sleeve, trying not to let any sobs escape. The white heads in front of her were bobbing in the swell of the music, like so many faded bottles washed up by the tide. They didn't register her distress or miss a beat when Mrs Willoughby made her entrance, rattling her keys at the door, and, with a face of thunder, advanced towards Mr Aranovitch.

Jake had his small office door locked, his head down, and his phone on 'silent', while he worked through bales of Endicott versus Endicott files. It was amazing that so much argument could accrue from such a tiny sliver of matter as one man's semen. He tossed irrelevant photocopies into the recycling bin and tidied injunctions, affidavits and court rulings into piles marked – *evidence, reference, further research, rulings and invoice items.* He couldn't work out why the desk was vibrating with his efforts until he realised it was his phone signalling a call. The phone jigged, then slid across the Formica top of his small desk. He glanced at the number calling, and realised it was Angie's. He grabbed the phone, pressed answer. She'd gone. He rang the voicemail. Angie's voice wavered slightly.

"Hello, Jake." There was a pause and some sniffing. The voice continued as if it had a cold. "This is Angie. I don't think this is fair on any of us." There was a longer pause, something indistinguishable. Was it a cough, or a sneeze? Then an old man's voice he couldn't recognise, in a foreign accent.

"I am leaving, straight away now, Frau Villowbean. There is nozink you can do to stop me." A clock chimed, a door banged. Or was it a gunshot?

"What's going on? Are you alright?" Jake shook the receiver.

Angie's voice returned, this time more clearly. "I hope you realise your dream, Jake and become a judge." Then there was a sound – it seemed to be behind her – of a car's tyres turned on gravel, and a woman shouted. There was a small snivel, close into the receiver. And then something that could have been: "Goodbye." The phone went dead.

Jake shivered, tossed the phone away, and began kicking his feet into the wall opposite him.

This had to be Fiona's doing. She must have told Angie he'd sent a substitute and Angie had jumped to the conclusion that he was bailing out. "Fuck. Fuck fuck."

Derek fancied himself as a waiter, which was just as well. He glanced at his face as he passed the gilded mirror by the cash register; his cheeks were flushed, his eyes bright, his collar white. He had to admit that being trussed up like a turkey suited him. He paused, still; the two champagne cocktails on his tray carried on bubbling. He moved them sideways to see his whole suit. If he pulled in his belly, it fitted him more or less. That would soon go with all the running around. He scanned the dining room with the eyes of his old profession – a wallet on table six, a laptop on the floor near the Men's, a handbag open by the Ladies', a mink coat on the coat stand, ticket 22. Aware as he was of the CCTV camera, mining all this might have to wait. He tipped onto his toes, then sidled over towards table seven. It was when he put the glass to the left of the bird that he remembered her. It was Gregoyan's daughter. Only this time she was fully dressed, and wasn't miserable. She was starry-eyed, giggling at a joke the man opposite her was telling. She teased him about something, called him Eddles. Derek listened. No way this bloke was her husband. Boy, this girl gets around. He placed down the second glass, dusted breadcrumbs off her place setting, and reversed as quietly as a cat. He took a breath only once he reached the shadow of the gilded canary cage. Didn't want her recognising him and creating a stink.

It was while he was placing another set of drinks on a tray that Derek noticed the chief honcho chef of this establishment standing stock-still at the bookings-desk, looking at the happy couple as if he was considering having them both barbecued.

Chapter 34

Guy stared at Ray's back. It was hunched in front of the control panel, his whole attention focused on it. 'Harvesting its potential' is what he said he was doing. Guy wished he would stop, and turn around. Then he could try to tell him what he'd just been through. He couldn't bear to move any closer to the small viewing screen, which was flashing picture after picture of a naked woman with Fiona's head.

He felt distinctly queasy. Perhaps it was the crab chowder he'd brought back for their supper. No, it couldn't be. He'd sourced the crabs from Portlands in Ware on the Dorset coast. They were as fresh as the sea itself. Which was more than he could say for his wife.

"Stop this, Ray, please," was what he wanted to say. All he managed to do was groan.

Ray was humming 'God save the Queen', his knees tucked under him, a mess of wires and switches around him, relaxed, utterly absorbed.

Guy tried to picture a fully clothed Fiona here in this very room. But why should he care what she did here? He tried to boil down his feelings into something digestible. The fact that she'd humiliated him in his restaurant, in front of his staff, over the food he'd so lovingly prepared was the problem. He supposed she must have meant to enrage him.

As if that wasn't enough, she'd shouted to the whole dining room that it was her who financed each last mouthful of her lover-boy's *sorbet lavende anise*.

Money!

That's all any of them cared about.

What about his life-blood, his creation, his cooking? Did they have to lick his *orange en feu* sauce from each other's fingertips so flagrantly? It was he, Guy de Borzoi, or – to call a spade a spade – he, Gary Barker, who'd made the bloody pudding. Money didn't do anything but buy time and ingredients. Couldn't she at least give him that? He had a good mind to go back to his old name and fish, chips and blood pudding.

Ray's back muscles tightened in a way Guy longed to touch. But this was no time for anything erotic. Not between them at any rate. Ray had freeze-framed an image onto the small monitor. From the picture, Guy recognised her hat, at least. He realised he hadn't seen the rest of his wife for some time – if that was who it was.

She wasn't the easiest woman to get along with. But in his part of Birmingham her kind of money was something you only saw passing the allotments in a hearse. Auntie Lil had warned him:

"She'll use you like a toy. And when she's tired of that, her rich Dad will wipe his expensive boots on you."

If only he had. His father-in-law had never once deigned to come over, never mind dirty the mat. The old bastard only paid for their wedding on condition they feast their guests at the Armenian club. All those toasts in cherry-flavoured paint- stripper. They had such effect that Auntie Lil defied her arthritis, age and gravity and danced the can-can.

Guy jumped when Ray turned; he was grinning.

"It's all here. More than we need."

Why hadn't Ray checked first with him before lending

Fiona the flat? They were supposed to be edging out of trouble, not plunging into it.

"You just have to go over to the old boy, mention in passing that someone is blackmailing you with footage of your wife, and say that you need his help."

Guy shivered. This was unthinkable. Anyway, Ray himself would obviously be the prime suspect, so what was the point? "You must be joking."

"Joking? I never joke," said Ray.

"You approach him, then."

"Me? I'm not related to the man."

"If he sees his daughter's state of mind emblazoned on a screen, he'll blame me."

This seemed to give Ray pause for thought.

"Anyway, why is the restaurant losing money?"

"Have you heard of the recession?"

"Maybe the whole enterprise is a disaster."

"Are you saying that I'm no good at business and you're a mediocre chef?"

"No, I'm a very good chef, but you..."

Ray was glaring at him, daring him to go on. He couldn't. After all, Ray was prepared to dirty his fingers to support any terrine, soufflé or gratin whim he had. That showed good taste, if nothing else. No, he had to do his own quota of vegetables at the chopping board of life, so to speak.

Regarding Papa Gregoyan, he didn't know what he could promise. "I'll see what I can do," he said.

"And I'll mix us a cocktail," said Ray.

"I need some air." Guy slid open the door to the terrace.

He went out, leaned against the terrace railings and drank in the damp night air. Lights began to light up distant windows in random sequences. A line of geese carved a line across the clouds, honking. He wondered how they would fare as a *confit d'oie*. It pained him to think of so many goose-livers, out of reach.

Jake swirled his third pint of bitter around the glass. How had this happened? Another woman had dumped him. Angie was a nicer, more loving person than any of the others. But she'd still done it.

Well, he wasn't going to let it happen.

He was going to talk her out of it.

He tried her number again. Without leaving a message.

The drinkers left in twos and threes, umbrellas unfurling at the street door.

The Cock and Bull was emptying around him, his hold on a corner table no longer challenged. No newcomers were arriving to shout inanities in his ear. Was the doctor going to show up? This was the time he usually did. Jake had decided he needed his expert advice on women.

Now that he thought about it, perhaps he was exhausted after a session with the mad Fiona. God.

Where was he?

He downed the rest of his pint.

Another picture began to form – if the doctor got close to Fiona – even briefly – the coast to Angie would be clear.

The pub's smoke faded to a bitter taste in Jake's mouth. He finished his pork scratchings, scraping the last traces of salt from the empty packet. This was it. He had to reach Angie while he could still persuade her to change her mind. There was nothing for it; he had to find Angie's address.

On the far side of the room, Max was facing a bevy of young women, who surprisingly, on this occasion, were gathered like fruit flies around a peeled banana. Inexplicable. Could he have won the lottery and be sharing his secret technique? They must be students, Jake decided. He slid his empty glass along the bar counter and walked up to Max, who was flushed, tipsy, and seemed to have three rather pretty girls entranced.

"The only thing between Truth and Justice is the letter of the Law, and those signalled out to interpret it," Max was pronouncing. His audience were nodding in admiration.

Jake stared at them in amazement. Were they perhaps foreign and unable to understand him? He bowed at the girls. They ignored him. Well, he wasn't going to splay himself open for their rejection. He'd had enough of that for one evening. He turned his back on them and tapped Max's shoulder.

Max swung round, knocking a glass from a table. It tumbled to the floor and dripped, refusing to break.

Jake sympathised with it. "I need your help," he said to Max.

"But I'm spending a few precious moments here with my new fwwwiends… telling them that… it was me who made the difference between life and death…"

Jake suddenly had a vision of Max older, fatter, and in a judge's wig, delivering a long prison sentence. It was horrible. Jake grabbed the front of his coat and spun him round to face the door.

"The defining moment," said Max defiantly, "was when I flushed the spunk down the sink, replacing it with my own."

Jake was conscious of three dropped jaws as he marched Max into the street.

Chapter 35

"There was such a rumpus nobody noticed the rabbits had got into the kitchen." Angie looked across at Ted, who slumped over his computer. "Are you listening?"

He was humming to himself, not even pretending to be interested. She stared at him, furious. He was so impenetrable. And so bloody well turned-out. His silk tie was beautifully knotted; his shirt was uncreased. He didn't have a hair out of place. He looked like he'd come home from a holiday, not a stressful job.

How could anyone come back from work looking exactly like they had done when they left? But then she hadn't seen him leave recently. She'd been too busy getting Dusty off on her trip. And tidying up the storm Alex had left before going off with the Browns. Ted didn't do his share with the kids. Never had done. Oh, he'd help them with their maths or take them to Burger King if they asked. But they'd have to ask. She sighed. Did it matter anymore? Soon, they'd be gone altogether. In another year or two.

A whiff of coconut suntan lotion from family holidays, and suddenly she was standing at the reception of the Hotel Bellariva, Italian opera swirling from the radio, Alex and Dusty, tiny, still needing her, tugging at her arms, Ted banging the bell, dressed beautifully in unbleached linen, perfect for the occasion, signing the register with a flourish. What had happened to him? To them?

She began to tell him her story again, this time more slowly, as if translating it. "The rabbits, they'd got into the kitchen and were hiding under the sink. But, amazingly…"

There was still no reaction.

She breathed in, looked hard at the darkness beyond the window, holding back tears. "I was so terribly worried that Mrs Willoughby would…"

Ted was tapping away on his laptop, as far away from her as Italy-out-of-season, or the moon.

She resolved not to get irritated. Instead, she would sit quietly, companionably, and dwell on the peaks of their relationship without kids interrupting. The only thing was – their shared landscape didn't have peaks anymore. At best, it undulated slightly. Alright, she would try to remember something important from this simple shared evening. Hmmm.

Where should she start? Ted had been as late as usual, blaming work. He'd whistled under his breath, and hadn't looked stressed. In fact, he'd worn an air of triumph, rather like the shiny briefcase half-open on the floor at his feet. He'd eaten his microwaved fish pie and peas with gusto, and had searched for a second helping. This was highly unusual, now that she thought about it. Normally, he only did this when Arsenal won an away game. There wasn't any more pie so he'd made do with celery, rice-crackers and a second glass of Chianti. (Oh, dear, she'd been very sloppy with the shopping recently.) Crumbs were on the plate by his side; there were only dregs at the bottom of the wine glass. He was now making a low noise like a dish washer. Humming a tune perhaps? She couldn't recognise it.

It wasn't as if something was missing between them; it was rather as if something had been added, an invisible barrier like a skin, separating them. Whatever or whoever it was, she had to get rid of it. Jake's face appeared in that space beyond the window. And hovered. She blinked it away.

She didn't pay any attention to a tapping at the same window.

"Shall we go to bed now, before we're both too tired?" she said.

He laughed. Not unpleasantly.

"Why is that…" she tried not to show hurt in her voice, "…funny?"

"It's some idiot's proposal that hospitals offer a lottery scheme for beds and surgery," he said, pointing at his computer screen and chortling.

He didn't usually laugh after supper.

She began for the third time: "Mr Aranovitch received a standing ovation at the Home. Well, those who could stand, did. The others banged their Zimmer frames, or used their teeth as castanets, and whistled. He promised he would come back to Vetchling with a coach and take them all to Baden-Baden."

Ted shifted his position – a little stiffly, she noticed.

Had he been exercising? He hadn't mentioned resuming his gym regime.

"Mr Who?"

"Aranovitch."

"Do I know him?"

"He escaped. Don't you remember?"

"Hmmm."

"I went to Baden-Baden to bring him back."

"Poor man."

"Not poor man at all."

Was her husband accusing her of being anything less than a humanist?

"Don't blame him, trying to escape that bloody Willowberry woman I should think. He must have gone to some trouble to escape. Why bring him back?"

"He didn't come back."

"Good."

She noticed that Ted let out a small cry as he moved, as if his back hurt.

"Shall I book you an appointment with the osteopath?"

"What? Why?"

If she didn't know him better, she'd have said he looked furtive.

"Your back is hurting."

"Whatever makes you think that?"

There he sat, ignoring her, as if their marriage was some sort of listed building. Would he carry on not noticing her if she tipped him off his comfortable chair?

"Because you don't seem to be yourself," she said.

Jake had one foot on Max's shoulders, the other dug into plaster under a ledge, his knees apart and straining. Through the lit, double-glazed window, Jake could see Angie open and close her mouth like a goldfish breathing out of water. Each exercise of her jaw appeared crushed by an outside force. Each effort grew weaker. He longed to tell her to stop trying. On the other side of the room, he could see a profile set in a pool of light. The expert witness himself.

Under him, Max was jigging about, agitated. "Why don't you come down and ring the bloody bell like a normal human being?"

"She's in the doctor's front room, staring straight at me.'

"Fuck."

"Why didn't I listen when she told me her husband was involved in a trial?"

"Get down, dammit."

"I can't."

"Why not?"

"Disturbing her home life. It wouldn't be fair."

"My shoulder's going to fall off."

"You're going to have to ring the bell…"

"Me?"

"…And distract him, while…"

Fiona took off her hat and leaned her face against the cool window of the taxi, half closing her eyes, sated. The city's streets blurred into red and yellow, dark figures picking their way across neon-lit paths with long-legged shadows like ants on missions. Hip-hop belted out from the car nearest them and Beethoven crescendoed a little further along. Wait 'til she told Angie about this lovely new man.

They weren't moving. She opened her eyes. Commercial Road was a log jam.

"Has something happened?" she asked the driver.

He looked over his shoulder at her, lime-green-turbaned and sympathetic. "You could alight here, and take the Docklands train."

"Train? Certainly not. Just carry on." Guy wouldn't be home yet. The flat would be humidified, heated and empty. She caught the taxi driver giving her an anxious glance, nodded at him, smiled.

He nodded, smiled back, nodded again.

She gazed out at the lines of brake-lights studding the grey stone buildings with red; the vans and cars and buses that owned them carrying lives home or further, wherever that was. She peered at her driver's beautiful furls of lime-green turban and saw cities built of ancient brick, glass and steel, crumbling wooden shacks, pagodas, on plains, astride rivers, perched on milky white mountain peaks, and suddenly felt linked to all humanity in a surprising leap of affinity. Her spirits soared, bringing with them a new idea for a hat – a city-at-rush-hour hat. Her city. Its body would be from tarmac-grey felt, cross-stitched with white road-markings. She would stick a London bus to its rim and hang a small silver bike at an angle where it could dangle, tinkle and catch the light. There'd be no cars or taxis – as a concession to global warming. A traffic light could protrude from the crown, sprouting magenta, orange and green pompoms, and bleep, if pressed. She could think of the very client who would buy it – the harridan in London Transport with pathological hat cravings.

She must have laughed aloud again.

"You are very happy this evening," said the driver. "Have you had some good news?"

"Hmmm, yes," she said, her mind drifting back to Casier aux Homards, Eddles's hand on her thigh as he chose an appetiser. She and Eddles had been introduced to Claude, the lobster, before having him grilled to perfection. Eddles hadn't actually said anything but she could feel that he found it distasteful. She would take it up with Guy at the next opportunity. No more nicknames for the crustaceans. And there was the whelk-and-cockle wallpaper. She'd never noticed how frenzied it was, before. Guy needed help with the décor, with the dishes, the staff, and everything; she could see that, now. Especially since she was funding it all.

Things had been a little less controlled at the cloakroom desk, where Eddles had made a meal of wrapping her coat around her, behaving more as if he were disrobing rather than robing her. It was exquisite. She caught the cloakroom assistant averting his gaze. That would get back to Guy. How could it not? Unlike Jake Horribilis, Eddles wanted to arrange to see her at the same time and place the next week.

There was just one little problem; of course next week, he'd be meeting Angie, not her. She'd completely forgotten to tell him.

She would have to explain to Angie in words of one syllable.

Now.

Outside, the traffic began to move, cars passing them on either side, horns tooting as if clearing their throats, the smell of diesel. Hold on a moment – was that Daddy's limo, on the other side of the road, in the bus lane, travelling east? His journeying this far from Knightsbridge could only mean one thing – he was on his way to see her.

"Please turn the cab round, and head for Mornington Crescent," she told the driver.

She felt the cab slow down, take a jerky turn to the left, stop; and then, with a wild tooting and screeching of brakes, they were travelling back the way they'd come.

Chapter 36

Derek found himself back in the silent limo. Only this time he was right next to Gregoyan. Not very comfortably, it had to be said. He stole a sideways look at old Money-bags beside him, in his Savile Row finery, his crinkly old neck smelling of musk. By contrast, his own waiter's whites carried a whiff of fish. Well, bloody served Gregoyan right. He'd hauled him out of the restaurant before closing time and hadn't given him time to change. He'd only just had a moment to wash his hands.

So, here they were: Tweedledum and Tweedledee cruising along Commercial Road again in the limo. What was it about this time?

Derek took another peek at Gregoyan. The man had such unblinking eyes. And a way of holding his own hands as if he was meeting himself for the first time. Derek didn't trust Gregoyan as far as he could do him over, that was for sure. For the record, he wished he could do him over, and live long enough to count the proceeds. Fat chance. He edged away, and stared out at the passing pedestrians. Traffic was so bad he could have picked their pockets clean by rolling down the window and sticking his hand out.

A loud *twaap* made him jump.

What? But Gregoyan was only cracking his fingers.

"What do you have for me on de Borzoi?" he asked.

"Runs a tight ship," Derek said, cautious as an old duffer crossing the Edgware Road.

"Ships. I know all about ships," said Gregoyan, working the word around as if it was a ripe peach. "I own most of them. If unmanaged, they ooze oil, breed lawlessness, hide stowaways, catch fire and sink without warning." He jabbed his head at the window, and the river. "And my son-in-law is no sea captain."

Why was old Elijah so obsessed by his son-in-law? Why wasn't he worrying about his nutter of a daughter, shagging anything on two legs, as far as Derek could make out? Okay, so maybe her hubby was more than friendly with his business partner, but Derek had no problems with anyone being gay; it led to rich pickings.

He returned his gaze to his window, and to the window of the cab opposite. It was tooting and doing a three-point turn in a space too small for it. Hang on a minute, wasn't that Gregoyan's daughter's face flattened against its window? There was no mistaking that feathered hat. Bloody woman was everywhere. Old Signet Ring's attention was also taken with the cab's manoeuvre. He was muttering something foreign.

"That lobster-pot diner's the same as anywhere else," Derek ventured carefully. "Everyone's on the take." This should square all the angles, he hoped.

With a grinding of gears, the cab passed them on the other side of the road.

Old Grey Eyes turned back from the window. "The staff or the owner?"

Derek slid around in his seat, uncomfortable that he was being coerced into saying something against his new boss. De Borzoi – for all his airs and graces and his assumed name – was in fact just a simple Brummie boy, creaming fat from folk who could do with a diet. And, anyway, Derek was beginning to like being a waiter; it offered opportunities. If he had to give the impression he was doing something, this wasn't bad. "I don't know any names and addresses," he said. "But the grub's good, and the punters like it. You should try the *Tatties Bruges* – best chips I've ever eaten."

Gregoyan flicked the intercom button.

"Turn around," he told his chauffeur. "And…"

Derek felt the iron hand on his wrist.

"I haven't finished with you yet."

The bell sounded through the house like an alarm. Angie glanced up at the clock – a quarter past ten. They weren't expecting visitors this evening. Had something happened on the street? Dusty'd come in an hour ago and Alex wouldn't be home 'til one at the earliest.

"I'll get it," she said to Ted.

The automatic light came on in the porch shining on two figures. She unlocked the Chubb.

A tall young man with bulgy eyes stood on the mat; he was out of breath, wore a ridiculous bow tie and had bits of ivy in his hair. His companion was partly obscured by the Mahonia bush with which he seemed to be tussling.

"Is Doctor Gold in?" asked the ivy-leafed young man.

"Why, what's the matter?"

"I need to consult him rather urgently about a case we're working on."

He was sweating and seemed hesitant, nervous even.

"Who is it?" called out Ted from inside.

"Some of your people," she shouted back. "Can't it wait until the morning?" she asked the young man.

"Sorry, but it can't," said his companion, who now stepped

forwards into the light. His voice set her heart flapping like canvas sails in a gale.

"J…" She coughed violently, remembering just in time that she should not, on any account, admit to knowing him.

Ted's footsteps reached them. He touched Angie's shoulder, pushing it gently to one side so as to be able to see who was there. "Max. Jake. What's up?"

Ted knew Jake? Angie was reeling.

"Something's come up. The sperm specimens. There's another sample, only…" said the tall young man.

"What?"

It was Jake who nodded.

Angie felt faint. Jake avoided her eyes.

"I thought we'd finished with the wretched stuff."

"Sorry, sir."

"You'd better come in." Ted walked away abruptly, leaving the door open.

The tall young man followed him, disappearing from Angie's view.

Jake hovered on the threshold, appearing to stare at the crack between mat and step. Angie was aware of the voices in the living room. Time forgot to pass. Angie stood with her mouth open.

"I wanted to…" Angie began, uncertain of what she was trying to say, just that *want* needed to be part of it.

Jake put a finger on her lips, softly, then followed his friend.

She stayed in the hall, desperate to catch her breath as she stared out at the main road beyond the trees where traffic blinked from behind dark leaves. The world seemed more vivid, every sound alarming. A door banged shut inside the house, disturbing a bird in the creeper above her. There was an agitated chirping, twigs and leaves scattered, and a tiny egg fell onto the garden path, breaking into two, the tiny yolk spilling out. She looked at it in horror for a moment, then closed the door softly, and willed herself back into the living room where the three occupants had their backs to her.

Jake and his friend were on their knees in front of the coffee table, rummaging through the contents of Ted's briefcase. Papers already lay strewn on either side of them, along with twigs and leaves. Anyone would think they'd been up the creeper. Ted was standing over them, hands folded.

"I've just thought of something," said Jake's friend.

Angie held her breath.

"Yes?" said Ted.

Even he seemed uneasy, Angie thought.

"Did he ever say he loved her?"

Angie's jaw dropped, but luckily no one noticed. She gave her cheek a sharp pinch.

"Not as far I can remember. The nurse gave him some Playboy magazines, put him in a darkened cubicle, and told him to get on with it. After all, it was only his count and its mobility we were concerned with. The nurse herself… wasn't involved."

"If you could remember him loving her, in words or otherwise, we might get an appeal," said Jake's friend.

"I'm sure it's not something a woman would forget," Jake added, softly, surreptitiously looking round at Angie. "And what about her? Did she ever love him?"

Angie sank into Ted's armchair, releasing all its air, and tried not to catch Ted's eye. Instead, she stared hard at Jake's friend.

"It doesn't matter what she felt about him. All that mattered to her, was… you know what I mean." Now Jake's friend winked at Angie in a way that horrified her. Who did he think she was?

And more importantly, who was he? A colleague? A friend? What did he know? It was overwhelming. She closed her eyes. Perhaps she should disappear before anything worse happened.

"There is a reference here to his suggesting they made love on the sofa, while watching the FA cup final," said Ted. "I think it must have been just after Arsenal scored…"

There was the rustling of papers; a piece must have escaped.

"If we get an appeal, the case could come and come, sorry, run and run," said Max.

"I don't know… it could take me away from my family." Ted flashed a grin at her. She tried to loosen her lips enough to grimace back at him.

"Think of the satisfaction you'd get," said the young man.

"Who would?" asked Jake, rather too quickly.

She took a deep breath, and strained every muscle in her body to ask:

"Shall I make us nice pot of tea?"

"Or something stronger?" asked Ted.

"Now you're talking," said Jake's friend.

"I'll do it." Angie had to make every movement separately in order to reach the drinks cabinet without screaming. She made it and held the counter with both fists, her back to the room.

"Do you all work together?" she asked, hoping her voice wouldn't betray her.

"Sorry, I should have introduced you," said Ted.

She made a supreme effort to turn towards him, and smile.

"I'm Max." The tall young man waved.

Was he leering, or was that how he always looked?

She splashed ten-year-old malt into a glass and wondered how she was to carry it, with every part of her trembling.

"I'm Jake," said Jake, in a low voice, from the furthest corner. "I would rather have a cup of tea, please."

"Oh," she mumbled, barely audibly and staggered from the room, grateful he'd given her the chance to leave, praying no one would follow her.

In the kitchen, she grew calmer, setting cups on her favourite Andy Warhol Marilyn Monroe tray when she heard Jake's footsteps. He cleared his throat; she could smell his aftershave. It was cheap but heartbreaking.

"You know my husband?" Her voice sounded shrill.

"Let's talk about it next Thursday." There was something entreating in the way he fingered her elbow. His shoes met each other at the toes as he edged forward.

She felt his breath as he took the tray and leant backwards so as not to let him touch her.

"Only if you promise to…" She faltered. See Fiona again? Never see her again? Pretend he didn't know her, Angie? Shout out that he did know every nook and cranny of her and wanted to go on knowing her? Exactly what did she want him to promise?

He left, walking backwards.

She switched off the kitchen light and turned left in the hall, stumbling up the stairs to throw herself on Dusty's bed. Then, drawing the duvet over her head, she sobbed.

Chapter 37

Fiona climbed out of the taxi and emptied the contents of her purse into the taxi driver's open hand.

"Keep the change," she said.

The taxi sped away.

The street was lit by only one or two period streetlights and, apart from the pounding of her chest, it was quiet. She scanned the row of identical terraced houses separated from each other by neatly barbered hedges or stubborn brick walls.

What number was it? Twenty something? Forty something? Which one was it?

The last and only time she'd been to Angie's place, she'd been sozzled.

It couldn't be the one with the fancy garage – Angie didn't have a car. Or the one with grinning cats engraved into the masonry – Fiona would have remembered those.

She carried on walking until she recognised a chipped yellow gate and remembered that the house was half-consumed by greenery. Pushing open the gate, she stepped over some broken flowerpots and dislodged ivy.

On the doorstep, she paused. How was she going to put it?

"Angela, you've broken all our rules." That should cover it.

"But…" She would give Angie time to feel bad, cry and beg forgiveness and offer her something to drink, then and only then would she say… "Just this one time I'm going to forgive you." She'd have to give Angie both cheeks to kiss, before… "You like that appalling Jake." Angie would deny this of course. Perhaps she'd leave out the 'appalling'. "So I'm not going to hold that against you. I'm going to give you both my blessing."

Then they could both get tiddly like the last time and amend the rules slightly. Rule number whatever could have a sub-clause that allowed to Fiona to have a new man all to herself. Eddles. Of course, they could carry on sharing the flat, on alternate Thursdays, but bring their own supplies – the men. They might even cobble together a foursome and play Strip Scrabble in two teams. Right. She drew her shoulders back.

There was a light on in the front room; someone must still be up. Damn, what was Angie's wretched IVF husband called? She stood in front of the window, unable to see anything but the grape mouldings on the lit ceiling. She used a thick branch of wisteria to pull herself onto the ledge and peered in.

There were three men in the room, their backs to her, half obscured by a side table, concentrating on some documents spread out on the table. This wasn't surprising; men were always doing something incomprehensible. One of them picked up a piece of paper and turned towards her as he examined some detail; his face contorted into a sneer. She didn't like his gangly limbs, his expression, his squinting eyes, or the way his leaf-stained shirt swung loose from his trousers. She wished she'd brought her reading glasses to get a better look. If this was Angie's husband, he was rather young, wasn't he? And unattractive. No wonder Angie had wanted to share a lover. But where was Angie? There was no sign of her in the room or the corridor beyond it – but that was her basket tipped over on a side table, its contents spilling out. Perhaps she should give Angie's mobile one more try. She balanced herself against the windowsill, pulled out her phone, and clicked on the number. Miraculously, she could hear it ring – there it was on the table under the standard light. Another of the men turned and the light shone right onto the face of the awful Jake.

That was a shock.

What was he doing in Angie's house?

This was definitely against all the rules.

Unless...

Something dawned on her.

Angie knew Jake already. All this 'candidate' nonsense was sheer make-believe. The cow.

Fiona dropped down from her perch. Stepping back, she looked up to see which room Angie could be in; the top light was on. She picked one of the muddy boots, and hurled it at the top window, hissing:

"Angie Riley... come on out."

The boot fell back and nearly hit her on the head. A tabby cat appeared on the neighbour's wall, stared at her. Angie's house stayed curiously quiet and leafy. Well, she wasn't going to ring the doorbell and make an undignified appearance. It would look like she cared. She stormed back down the path, sending the flowerpots flying, and caught her sleeve on the gate.

"Fiona Seta Elena Gregoyan," said a voice in front of her.

She froze.

"Daddy?"

He was standing on the pavement, his limo parked behind him on the kerb, its headlights dimmed, its engine purring. What the hell was he doing here?

"Get in, my dear. We must have a little chat."

That's all she needed.

A man in a waiter's apron opened the door to the back of the car. He looked vaguely familiar. Where had she seen him before? All her fears ganged up on her. If she weren't careful she would embarrass herself by bursting into tears, which never brought the best out of Daddy. He admired self-discipline, not unrestrained hysteria.

Fiona reluctantly accepted Daddy's arm and sank into the comfort of the leather seat. He slid into the seat beside her. The waiter disappeared somewhere into the dimness of the rear compartment, and the car peeled away from Angie's street.

Guy tossed and turned in bed. The flat felt strangely crowded, the mattress lumpy. He just couldn't get comfortable. He felt sick to the stomach. Even Ray hadn't managed to reassure him. It was one thing to distract Fiona from everything he and Ray were cooking, quite another when she seemed to have learnt how to spin her own sugar, so to speak. Didn't Ray realise that he would be just a little upset? He gazed at the part of Ray's head that protruded from the pillow. The forehead was long and wide, cresting down to a shell-like ear; an eye was half-closed behind thick eyelashes. He reached out and stroked the brow, feeling the hum of his brain under his fingers like a machine that was never switched off. He had a sudden repulsion, like when a *tarte tatin* was overcooked.

It had been a confusing day. And it was time to go home to his wife, if that's what he could still call her.

How was he supposed to carry on behaving as if she didn't exist, when he now knew so much about her…what could he call them?…inclinations? His new understanding changed things.

Guy tried to relax by doing a bit of stocktaking. One – he

didn't have a wife, in anything but title. Two – he wouldn't have a restaurant if he didn't have a wife. Three – he wouldn't have a rich father-in-law to fall back onto if he didn't have a wife. Not that his rich father-in-law was the sort of man you would want to fall back onto. However, exactly what was in his store cupboard?

Ray.

Would Ray love him if he didn't have the wife, the restaurant and access to credit?

No, was the short answer.

What else did he have? Anything bottled or even freshly picked?

A very small voice inside him whispered – talent.

Another voice shouted – of what relevance is that? He laid his wonderful culinary creations before people who were too busy, or too full, to taste them. Dishes flashed past him, from a golden time – John Dory fish-balls he'd made for the Working Men's Christmas Party at Wolverhampton, which had brought cheers from men used to jeering; the pancakes for the Nuneaton UFO Society's thirtieth birthday the same year, which were the talk of the extra-terrestrial seekers community; the picnic for the Vicar's Away Day, where he'd used all local ingredients, and there'd been salmon in the sermon. He felt tears brew in some Brown Betty part of his soul. He had to admit that Fiona had built him up from someone whose ordinary, bargain- basement fish-balls were wolfed down by working men to having the same dish written up as *Bal de John Dory* in gourmet magazines.

But, what was he without her?

He might be able to fool everyone else with his *Carree d'Agneau d'Avignon* and his *Cotelettes Composees,* but, as far as he was concerned, they would always be lamb stew and grilled chops.

He let one foot drop out of the covers. It hung in space,

between the sheets and the carpet.

He had to reclaim the Gary Barker out of the ruins of Guy De Borzoi.

He was disentangling his other foot from the sheet when the door buzzed.

Chapter 38

Ted watched them go through the front garden to the gate. It squeaked as they left, as if in protest. Needed oiling. The garden path was strewn with dislodged ivy and broken flowerpots. It could do with a bloody good sweep. He was about to raise an arm to wave goodbye to the young men; but they didn't look back. Once they were in the street, they broke into a run. Must have seen a C11 bus arriving.

This had, after all, been a very productive meeting. Very. Perhaps Ina Endicott could get rights over her ex-husband's issue after all.

By God, these young men would make fine lawyers one day, such diligence, and such energy. Bollard's ferreting out an ancient High Court ruling meant months more work for all of them. He could treat himself to taxis for a year on the fees alone.

He sighed happily and turned back to the house. He won so few battles in his work; it wasn't his fault; the odds were stacked against him. Older women had low ovarian reserves and high expectations as well as healthy bank accounts. So much of the progesterone, oestrogen, dehydroepiandrosterone, syringes, swabs, paper towels and bedside talk brought so little new life into the world. He wished he could tell his clients the truth: that their lives were short, their chances slim, and there were other pleasures in the world besides the cry of a new baby.

It was chilly. Or perhaps he was tired. The air was cool and smelt of diesel fumes from the road. A wind was tugging at some loose branches, and making the wretched gate creak. He nosed some of the leaves from the path with his shoe and headed for the kitchen, where he rummaged for the WD40 spray-can.

Fiona sank back into the plush leather seat, letting the street lights blur past, feeling she urgently needed something she could wrap around her head, her face and her emotions. An invisible hat. That was it. What would she call it? Mystery? Sleep? Silence? It would have a trilby base softened with midnight-blue chiffon, and sprout a black ribbon from its crown, rippling all the way to Mount Ararat and the nineteenth century. It needed to be light so that she could carry it everywhere and wear it every time Daddy reclaimed her.

Daddy sat facing the other window, swinging his worry-bead chain.

This must mean he was going to disinherit her, again.

Should she bring up Varushka?

Daddy let the worry-beads fall onto the seat; he took her arm.

His fingers felt knotted and shook a little.

"What's the matter, Daddy?"

He didn't seem to be able to speak. Was he ill? She turned and peered through the smoky glass at the aproned man in the rear compartment for clues. Where had she seen him before? She leant back to get a better view. The bruiser's nose and crooked teeth! Of course, he'd been at Guy's: the new waiter! She smiled rather weakly at him. His lips didn't respond, but one eyelid drooped. Was it a wink? Or a twitch?

Leaving her with that unsettling sign of having recognised *her*, he turned away to look out of the window and she saw the clawed tattoo snaking around his neck! Oh, no! He wasn't just a waiter; he was the gardener at Ray's flat. The one who'd sat on the bed and offered a Scrabble solution.

He couldn't be both.

Or could he?

He had been both. It could mean only one thing – the man was working for Daddy. Then Daddy must know everything. Droplets of sweat began to trace lines down from her armpits. Naked games with someone you hardly knew were one thing; nice Eddles was another. Urbane, gentlemanly, keen on lobster thermidore. Daddy would see him as a direct attack on the family honour. Not like Guy who he was comfortable despising. The ring clinked against Daddy's knuckles. She dared not look at him.

He wasn't going to cut her off, was he?

She sat as quietly as she could, trying to contain her fears. In the darkness of her mind, they were mushrooming.

Daddy let out a low moan. Was it possible that he also was suffering? He wouldn't have her to persecute anymore. For goodness sake, get a grip, she told herself. She didn't want to have to feel sorry for him as well as herself. She'd never manage both.

She tried not to panic. Would Daddy stoop so low as to seize ownership of her flat? She imagined its contents being packed into huge containers and driven away, along with Guy and his cooking utensils, into a storage facility somewhere beyond the M25. And her shop? She bloody wouldn't let the bailiffs in. Not until she'd done the finishing touches to the Hat of Anger at least. Even then she'd cling onto it as some brute tossed her other creations into his pick-up truck where they would sag among grimy rope coils and dog muzzles, their colours running in the rain. It would be raining. And she'd have to run down the street, hatless, in odd shoes, chased by the local kids all the way to the Council Housing Office, to stand in line.

Don't be ridiculous, she told herself, you have a perfectly viable business that you've built yourself. Even if Daddy helped you at the beginning. And if the worst came to worst, you could begin it all again by recycling hats from rubbish left on skips and selling them at car-boot sales.

The limo was drawing up to the kerb. She saw they had landed outside a block of modern apartments behind wrought-iron gates. With a sickening feeling she recognised the place only too well.

Yes, this was it. May as well face it.

"So, you know," she said in a low voice.

"Yes."

"I'm sorry, Daddy, but we all have to live our lives our own ways." Boy, this was brave. Well, she had nothing to lose.

"Not if you have to lie to sustain such a life, Elena."

"Daddy! I don't lie to you." At least, this was true. She didn't see him often enough.

"My poor child. Not you."

What was he on about?

"Not me?"

The gardener-waiter opened Daddy's door and helped him to his feet. And round to her side of the car. Her door swung open. Daddy stood looking down at her.

"There is something you have to see with your own eyes," he said, and spat into a bush.

There was no other course but to follow him into the foyer.

Chapter 39

Angie smelled Ted before he entered the bedroom; he exuded good wine, surgical soap, and a determined look she knew only too well. He launched himself out of his clothes with one swift movement, leaving them in clumps at his feet, before diving into the bed beside her. His arm brushed her, his legs snuggled down next to hers. His skin felt softer than usual. She caught a whiff of something different, but familiar – a spicy scent she knew very well, but couldn't place. What was it? He began humming again. He'd been out of tune all evening. He never usually showed any interest in music after work. Now he was searching for her feet with his, and giving 'The Look of Love' a rasped airing. Oh, God, making love to Ted would be a muddying of everything she'd just renounced with Jake, wouldn't it? But, exactly what had she renounced? In fact, by being muddled and silent, hadn't she just promised to see Jake again next Thursday? What was the opposite of a renouncement? An announcement? She felt trapped within the confines of a Rubik's cube. Green, yellow, red. And black.

Ted's body was pulsing with an intent she hadn't witnessed for ages.

She looked heavenwards for some sort of perspective. A slice of night sky showed through a gap in her striped curtains. Even the stars looked diffuse and indecisive, uncertain as to whether to shine though the dark or disappear into it. Oh, dear! Betraying her feelings for Jake was one thing, doing this with the curtains open was another. She rose, went to the window, closed the curtains tight. Then she climbed back into the part of the bed furthest from Ted.

Ted didn't seem to get the hint; instead he leaned his hairy leg against her thigh. She sighed loudly. This was meant to convey that tonight was inconvenient for her. He didn't move away, but laughed amiably, pushed her nightie up and placed his hand on her belly. He appeared immune to the bedroom signalling language they'd developed over twenty years, stroking her belly in rhythmic circular movements. She had no recourse but to use her sleeping-hamster position. She let her arms relax, held her breath, kept her gaze fixed at the slither of darkness beyond the windowpane.

"I was thinking…" he began.

"Oh," she said, trying to sound asleep.

Ted's hands moved up to her left breast. He began kneading it.

She was about to push his hand away.

"That Jake Bollard…" he said.

She froze. "Who?"

"You know – you met him earlier – the one with plenty of hair – charming, smart. We must have him round for dinner, so that you can get to know him better."

She gulped.

He moved on to her right breast and gave that a workout too. "Who can we pair him with? Do we know any gorgeous twenty-year-old women?"

What? "No, we don't." Thank God Fiona couldn't hear this conversation.

Not wanting to show him quite how bothered she was, she let his hand travel south, where it playfully tugged at her pubic hairs as if he was trying to tune an antique stringed instrument.

"I could ask Brenda. She'd be game," he said.

She wasn't laying a dinner table for Ted, Jake and that honey-voiced secretary who always patronised her on the phone. "Doesn't she have anyone of her own?" She couldn't stop herself pushing his hand away.

"She'll love him. He's really got something…" Ted was using both arms to pull her towards him. Her nightdress was beginning to block her airways. She sat up and threw the garment across the room.

He's got me, she almost blurted out.

"…A wisdom beyond his years…"

On the other hand it was a relief to hear someone talk positively about Jake. "How well do you know him?"

Ted was mounting her.

"Enough to admire his verve."

"His what?" This was very confusing.

"Oh you know… That's not to say he doesn't have a few emotional problems."

In spite of her whirling mind, her body was relaxing. "What sort of emotional problems?"

Ted looked around as if someone could overhear them. "He's terrified of women."

"Hmmm." She pushed Ted off and mounted him herself. "He was perfectly civil to me. And I'm a woman."

Ted gasped with pleasure. "No, no – in love, Angie."

Her movements were coming in bursts. In spite of herself. "In love?"

"Someone older and the world would be his oyster." Ted was coaxing her towards a climax.

"Oyster?" She felt the flooding tide of her own ocean.

Then she was overcome by desperation; she needed someone's reassurance – anyone's.

"Do you love me?" she asked.

"Of course."

She rose as high as she could over him, digging her knees into the mattress on either side of his hips, pinning his arms to the covers with her hands, just as she did with Jake.

"Say it," she urged through her teeth.

"Say what?"

"That you love me and that you'll never leave me."

"Relax, Angie, relax."

She felt tears well up unaccountably.

"But it's all so..."

"Is it?"

"You know what I mean..."

Everything rose and surged and finally released in her with a violence she hadn't expected and she shouted out the name that she stored hidden with alternate Thursdays.

She heard the *jay* reverberate around the room, shaking the windowpanes; the ake tinkled all the glass fronts of the family photographs before it dived, at the end of her breath, out of the window. She froze, appalled at what she had revealed, waited in dread for Ted's realisation to catch up with her.

But he was away, in a world of his own, jiving with the spasms of his own pleasure. He jerked and muttered something too. Was it also a name?

It wasn't hers. Whose was it? She stared at him, dumbstruck.

His eyes were flickering under closed lids. He epeated the name, with more yearning this time.

What was it he said? Lana? Diona? That was the name of a spring-cleaning company.

"Oh, oh…" he groaned. He put out a hand to touch her hair. She pushed him away.

Then it hit her. Like a short circuit. Or the ceiling falling down. She knew what perfume he was carrying, and whose name he was calling.

"What did you say?"

"I do. I love you."

She looked into the brown intelligent eyes that gazed back at her. They seemed to be twinkling. She wondered if hers were too. How little they knew about each other. They seemed both caught somewhere so sweet, so intimate, that it was tempting to share the experience. She could have asked him who? He could have asked her the same question.

"I love you too," she said, sighed, and closed her eyes.

Chapter 40

Fiona was determined not to show any sign of panic she walked down the corridor to Ray's apartment on Daddy's arm. How different it had been three hours earlier when she'd sauntered out of here on the arm of Eddles. Where the lighting had been muted and romantic, it was now dim and slightly unnerving, the building silent of anything but the alarming hiss of air-conditioning. At least Daddy had banished the gardener-waiter to the foyer, where they'd left him reading an old *Country Life* under the baleful eye of the porter. Now that she thought about it, could he have been paid to spy on everybody?

Daddy pressed the bell. The door jolted open, revealing Ray, in a dressing gown. His jaw dropped. He stared at Daddy, then at her.

"Is Barker here?"

This was the first time she'd heard Daddy call Guy by a name. Even if it was fifteen years out of date.

Ray took a few steps backwards. "Good evening, Mr, er, Gregoyan, er, Mrs de Borzoi..."

"You heard me."

"Did I? I'm terribly sorry, but could you repeat what you just said?"

Daddy wasn't doing anything of the kind.

"Guy," said Fiona, desperately. "That's who he wants."

"Who?" There was a long pause as Ray seemed to try to recall someone he'd once known, then he cleared his throat loudly. "Ah, yes, your husband has just...."

Daddy was already marching past him into the living room. Fiona heard a clash of cymbals.

"...Been finalising next week's serving rotas."

She followed Daddy, edging past Ray.

"Guy," called Ray, in a high, shrill voice.

Guy obliged by appearing, naked from the waist up, a razor in one hand, half of his face covered in shaving foam. On seeing Daddy, he quick-stepped back to the bathroom, a wanton trail of foam in his wake.

"He needs a shave more than once a day," said Ray waving his arms as if a swarm of wasps was attacking them. "Happens more at this time of year."

Ignoring him, Daddy headed for the sofa, where he sank like a ship, his hands knotted around Mummy's gold chain.

Fiona couldn't help noticing that the room seemed smaller and was unusually messy; half-full cups and glasses lay about; the coffee table was covered with CDs, the floor strewn with computer printouts. Even Arthur's control panel was exposed. She picked her way over wires and cleared room for herself on the other side of the sofa from Daddy, opposite the open bedroom door.

"...Don't you find yourself growing hirsute in humidity?" Ray continued to no one in particular.

"I have come to make you both an offer," said Daddy.

Ray's shoulders seemed to soften slightly. His eyes gleamed.

"Offer?"

What on earth was Daddy talking about? Fiona was going through all the possibilities in her mind when she thought she caught an image of her and Eddles on the far bedroom wall. It couldn't be that art installation's idea of a joke, could it?

"What offer, Daddy?" she asked, half-standing in her attempt to block his view of the flickering images.

The installation launched into Winston Churchill's 'we shall fight them on the beaches'. This seemed to grab Daddy's attention. He stared past her.

"One he won't be able to turn down," he said grimly, turning to Ray.

"Guy!" called Ray again.

She noticed he was doing some sort of sign language at a mirror in the hall and took the opportunity to edge towards the exposed art installation control panel. She stretched, but was too far away to reach the top red button.

"Damn!"

"Quiet now, Fiona Elena." Daddy stood up to tap on the partition wall. Then he paced carefully in one direction, counting his steps, as if measuring the size of the room. "One hundred and ten. Good, good," he said, before stopping at the window and peering out.

"Coffee? Or cognac? Or both? I'm certain he'll be back in a jiffy," said Ray, not sounding certain of anything.

What the hell was Guy doing? Taking the razor to his jugular? Fiona thought she could make out several naked Angies breasting the picture rail in the bedroom, the matching number of Jakes beneath them. At any moment they might intrude into the living room.

Luckily Daddy was now taking stock of the sun's position by measuring it with his thumb. Trying to calm down, Fiona began an imaginary count of her hats.

"Why don't you have something to drink, Daddy," she said, when he threatened to return to the sofa and a view of the bedroom.

With a dismissive wave of his hand he bent down to

examine a crack in the plaster above the skirting board. He scraped along it with his fingernail as if testing for damp.

"Or armagnac? I have an excellent bottle," Ray persisted.

"I'd like some," she said.

Ray almost ran to the drinks cabinet.

"What is there to like about it?" asked Daddy.

"I quite like the effect it has." How strange. He'd never been interested in her tastes before.

"The effect?" Daddy frowned at her, then peered around him.

"It's warm, and smells nice."

He reached out his hand to pat the nearest wall. "Dry, I'll grant you," he said.

Ray arrived at Fiona's side with a small glass filled to the brim.

"Dry? I suppose so." She sipped at her drink.

"Water?" Daddy asked Ray.

"Yes, yes, water." Ray raced over to the drinks cabinet and back with a jug and glass. He poured some for Daddy, his hand shaking, and offered it to him. "You did say water, didn't you?"

Daddy seized the glass and examined at it as if looking for tadpoles. Then he put it down on the table in front of him, untouched. "This is the fourth floor. How good is the pressure?"

"Er… we, sorry, I have a power shower which works perfectly alright."

"Lease," Daddy shouted, making Ray jump.

"Lease?"

"How long have you got left?"

Under his tan, Ray was growing very pale. Was Daddy referring to Ray's lease of life? And had Guy escaped? She had an image of him escaping Daddy by climbing down several beautifully knotted Egyptian sheets. She slugged down a mouthful of the brandy and was horrified to see that a kaleidoscope of blurry random mating couples were filtering out through the bedroom door and taking purchase on the skirting board.

Fortunately, all Daddy's attention was now on Ray, who he seemed to assume was deaf as well as stupid. "How long?" he shouted, even louder than before.

Who were *these* new figures rooting along the skirting board? Did Ray hire out the apartment every afternoon to different people, then blackmail the users afterwards? Art, my eye.

"The lease here?"

"Yes, damn you, man."

While they were busy trying to understand each other, or so she hoped, she grabbed Daddy's glass, tiptoed over to the exposed installation control panel and poured the water over it.

The panel sparked, fizzed, the sound died. Light dimmed to a single bulb. Apart from the hum of traffic and Daddy's heavy breathing, there was now silence in the room and darkness on the bedroom wall and skirting board. She'd done it!

Neither of the men seemed to notice.

"Ninety-nine years." Ray sounded frightened.

"Then name your price," Daddy shouted.

"My what?"

Fiona felt like a child on one of Daddy's business trips to oil wells, ignored, patronised with sweets, overhearing a deal she didn't understand.

"The price this apartment would fetch on the open market."

"But it's not for sale."

She was relieved to see Guy appear; he looked flustered, but dressed, the silly man, even if his shirt buttons were out of sync. She waved weakly at him.

He grimaced back at her while tugging his shirt rather unsuccessfully. "Why, hello Father," he said weakly.

"You cheating, lying piece of manure," snarled Daddy. "The only reason I am here is that my daughter likes this flat."

"Does she…?" Guy gave her a desperate look.

She felt she had to say something.

"But Daddy, I don't especially like this flat…"

He turned to her, his eyes bulging. "Yes you do, Elena."

"But…"

"Mr Gregoyan, I do think you should listen to your daughter occasionally," said Guy, softly.

This was brave of him.

"My business partner simply came in to finalise his employment rota. Is there a law against that?" Ray was shouting now.

"Shush, Ray," she said weakly.

"Carrying on as they do, these men are an insult, a grave insult to our Gregoyan bloodline."

"They've got nothing to do with the Gregoyan bloodline."

"So we must do what the Gregoyans have always done." Daddy made a hissing sound. "Destroy our enemies and take their horses."

"Oh, Daddy…"

"I'm only thinking of you, my dear," he said softly and tenderly to her, which was confusing. Then, to Ray, he bellowed: "Name your price."

"Please, somebody, tell me what is going on." Guy stared at her for clarification.

"I only said I liked this apartment, Daddy, because I could share it with someone." Unable to prevent herself, she reached across and rearranged Guy's buttons. "You see, I know Ray's a bastard."

"Easy on," protested Ray.

"And that Guy is weak."

"You *knew* that they...? You *accepted* this...?"

The worry beads dropped to the floor.

"There," she said to Guy, patting his shirt back down.

"Thanks, doll," he whispered, looking relieved that at least something was in the right order.

"Yes. Why don't you ask me what I want for once?"

"Four million for the flat..." said Ray.

"Isn't anyone listening to me?" she shouted.

Guy put a hand on her arm and squeezed it.

"And two hundred thousand for keeping quiet about all this," persisted Ray.

"Stop it, Ray..." said Guy.

"You will spend the rest of your life regretting you said that," said Daddy.

"If you ever bothered to listen, I would tell you, Daddy, that all I ever wanted was a proper Dad who takes me to the theatre, or the cinema, or lets me take him to the river or the park. A Dad who comes to Sunday lunch even though he knows I can't cook very well." Furious, she brushed away a tear.

Daddy wasn't looking at her; he was staring at Ray as if he was going to have him freeze-dried and packed into one of his shipping containers.

"But go on, Daddy, make your ridiculous deals and alien-ate the only person who could possibly really care about you."

But Daddy was hell-bent on his present mission of destruction, one that had nothing to do with her, or any-thing she wanted. She realised it had been like this as long as she could remember. And that she was powerless ro change it. She found herself missing her mother, Angie, Rudolfo, and, actually, in a strange sort of way, Guy.

She rose, gave him a peck on each cheek and left, slamming the door loudly behind her.

Chapter 41

Angie was pushing a supermarket trolley down the aisle of Sainsbury's, and was surprised to find Jake beside her. Dad was grinning at them from the label of a tin of tomatoes – which was strange because he never grinned. Her mother was her own life-size person, but was talking to a nodding cat featured on a cereal box. She carried on wheeling the trolley when a red bottle attracted her attention. Eerily, she could see that inside it was Ted, in vinegar, and next to him, a veiled woman preserved in olive oil. A miniature Dusty was sizzling in one of the display frying pans, with her sunglasses on, and a tiny Alex was hacking his way through a jungle of asparagus with a machete. The cash registers played a tune she seemed to know. She clutched Jake's hand to pull him towards the tills.

Then she woke up, tugging at the bed cover.

The clock said six-thirty.

She put out her hand.

Ted was there, his back to her, breathing evenly, the duvet pulled up to his neck. No hint of that unfortunate revelation last night,

She moved in closer, sniffed at his skin.

It was faint, but it was there – Fiona's perfume. Of that she was certain. The smell was as distinctive as her flowery handwriting. It summoned something ice-cold like grapes, but on a balmy day.

Fiona was the name he'd cried out last night in the heat of passion.

Ted moved, muttered something. She laid her hand on his back, the back that belonged to her perfectly serviceable husband – as dependable as a winter coat on a spring day – a bit heavy to lug around, but you never knew when you might need it.

And all the time he'd been canoodling with Fiona.

Is that why she wanted to set up the timeshare?

But Fiona showed no sign of knowing Ted. In fact she never remembered anything Angie ever said about him, including his name. She had certainly never introduced them to each other. How could they have met?

Fiona was always consulting doctors.

Ted was a doctor.

Fiona was supposed to be her oldest friend even if she wasn't her best one.

The two-timing bastard. She felt a sudden urge to slap him,

He let out a small snore, then went back to breathing deeply and calmly.

Angie slid out of bed, her heart a stranger, and put on her dressing gown.

She passed Dusty's empty room and closed Alex's door so that the cat wouldn't get into his room and sharpen its claws on the wicker chair. The whole house felt like a departure lounge for people booked on different flights.

She padded on to the bathroom, dropping her gown onto the tiles before switching on the shower and letting it run. She watched the steam rise, clouding the frosted window pane which separated them from the ivy-covered wall dividing her back garden from the coffee shop in Delancey Street, where the first customers would be downing espressos.

Fiona and Ted. Ted and Fiona. They sounded like a couple she knew. She should have known.

That night on the timeshare barge.

Ted must have known Fiona would be there and didn't want her and Fiona to meet. He made sure they were late and hadn't expected Angie to jump aboard like she did. She didn't usually do things like that.

Angie stepped under the hot water and let it pound her skin with small jets of heat, trying to gather some warmth.

They must have cooked up this whole timeshare scheme to throw her off their scent. What an idiot she had been. And Ted knew Jake already. Of course he did. Ted had sent Jake to that apartment to entertain her. And Jake had done it so beautifully. This hurt. It hadn't seemed like an act; he was so convincing. But was it? Her cheeks burned. She began to cry, sniffing, then started scrubbing her scalp, tugging at tufts, not caring if she looked like a Mohican. After all she was only going to work, where her wards wouldn't notice if she'd turned into Beelzebub on ice skates, as long as she got their Zimmer frames, commodes and mashed potato delivered in the right order.

She scrubbed her left, then her right arm, working her way into her shoulder. She thought of Jake's bright, uneven, sad smile, his hot dusty touch, the downy hair on his back, his soft way of working to the heart of her. She rubbed at her skin ferociously, trying to remove any trace of his, or Ted's, or anyone's, touch.

Jake woke up early, grinning. The trip to the doctor's place was a coup; Angie'd promised to see him again Thursday. Well, she hadn't actually said she wouldn't. Same thing. Seeing her there, on her own turf, somehow, he felt like he owned her. From now on, whenever Carruthers barked at him, he'd think of her curves spilling over the proverbial three-piece suite. Or her standing in front of her own door half-hidden behind ivy, looking at him in that baffled, sweet way that he'd grown to rely on. Mind you, there was a slight drawback. There was the doctor and the court case. If he wanted to hang onto his unpaid job, there was some urgent research to do to get that situation reviewed.

He threw himself clear of his blankets and last night's toast, shook out a pair of boxer shorts before donning them, and rummaged through the pile of laundry, which he used to cocoon his laptop. He switched on the monitor.

The screensaver marched a row of penguins across ice, then gave him several options: A Nuevo Tango download, 5 new crazed-looking friends on Facebook, and an update on his credit rating which went some way towards denting his confidence.

Taking a deep breath, he started a new file, typed in the words: 'fresh sperm sample', paused blankly, then felt exhausted. He needed coffee and a change of scene. His journey to the kitchen consisted of three steps and a turn towards a shelf.

There he found the jar of very fancy French stuff he'd filched from chambers. Actually, now that he thought about it, it came at the same time as Ted. Ah, never mind. And there was still a scraping of St Ivel left at the bottom of a tin.

He switched on the kettle, which hissed malevolently at him. What a mess the place was in. He had to do a major blitz before inviting Angie anywhere near the place.

He'd have to throw out the spider-plant, for starters, stuff his books under the bed, and liberate a pillow from its job as a draft-excluder. He stirred the powdered milk in a murky, clockwise direction, sat down, and stared at his computer screen again.

The case needed a new direction. Some bullet points. One to ten. Beginning with what? He punched out: 'future directions'. There he paused, his hand on the mouse. Thursday was aeons away.

Then a new thought intruded, overshadowing all the others.

Was it this Thursday or next when Angie had agreed to meet him?

Angie chained her bike to the railings and removed the helmet from her untidy hair. It was a beautiful sunlit morning, scored by blackbirds and honeybee frenzy over the buddleia flowers. She strode towards the entrance of Vetchling Grove, pausing to watch a robin pull a worm from the damp soil around the rose bushes. As if she had all the time in the world. Well, she did – she was early on this morning of the beginning of the rest of her life and she was husband-less, lover-less, and friendless. While she was at it, she was going to change all her habits. She rummaged, then switched off her phone. There was no one she wanted to hear from.

She drew a deep breath, looked about her. The garden was thriving without any complications. It wasn't worried which flower was open for bumblebees, or which bird chose which song. It just got on with its business. This is the new me, she decided. Lighter. Simpler. With no responsibilities.

She sailed into the building.

"Hallooo."

Silence. The entrance desk was unattended.

She coursed on into the dining room, which also seemed empty until she noticed Mrs Willoughby, standing, staring out of the window, her back to her.

"Morning," cooed Angie.

Mrs Willoughby's back seemed to shudder.

Angie raised her voice: "All quiet on the Western front?"

Angie had had enough of these sulks. It wasn't as if she had done anything wrong. And there didn't seem anything that needed her urgent attention. The room was orderly and peaceful apart from an array of detective novels scattered over Mrs Willoughby's desk. All the breakfast places were laid, spoons and straws neatly placed next to the cereal bowls and smeary glasses of water.

Then something struck Angie. She checked her watch.

"Where is everyone?"

As regards rudeness, this silence took the biscuit. "Don't worry. I'll pop upstairs and see what's happening."

"You do that."

Angie didn't like this tone one bit. All those detective novels can't be good for you. Leaving the morose Mrs W at the window where she seemed to be studying cloud formations, Angie took the stairs two at a time.

The first-floor corridor was quiet. All the doors were open. Inez, one of the nighttime carers, was sitting on an upside-down bucket, her head in her hands.

The inmates couldn't all have died in their sleep, could they? Or worse – been poisoned by the fish pie. That was an all-too-likely disaster waiting to happen.

She peered into the first room on the left. Mrs E's bed was neatly made up, which was strange for so early in the morning. Angie entered the room and looked around. And Mrs E's brocade slippers were at the foot of the bed, rather than in the usual place, on her feet. Where was she? Had she chosen last evening to shuffle off her mortal coil? She'd seemed fine the day before. And no one had reported seeing any rabbits.

Angie opened the cupboard – there was only a threadbare old dressing gown, a green cardigan and some empty hangers (Mrs E was a snappy dresser). She checked the shelf above the sink. There was an empty space where she expected to see ENO's Fruit Salts and teeth in a jar. Then she looked up and saw that the pink leather suitcase was missing from its place at the top of the wardrobe.

She stepped back into the hall, and entered the next room, then the next and the next. All were empty of their residents, teeth and suitcases. The only inmate to be found was Sid, Mr Aranovitch's goldfish, whose tank had been moved to the corridor. One fish eye looked back at her, with an air of world-weariness, then turning to swim the other way it treated her to a stare from the other, slightly cloudier eye. Thank God Sid at least was still in the land – well – water of the living.

By now thoroughly alarmed and not wanting to begin a conversation with Inez in holiday-Spanish, Angie ran past her, raced back down the stairs, and back into the dining room where Mrs Willoughby was still mulishly staring out of the window. The clouds outside had thickened. There was a storm brewing.

Getting her breath, Angie waited for Mrs W to say something. It felt like a whole fortnight before she cleared her throat and said, without turning, "Your Mr Aranovitch…" She waved her arm at the world beyond the windowpane. "Do stop behaving as if you don't know."

"Sorry?"

"He planned it very well…"

She didn't seem in the least bit interested in making herself clear.

"…Sending a luxury coach, a four-course picnic, three bottles of schnapps, and a doctor. Taking the passports from my drawer. Saying he had your authority."

"My what?"

Mrs Willoughby turned, finally, to face her. Her lipstick was smeared and she had a strange glint in her eye. There was a strong whiff of schnapps on her breath. "That's what he told the night staff."

"But where are they?"

"Well, if you don't know, then I don't know who does..." Mrs W's voice was slurring.

Angie realised her mouth was open and closed it.

Mrs W yanked at her pocket, swaying on her feet.

Angie overcame her natural desire to help her, to help anybody.

With a cloth-ripping sound, Mrs W extracted a set of keys, which she threw at Angie, while yelling, "You better sort this out!"

Angie looked down and recognised the keys to the Home's mini-bus.

Fiona stretched out sideways in bed. It was cool, uncrumpled and acres long. No Guy. She felt a tad aggrieved. It would have been nice if he'd come home last night. After all, they did have a bit of a history. Especially with Daddy. And if she never saw him again, she might miss him.

She pushed against the edge of the bed with her toes, screwed up her eyes, and tried to remember him at the beginning, before they'd become acquainted, when he came in off the street, dripping rain, his motorcycle helmet balanced on a pizza box soaking the pepperoni beneath.

"Adds to the flavour," he had said in a phlegmy Midlands burr she'd found unaccountably sexy. She always fell for men she couldn't understand.

Everything about him was wet, really. His forehead, hands, cough, place on the pillow. His cooking was never dry or crispy; it oozed, drooled and gurgled with sauces in various stages of steam, bubble or ice. But it did smell good – mostly. She'd miss that.

No, she wouldn't.

His restaurants sold his food. She'd take Eddles there once or twice a week. Just to rub it in. Perhaps meals at Casier aux Homards could be part of the divorce settlement. On the other hand there was something good in having a 'husband' to add to official documents and party invitations. Wasn't there?

With a wonderful rising feeling in her solar plexus, she realised that she wouldn't miss him at all.

She rolled sideways, like a child down a grassy hill, until she tumbled out of the bed and onto the carpet. From there she gazed up through the slatted blinds.

The sky was bright blue and festooned with streams of jet-clouds. A plane's wing glinted, heading for the City Airport. Standing up, she pulled the blinds up so that she could have full sunlight on her naked body and get a better view of the river, far below, where canoes were racing in rows like melon slices.

"Goodbye," she said aloud.

It would be cowardly of him not to contact her at all. Perhaps he would wait for the heat to die down before he came to collect his copper pots. And there was no way he'd leave his precious saffron behind.

Daddy would have stayed on in Ray's flat. She'd witnessed his methods working on sultans, priests and generals; she didn't need to see it work on Guy. She could picture the whole scene.

"Barker, you wouldn't want to leave the kitchen before your time," Daddy would say. "A waste."

Which of his stock of plagues would he promise? Cockroaches, rats, frogs, salmonella?

Or would he simply have the land redeveloped under Guy's feet?

"This city needs a new motorway. Here."

Then Daddy would go very quiet, sucking his teeth, and draw out wads of notes, looking baffled as if he didn't know how they got there. He would stuff them back into random pockets, letting one or two notes drop. He'd wish Guy good health, and say it would be charming if they could have dinner after the decree nisi. When he left, he wouldn't bother to close the door.

Suddenly she felt anxious. The flat! The door really was closing on it. Where would she meet Eddles? With horror, she realised she didn't have a phone number for him. Or his full name. She'd told him to come to the same place at the same time on Thursday. And he'd smiled. She hoped it was compliance. And if she didn't get hold of Angie, it would be her he'd be meeting. And Angie seemed to have a new way with men…

Fiona made strong black coffee and left it on the bathroom shelf while she showered, splashing and singing – 'Love Is a Many Splendored Thing'.

There was no one to give her a silencing look as she emerged from the bathroom, naked and wet. And no one to comment on her choice of figs and cream for breakfast, which she ate in her midnight-blue camisole, dipping the figs in the cream and slurping at them as noisily as she liked. She chose a bright green skirt and a deep magenta blouse for the day, adding a chunky silver and amber necklace which didn't really go with anything, but she felt she needed an anchor. Guy had brought the jewel back from Morocco on a harissa-paste-seeking expedition. She looked severely at herself in the hall mirror, and added a green felt hat adorned with pink berries, but decided against that. She tried a red-feathered cap, but took that off too. Eddles said she had lovely hair. She shook it loose and went downstairs in the lift. Tipping the porter with a ten-pound note, she walked to work.

Chapter 42

It was later in the day when Ted got the message. He was in the cool room, labelling sample bottles for the court clerk.

Angie's tone was urgent, breathless, like when the kids were late home or she'd gone into overdraft at the bank.

"I'm on the Rhine Autobahn, in case the kids were wondering…"

"The what?" He couldn't connect what she said to anything on the A12.

"…In a lay-by, eating pretzels."

"Did you say autobahn?" This sounded strangely familiar. "How on earth did you get there?"

"Don't worry, I haven't taken the car. I've got Vetchling's mini bus. Resting the engine, which is overheating."

"You're in Germany?" He heard paper rustling and the scratch of worn windscreen wipers. It must be raining wherever she was.

"They're gone."

What was she talking about? "Who?"

"All of them."

She wasn't making sense. "All of who?"

"Mr Aranovitch has become the Pied Piper of Vetchling Grove."

"Are you alright?"

"Don't worry; I won't come back in a hurry. I wouldn't want to get in the way of your smutty little affair."

"Smutty?" Was he hearing correctly? Surely something was wrong with the line. "Sorry, could you repeat that?"

"Yes, your sleazy little Thursday liaison."

"Sorry?"

The reply, if there was one, could have been drowned out by blood rushing through his ears. When he'd got his senses back, he heard:

"Remember to pick the kids up at the station. They'll be on the same train."

Then a click.

Ted stared at his phone. He didn't feel irritated, as he usually did, with Angie's lack of chronology. The way she connected things irrationally. His pulse was racing too hard for that.

Had she really said what he thought she said? His heart thudded randomly; he had difficulty pressing the buttons on his phone; somehow his fingers couldn't seem to do what he wanted then to do. When he pressed 'Angie' he got a foreign-sounding ring and no reply. Pied Pipers, autobahns, overheating? Had she really gone abroad? Or was she sitting in the car right outside his clinic, with the windscreen wipers on, about to make a scene in front of his clients?

Liaison?

Hardly. It was no more than a flirtation, completely above board. All conducted in a restaurant. Under the eyes of Joe Public.

But if he was honest with himself, he'd wished it could have been a lot less public and more intimate. Jake's extra woman was rather, well, unusual. Alluring. He'd been, well, invigorated, as if he'd experienced an electric 1,000 volts.

He wasn't himself. He couldn't be. He'd been under enormous stress – a nerve-wracking court case that unwanted press attention, the IVF lab break-in, not to speak of his wife's strange recent behaviour. It had all taken its toll, made him take up cooking supper and visiting the sympathetic Cuban woman at the dry-cleaners.

He found himself staring at the blindingly white walls, the gleaming stainless steel shelves, the military rows of glass jars as if he was seeing them for the first time.

Angie had found out.

How?

The porter in the building? His BlackBerry? Had she somehow seen him with her? He cast his mind back over all the people in the street, in the restaurant and couldn't remember anyone either of them knew. Yet, somehow, mysteriously, Angie knew. Sixth sense?

Maybe it was just as well. But then there was nothing to feel too guilty about anyway – it wasn't as if they had been off to St Tropez for a weekend together, was it?

He was no good at secrets. Especially this sort. It would slip out, trip him up eventually. Better to get it bottled, labelled and stacked away in the right rack.

What was he thinking of?

He'd have to come clean. Apologise. Order some flowers. A bouquet. Red roses. No, too obvious. Something quieter. Freesias. They didn't droop and shed petals. And not too big a bunch. Size could denote guilt. Desperation.

Angie hadn't said when she was coming back. If she was coming back. The last time she took off to Germany for a day, she reappeared a week later in a very shaky state. All he'd managed to get out of her was a diatribe about some odd psychiatrist.

He felt in need of someone to talk to. Nigel for a pint? His sister? Bollard? No. Much better to see someone unconnected to work.

The person he really needed to talk to was, of course... but no, that was the one thing he couldn't do.

Or was it? Could he possibly give Fiona a call? Nice name, Fiona. Jake had said she was fragile. Didn't want her having a nervous breakdown on his account. Since he was going to have to come clean to Angie, and apologise, he may as well make a job lot of the whole business. His spirits lifted.

There was that oyster bar in Islington. Off his beaten track. Yes.

Then he realised he didn't know how to contact Fiona. Except through Jake. Could be embarrassing. But she'd said something about meeting him at the same place at the same time. Thursday. Seemed like a very long wait.

He looked down at the plastic screw-top tubs he was holding. Couldn't read the label; it was smudged. Did it say Earle or Endicott? He squinted at the slimy contents of the test tubes. IVF wasn't much fun for either party, if you thought about it.

The sun was out but the bench outside the Vetchling Grove Retirement Home was damp. Jake worried about his trousers, his sanity, and why he was always sitting on wet benches. There was the new case of Ken Endicott bringing proceedings against Ina Endicott, which was doing his head in. And there was the fact that Angie wasn't replying to his voicemails, texts, or telepathic messages. Could this gloomy place really be where she worked? It was like Rosalba all over again, and it hurt.

There were lights on in the small barred windows, but no sign of her. In fact apart from some rabbits bounding across the lawn, there was very little sign of any life at all. Maybe old people spent most of the day sleeping like matron at the Barnardos home.

Was that a glint of something at the front bay window? A

telescope? He looked over his shoulder in case there was a mugger or a predator of some sort about. He couldn't see anything worth staring at – unless she was watching the rabbits. It was definitely a woman with a pair of binoculars. Could she be spying on him? Why? It wasn't against English law to do one's legal research on a laptop in the sun, was it? This garden was open to the road with a low hedge and a rusted gate. There was no sign that said anything about 'private property'.

The door was opening and a woman came into focus and grew legs. She had tight curls, an angry face, and was waving a bottle at him.

"Hey, you!"

She sounded drunk. He tucked his laptop into the front of his jacket and ran.

Fiona reached over for the box, smoothed it down and turned to Ina, who was waiting expectantly. Poor woman; this court case must have taken everything out of her. Fiona teased open the tissue paper and revealed the hat. With its brilliant scarlet and black taffeta trims, and its jutting sharp spun-steel arrows pointing out in four directions, it was one of her finest creations.

"I've called it Voltan, the husband-enrager."

Ina seemed a tad underwhelmed.

"You'll be the *true* belle at court," said Fiona, lifting Voltan from its wrapping and placing it on Ina's rather large head.

They both turned to the mirror. Ina was a short, round-faced bespectacled woman underneath something from the Trojan War. Instead of rising to the occasion, she was blinking. She didn't appear capable of understanding Voltan's full potential.

Fiona had to make things clearer: "The thing to do is shake

your head a little."

Ina cautiously shook her head, setting off a device that clashed the metal rods against each other, emitting a cascade of bangs, clangs and tinny clanks.

"Gracious me."

Couldn't she say anything more expressive? No wonder her husband left her.

But then slowly, Ina grinned, revealing a row of sparkling, sharp, ferret-like teeth.

The Baden-Baden sky was emitting a steady drizzle onto the surface of the spa pool. The place was steaming with hot flesh and chatter, but no one seemed to be in charge. Angie sheltered under her generous Vetchling Grove umbrella, at the edge of the waters, in her best work clothes, trying to pick out the features belonging to her wards among the flushed naked figures bobbing past her in a continuous stream of bubbles. Were those Mrs J's copious white bosoms, loose and bouncing, as she splashed the back of a young Adonis? Without her signature grey cardigan, spotted headscarf and thick glasses, how could Angie tell? She gave the umbrella a sharp shake, wiped condensation from her brow with her other hand, and squinted harder. The laughing young Adonis could just as easily be Fiona's Frederick from the zoo. His shock of red hair looked identical. As did the freckles peppering his pale skin.

And did that abandoned Zimmer frame on the far steps belong to Mrs E? Mrs E wasn't allowed hot baths at the Home at all, on account of her high blood pressure. Could that be her – the very wrinkled lady among the tropical plants, singing *Edelweiss* in a croaky voice? That could give her the very stroke they had all been trying to prevent. Angie had to get her away from the palm fronds as quickly as possible and hose her down with cold water.

She looked around for assistance, walked over to the glass-window partition, and peered through.

Aha! A large white-coated person was just visible in front of a wall of tall thin steel lockers.

Angie tapped at the glass with her umbrella. "Please."

It seemed to take forever for the woman to turn around and see her. Then all at once she seemed activated as if by a remote control switch, waving both arms. '*Verboten*' was the only word Angie understood. But at least the woman was rushing to the partition door.

Angie waved at Mrs E. 'Help. Out. Out. Urgenttung.'

The woman didn't pay any attention to Angie's gestures; she burst into the bathing Saal, red-faced, glaring.

"Remove your clothes," she said.

"I have come from England to…"

"Immediately."

The woman could have been related to Mrs Willoughby; she pointed at a sign in several languages: 'No clothing allowed in the bathing hall' was the English version.

The attendant glared, as she waited for the arrival of Angie's clothes into her outstretched arms.

"No, I…" But perhaps it would be easier for everyone if she obeyed. Mrs E needed immediate attention. After a quick look around to see if anyone would notice, and using the Home's umbrella as a screen, Angie undressed as discreetly as she could. The attendant tossed the clothes over her arm, where they hung like old grey bunting littering the final moments of a political rally. Not content with that, the woman held out her hand for the umbrella. This was a step too far. Angie was not parting with this remnant of Anglo Saxon modesty, the one remaining symbol of the Home's authority. She used it as a portable screen.

"There is no sign that says you can't have an umbrella,"

Angie said and glared back over the top of the umbrella. The woman seemed to accept this, handing over a rubber-banded key, before stomping away towards the lockers.

Angie gave a sigh of relief. It was the first success of any kind she'd had for days. Gingerly proceeding forwards, angling the umbrella in front of her like a shield, she parted the fronds and scanned the steamy horizon for Mrs E, or her *Doppelgänger*, no longer visible. Well, there was nothing else for it. No other help was available. She slid down into the bubbles, immediately losing her footing as a strong jet bore her away, sweeping the umbrella downstream, ahead of her. And into the mizzle she shouted:

"Mrs Endemion, it's Angela Riley, Vetchling Grove." (Which on reflection didn't seem to have the slightest effect.)

More figures splashed past her, their voices so distorted by the gurgling that she couldn't even tell what language they spoke, the steam obscuring their features. She thought she saw Mrs S's face cruise past, framed by a fuchsia-pink bath cap. And almost fancied she heard Rudolfo Mirando singing an aria from *Die Fledermaus*. His great bulk loomed out of the steam, its shadow taking up most of the far wall. She must be imagining that, surely?

"Mrs Endemion," she shouted again, as loudly as a mouthful of warm, sulphurous water would allow. No response. Or none she could isolate. Oh, God, perhaps Mrs E had sunk below the bubbles already. She was giving up all hope of being able to pin anyone down when she imagined she saw Mr Aranovitch sailing towards her on a stylish inflatable penguin.

Or was he? It was becoming awfully hard to keep hold of reality.

"Angela," said a voice very like Mr Aranovitch's. "You received my message. I'm so delighted you could grace us with your presence."

She launched herself at the penguin and held on.

"Mr Aranovitch." She was close to tears.

He nodded sagely at her through the mist.

"You have to help me," she said.

With a wink, Mr Aranovitch disengaged himself. "You worry too much. Enjoy life a little more." With a splash, he and the penguin were gone.

No friend, no lover, no husband, no Mr Aranovitch, no penguin, no help, no umbrella, and, without retrieving her wards, very soon she was sure, no job.

Hanging onto the side of the bath, she inched towards the tropical plants, sweeping her feet hither and thither along the bottom to check if any of her wards could be marooned, unnoticed. The bubbling amongst the greenery was less intense and there she rested for a moment, wondering how to phone the Home for reinforcements. This was where she saw the trim haircut and little else of Dr H, who was deep in conversation with Mrs S.

Angie tried to reach them, but the jets propelled her on past them and to some steps leading to another *Saal*. Not daring to look back, she lifted herself out, dripping and panting, onto the cool tiles and followed the arrows.

Chapter 43

"Court rise," boomed Judge Stead.

Jake felt Max dig him in the ribs, propelling him to stand.

Several loud wheezes from further down the bench suggested Carruthers had also been launched onto his feet.

"The civil case of Kenneth Endicott versus Ina Endicott for the theft and illegal use of Kenneth Endicott's emission."

A few coughs and more wheezing and they all sat down again. The opposing barrister flurried up to the bench with his papers. Carruthers muttered something. It sounded menacing to Jake. So much so that Dr Gold turned around with a pleasant smile on his face. Somewhat baffled, Jake couldn't help noticing that Dr Gold appeared more relaxed than usual.

There was a metallic clinking sound at the back of the courtroom.

Jake didn't pay any attention until he saw Judge Stead drop his gavel.

The barrister, too, was staring at the door, open-mouthed. Benches squeaked as people turned to stare.

Jake turned, too.

Ina Endicott was standing stock still in the doorway. This seemed strange to Jake, as normally the woman was neither still nor silent. Then he realised the cause. Some sort of steel-coloured wide-brimmed contraption had wedged her head in the doorway. Was it a weapon? Some sort of bizarre helmet? Or could it possibly be a hat?

Attendants were racing to the rescue. She waved them away, looking awfully like an insect caught in a spider's web. Then she put on a frightening smile as if being head-locked by metal spears in the doorway of a courtroom was something to be envied, and gestured that the proceedings could continue.

Church bells woke Angie with a start. Where was she? Light blazed in through a tall window she couldn't remember seeing before. The sky was framed by limp grey velvet curtains and hosted a hot-air balloon in its watery blueness. She could make out the words *Wumag Texroll* on the banner. Germany. That's where she was.

She turned away, pulled the cover up over her eyes. It was made of a crinkly material and smelt of coal tar soap so she pushed it away again.

It felt very difficult to summon the strength to get up. Her body ached, her eyes stung, her skin was prune-like. It was all coming back. In her efforts to locate all her wards, she'd plunged through hot pools, cold pools and fronds. She'd been boiled and iced, exfoliated and oiled. All in the name of Vetchling Grove.

And her wards – had they been in the slightest bit grateful?

No, they'd wanted to stay forever in that steamy paradise. And she'd had to lure them away finally by stealth by using the very person who'd tempted them there in the first place – Mr Aranovitch.

She'd never have managed to herd them all into their clothes and the Vetchling Grove mini-bus without his help.

They would follow him to the ends of the earth. And that's exactly where he'd promised to take them next, even placing a 'destination – end of the earth' sticker on the front windscreen.

Her wards. She sat bolt upright. She hoped to God they were still asleep in the locked bedrooms of this small hotel. She'd secured them in their en-suite twin-bed rooms. Illegal, but necessary. She eased her aching body out of bed. Argh, she could hardly move.

Wearily, she climbed into the same clothes she'd been wearing for a week, staggered out of her room and tapped on the next door.

"Mr Aranovitch," she whispered, "are you ready?"

The door opened. Mr Aranovitch was dapper in a linen suit, his violin case at his side.

"Good morning," he said, beaming with health. "How lovely you look."

"You will help me get all your friends downstairs, won't you?"

"My friends? Oh, yes, I see! Of course, relax yourself. It will be a pleasure."

Breakfast was done in stages. Mrs E couldn't have coffee. Mrs S couldn't have bread. Mrs V couldn't find her teeth. There had to be fried eggs without the yolks, porridge without gluten, bread without crusts, and milk that was neither too hot nor too cold. It took an age to get everyone down the steps, into the mini-bus and on their way. Mr Aranovitch chose Schubert to accompany them, and then something by Richard Strauss. They'd reached the only hill in Holland when Mrs Willoughby rang. Angie used the hands-free.

"Someone from the press has been snooping."

Angie seriously doubted whether a few old people making an unscheduled journey to Germany would hit the front pages of the Daily Express.

"I'm sure there's nothing to worry about, Mrs Willoughby."

"There are no buts about it, I apprehended a young man skulking about in the grounds, taking notes."

The reception was intermittent. Her voice was slurred. Angie suspected Mrs Willoughby had commandeered the schnapps again.

"Did you say a young man?"

"You heard me. When I pinned him down, he claimed to be a friend of yours. And was looking for you. An unlikely tale. He's much too young. There's only one explanation – he's from the tabloids. They're onto this. If he shows up again, I shall discharge the Vetchling Grove cannon and bury him in the vegetable patch."

Oh dear. Angie made a mental note about duty free. Mrs W would be furious if they didn't bring back their full allowance.

Mrs W gave a mirthless laugh. "I expect you to hold a press conference and sort all this out the minute you get here."

Before Angie could gather her wits, the line went dead.

"What does it say?" asked Carruthers.

"Before or after section 7?" Jake was trying not to get irritable.

"Read section 7 again."

Carruthers began to pace up and down the tiny room.

Jake looked up at his twitching eyebrows and wondered how he was going to get out of range of that fierce stare, escape the sweltering room, board a tube and get to Ravensville Mansions by two. He hoped against hope that Angie would turn up. Stifling a scream, he read for a second time, "The Authority shall send a draft of the proposed first code of practice under section 25 of this Act to the Secretary of State within twelve months of the commencement of section 5 of this Act, or risk disqualification…" He was conscious of the clock chiming half past one.

In desperation he speeded up, spitting out the words like errant fireworks.

"…A failure on the part of any person to observe any…"

Carruthers footsteps quickened in time with Jake's pace, until he was pounding up and down the room like a swimmer drowning in a fish bowl.

But Jake seemed no closer to freedom.

"…Provision of the code shall not of itself render the person liable to proceedings…" The ruling went on and on. He decided to change tactics and slowed down his pace to a boring drone, letting the words bump into each other like an insomniac's sheep. But Carruthers wasn't getting sleepy. He tried another approach. "A licence committee shall, in considering whether there has been any failure to have a glass of good claret with lunch…" he peeked up.

"Claret? Good Lord, what time is it?" Carruthers stopped, drew breath, and looked at his watch. "Ah, that reminds me… Chop chop, Bollard. Back in an hour."

Jake had grabbed his jacket and was taking the stairs two at a time before the QC could change his mind.

Fiona was furious with Angie. Why wasn't she answering her calls? Who did she think she was? They hadn't spoken for four days. What was going on? All she could get from her wretched phone was that metallic bark the bloody things emit when they're abroad. It was against rules seven to thirteen, but, to hell with it. She called Angie's work number.

She got the dreaded Mrs Wallaby, who was most unforthcoming and sounded as if she was sucking a large mint.

"I know she's away," said Fiona. "But when will she be back?"

"ETA unknown," said the ghastly creature. Whatever that meant. "And don't call here again."

That did it. There was only one thing to do. She had to get over to Ravensville Mansions, and wait there for Eddles. Even if it wasn't her turn, and against all the rules. Even now she could feel his smooth hands on her thigh. She applied lipstick the colour of burnt oranges, and plucked out a stray eyebrow hair.

Chapter 44

The sun blazed down on Fiona's unusually bare head, making her hot and bothered. It was the wrong day to be hatless but Eddles had admired her hair. She had managed to be fifteen minutes early and needed a good vantage point where she could see him arrive. She clattered through the wrought-iron gates and paused, shading her eyes to look up.

No one was visible on the roof terrace; the third floor windows were closed, the blinds down.

Was anyone there? Ray might be in. Or Guy. Even Daddy? Or all three. With lawyers, accountants, spirit levellers and measuring tapes, for all she knew.

She needed to maintain a low profile while keeping an eye on the gate. At the front, tall twenties pillars rose from neat topiary balls of privet. They wouldn't provide useful hiding places for anything but mice. Then she saw a bench, half-submerged in some azalea bushes but still affording a view of the entrance. Perfect. She went over to it, pushed aside obscuring foliage, sat down and waited.

Birds sang; a jumbo jet came near – it seemed unusually near; a cloud softened the rays of the sun. It was very quiet in front of the building; a haze of pollen made her nose itch. She didn't mind. For the first time in ages, she felt happy. Life was good. She'd discovered Angie again, lost another husband, and found the love of her life, or, at least, someone who could stand in for one. All because of that timeshare evening. And she'd only gone to annoy Guy.

She was growing drowsy when she heard a white van reverse into a parking spot in front of the building. *Easy Come, Easy Go Removals* said the van's logo in peeling red paint. Her view of the entrance was now obscured. Damn.

Two men with *easy come easy go* emblazoned on their overalls emerged from the van. They were both smoking. One was telling some story that had the second one laughing and coughing asthmatically.

She was just about to shout – "*move your van!*" – then she stopped. It couldn't be him, could it? Those tattoos looked awfully familiar. The bloody man was now a removal operative as well as a waiter, spy and gardener? She knew times were hard, but this was ridiculous. And where Tattoos went – if it was him – Daddy invariably followed.

She sat back down again pretty sharply and pulled the foliage back in front of her face.

Tattoos and his mate didn't pay her any attention. The punchline delivered, they stubbed out their cigarettes and sauntered up the front steps of the building. The glass doors swished open for them, which is more than they ever did for her.

If Daddy was in the building, she had to waylay Eddles. Damn, damn. Calm down, she told herself. A couple of magpies strutted past. A bee dived into an ornamental thistle with a hiss. Beyond the gates a car hooted. She jumped.

She heard the swish of the glass doors again. The two men in overalls reappeared in the entrance with something under a dustsheet they proceeded to carry down the steps. It took forever. "Hurry up, hurry up," she muttered. After what felt like an age, they laid it down on the forecourt, then disappeared back into the building.

"Oh Come on Eddles," she said, willing him to arrive while no one was about.

"The r of 'rumbustious'..." answered a strained, shrill voice from somewhere.

She looked around. The place was deserted.

"...Is on a triple word score."

It was her own voice. And it seemed to be emanating from under the dustsheet.

The men weren't reappearing, so she crept over, was about to lift the dustsheet, when she heard:

"I'll have your boxer shorts, thank you," in her own voice.

She dropped the sheet.

It was Arthur, the art installation. What was going on? Could Ray and Guy be leaving already?

Taking Arthur with them. With her voice entombed in his inner workings. She lifted the dustsheet again and peered at what was under it – a tangled mass of wires and a control panel. Why was it still working? This didn't make any sense to her. Could it run off a battery? With an everlasting life, like a vampire. What was it you did with vampires? She looked around for a stake. Hmmm. The wrought iron gate looked a bit immovable. If only she had the Hat of Anger. She reached for her hair instead, found a hairgrip, unpinned it, found a hole in the control panel and pressed the grip into it as far as it would go. There was a spark, a fizz, a bit of heavy breathing she didn't recognise, and the soundtrack faded.

She could hear the voice of the security guard in the foyer. Footsteps. Noisy voices arguing. What if Eddles turned up now? She ran back to the bench and shrank behind the foliage again.

From the corner of her vision, she saw the men reappear and try to heave Arthur into the back of the van. But to her amazement, they were suddenly peppered with large, coloured indigo question marks. She blinked, wiped her eyes. Looked again. The question marks were spreading. That could only mean one thing – in some odd malfunctioning way, Arthur was still alive.

She prepared herself for the appearance of Scrabble letters or worse. At this rate, her Scrabble game could become a permanent display at the Tate Modern. She watched, mesmerised.

But Arthur seemed content with expanding the size of its question marks to cover any shady spot within range.

"Careful!" shouted an irritated voice. Fiona recognised it as Ray's.

Nervous that he'd spot her, she leaned as far back into the branches as she could manage without toppling over, at the same time straining her neck to keep an eye on the entrance.

Ray scurried down the steps in the direction of the van, closely followed by Guy. They were both a little close for comfort. She rolled onto her tummy on the bench and squeezed herself through the gap between the seat and the first slat, letting herself down into the azaleas. There, a little stiffly, on a bed of dead leaves, she turned over and lay on her back, her eyes closed, as if she was taking this opportunity to sunbathe. After a moment, she raised her head a little to see if anyone had noticed her.

They hadn't. The question marks had multiplied and were coasting across the T-shirts of all four men. They were huffing and puffing as they pushed and pulled the installation, the van tilting. Guy looked thinner since she'd last seen him on that fateful evening with Daddy, and – she hated to admit it – more cheerful. He looked as he had when she'd first met him. Some of his hair seemed to have grown back. Oh my God! Was that a toupee?

She didn't notice the stylish chocolate-brown suit until it had sauntered up the steps and into the foyer. Eddles! She could see him through the glass, talking to the porter. There was nothing else for it – she rolled over onto her hands and knees, crawled round the end of the bench, stood up, brushed herself down as if she'd just taken a small tumble, then made a dash for the entrance.

"Let's go," she shouted through the closed glass doors. Then, as he didn't seem to hear her, she banged wildly on the glass. The concierge appeared from behind a potted palm to glare at her. Eddles turned, beamed, waved.

"Quick!" she yelled, waving at him to join her.

He walked to the threshold. The glass doors opened. He hesitated inside them.

"What's wrong?"

She was jumping up and down, urging him to hurry up. "My friend could be arriving any minute."

"Do you mean Jake?"

"No, no, my friend. This is her week for... oh, never mind, let's go."

He took a step backwards. "Calm down," he said.

She stepped through the doorway and lunged towards him.

"This is a residence, not a garden centre, madam!" The porter made a furious gesture at her trail of azalea foliage.

She grabbed Eddles's arm and tugged at it. "She could be arriving any minute from Germany."

Eddles's arm stiffened.

"Germany?"

"It's too complicated to explain but I don't want her seeing you with me, so could we just get out of here?"

"Where in Germany?"

"Oh, I don't know. Some place like... Flyden Flyden."

"Not Baden-Baden?" He seemed to go pale.

"Sounds right."

She got behind him and tried pushing him forwards. But

he seemed to have taken root.

"Baden-Baden has become very popular all of a sudden," he said.

She heard the lift chime in the corridor. The porter looked up, expectantly, towards the inner door. Any minute, they would no longer be alone.

Weaving her hands over his face, she pressed them hard over his mouth.

"Don't speak!" she said. "Come with me." He seemed to weaken. So she grabbed his arm and propelled him out of the glass doors. She was relieved to see the removals van was in the same place, rocking slightly. There was no one on the forecourt.

"My wife…"

"Not now," she said firmly as she pushed him sideways towards the shrubbery. This route could lead to the back of the building; from there she hoped they could exit the property without encountering anyone they shouldn't – her husband, his boyfriend, Daddy's chauffeur, or, heaven forbid – Daddy himself.

"…Knows."

So? What was his wife to her? "Don't worry about your silly wife."

But Eddles was dragging his feet. Perhaps he was anxious not to get his suede shoes dirty. In the past she might have felt the same. But not now. She kicked off her shoes, and left them where they fell, stepping into the flowerbed in bare feet.

"*Avanti*," she urged, keeping an eye on the removals van, which seemed to be tipping to the other side drunkenly. Chortling gaily as if this was all a game, she pushed Eddles towards an evergreen shrub which shuddered and spat out a pair of butterflies.

Jake ran past the zoo towards Ravensville Mansions. At the crossing he had to slow down to allow a procession of children bearing large monkey cardboard cutouts to overtake him. They were followed by a zookeeper and a policeman. There was a blast from a whistle, and a flash of red coloured the sky as balloons took off for the sun. He pounded on. At Ravens Crescent he realised he was at the back of the building, so instead of retracing his steps, he scaled a high brick wall, trespassed through an ornamental garden, squeezed through a gap in some bushes and arrived on the edge of the Ravensville Mansions forecourt.

He was flying towards the front steps when a voice called from behind him:

"You couldn't give us a hand, mate?"

He looked back. Apart from a van parked at an angle, there was no one about.

"In here," said the voice.

Jake reversed back to the van and peered in.

Two overalled men were struggling to right some piece of equipment. It must have been some sort film projector because pictures were pouring out of a light box onto the wall of the van.

He was about to excuse himself and escape when he noticed that the projections were small green frogs. He looked closer. They weren't any old frogs. They seemed to be an exact replica of the frogs he had on his boxer shorts. How could that be possible?

He stepped inside the van.

The minibus was making remarkable progress. It had stopped overheating and rattling. Angie decided it preferred travelling towards Vetchling Grove rather than away from it to foreign places. They were already within sight of London.

Open farmlands gave way to a patchwork of allotments; a leafy village was replaced by drab rows of thirties houses with bulging wheelie bins. The sun shimmered in windows and mirrors and forgotten puddles. They were nearly home, if you could call it that for any of them. Angie glanced in her rear view window at her wards.

Mrs S was still sitting bolt upright in the first row, beating her stick, nodding encouragement to the late lamented Lily on the empty seat next to her. "Keep in tune Lily, there's a dear."

There was no harm in Mrs S honouring her dead friend, whatever Mrs Willoughby said. Some friends were more dependable when dead. They couldn't steal your husband, at any rate.

Mrs E was harder to see – bent almost double at the opposite window. But she was in full trill. "…*A poem lovely as a tree…*" she sang as sweetly as if it was a love song. Miss Nesbit had moved back to the next row. She looked happy enough. Well, perhaps happiness was not her forte. What on earth was she doing? Her mouth was open; her teeth were bared. Aha, she was drawing a comb along her dentures. Quite tunefully, Angie thought.

There was a 'ratcha ratcha ratch…' coming from Jemima Sands at the back, who was shaking a plastic milk bottle half-filled with hairpins. So that's why she'd insisted on buying them in a motorway service shop. Alongside her, Evelyn Barnsdale was stretched out next to the luggage, fast asleep, snoring along, punctuating the chorus with grunts when the minibus veered or bumped.

All of them were keeping excellent time to Mr Arano-vitch, who was perched on the passenger seat, facing back, conducting them with a leftover half of a baguette he'd bought in Calais. Although he had no intention of return-ing to live at Vetchling Grove, he'd promised he would help

Angie get everyone back. And he was as good as his word, bless him. As long as he could then go back to Baden-Baden.

As for her own home? She dreaded getting back. There was Ted's seedy infidelity to deal with before she could kick off her shoes and take a long bath. The bastard. And as for what she thought of Fiona's duplicity? Well, that didn't bear thinking about at all! The road widened into two lanes. She whizzed past a three-wheeler she'd been trailing for miles.

"Play as if this moment is your last," Mr Aranovitch was saying.

An ache gathered like a puddle in Angie's throat.

One day she might be hurtling along in a minibus like this one herself, being delivered back to an old age home and fish pie every other Thursday.

Until very recently, secretly, deliciously, every other Thursday promised fragrantly laundered Egyptian cotton sheets, a view into the giraffe enclosure and Jake.

He hadn't acted like a man in the pay of anyone.

He was so earnest, and so poor. He'd straightened up and beamed when he came near her. And he'd risked a lot to come and find her at home, under Ted's watchful eye. Some of it couldn't have been in the plan. What he did in bed couldn't have been an act. That was impossible.

"From the heart," urged Mr Aranovitch.

And this was Thursday.

Fish pie Thursday. Her Thursday.

She braked.

The comb ceased, the plastic bottle fell, voices broke up. Mr Aranovitch's baguette appeared on the floor by her feet.

"I've just remembered something."

Tooting her horn, and waving one arm out of the window, she did a sharp right turn and crossed the river. She accelerated through amber lights, flew over the speed bumps, skidded around corners and stopped only at the sight of several giant cardboard monkeys crossing the road. They were followed by a crowd of kids and a distressed looking man in a dressing gown. He reminded her of someone. Could it be the magician who left behind those bunnies? What, another magic show? She wished magicians would hire proper venues and keep their props minimal.

"Hurry up, come on, come on," she shouted.

Chapter 45

Fiona could see Ray emerging from the back of the van. She had to hide.

"Darling, darling Eddles…" Wrapping herself around him, she pushed him deeper into the bushes.

"We really do need to discuss this," he protested.

For a romantic, he was being damned awkward.

She gave him a sharp shove. He overbalanced, crashing backwards. On trying to help him regain his balance, she tumbled with him until they both crashed into the corner of the building. It seemed like a good place to be, so she kicked at the branches behind them, so that they would spring back, obscure them, and they could settle in.

"…Before we…" He was still trying to speak.

"No more about your silly wife, whoever she is. This is only about us." To silence him, she kissed him violently. When she came up for air, she heard, "Fiona," before she plunged in again, his tie tickling her.

To hell with wives. And husbands. And Daddy. And rules one to a hundred. It was a long time since she'd kissed anyone so clean-shaven and strong, in the depths of a shrubbery. Come to that, kissed anyone at all. Perhaps she should join the Royal Horticultural Society.

There were footsteps on the gravel of the driveway behind

her. She ignored them. Branches shook; dead leaves crackled as the footsteps came closer. They came very near before they stopped. Couldn't the person see they were busy? She devoured as much of Eddles's lips as she could accommodate.

"Fiona... Seta... Elena?"

She went cold. "What?" It couldn't be.

"Is that you in there?"

His voice went right through her. What was he doing outside the building? And what was she to do?

She sprang away from Eddles, tried to pull her blouse straight and braced herself for the nineteenth century. This was it. She was about to be ritually disowned. In front of Eddles. Tears began to well; angry tears. What would he think? But he wasn't looking at her. He was staring beyond her. Men were always bloody well staring beyond her. Why was *Daddy* more important than her? Surely he didn't recognise the Gregoyan nose from the newspapers? Men were always recognising Daddy. So what if he did control the world's shipping?

All the big moments of her life were flavoured by Daddy stealing the show. At her last wedding he'd arrived in a helicopter, outnumbering her guests with his lackeys. At her mother's funeral, she'd been alone at the back of the church while he took up all the front rows with his board of directors. At her confirmation, he'd had a heart attack. He'd swung his worry beads through all family gatherings, and silenced any irreverent laughter with his finger or his stare. Before she could control her anger, she was incandescent; furious that he should appear, bringing his carpetbag views, his halting stride and his imminent threats of disinheritance into this precious bush-prickled moment. It was time to make a stand. Instead of letting him do it, she would disown herself.

"No, Daddy," she said evenly, astonishing herself. "It isn't."

She saw him open his mouth in fury. But nothing came out.

Eddles was clearing his throat as if he was going to speak. She put a hand out to silence him and kept her gaze firmly on Daddy.

"I want you to go away, Daddy, once and for all, and leave me alone."

Daddy seemed shrunken all of a sudden. His worry beads dangled from his left hand.

Jake was at the back of the van, a spaghetti junction of wires at his feet, wondering why the frog design on his best boxer shorts was replicating itself all over the walls.

There were four men on the other side of the van. Two were well-dressed, the others in overalls. They were all peering at a tangle of wires and switches.

"Excuse me, but..." Jake said.

They didn't pay him any attention.

"What do you mean, you don't know? It's got to have a switch," said the plumper of the two well-dressed men to the other. "Everything has a switch."

Jake tried waving both arms and shouting: "Hello!"

"If I knew where that particular accessory was, do you think I'd be keeping it a secret?"

One of the overalled men spat.

"Delightful," said the tall man, wiping down his jacket with a tissue.

"When did that have to do with anything?" said the man with the tattoos.

They were all glaring at each other, seemingly oblivious of the pattern that was multiplying all over them. Why on earth was the projector replicating his very own green frogs? It must be malfunctioning. And those frogs had to go. The one thing Jake had learnt at Barnardos was how to fix things. You had to or you froze, got wet, or contracted food poisoning.

"I think I know how to sort it out," he said, reluctantly.

"You do?" The plump man looked relieved.

"If you give me the screwdriver."

"Here," said the plump man.

"Right." Jake rolled up his sleeves.

The clock on the dashboard showed a minute past two. Angie sped through the red light, flew over another speed bump. Mr Aranovitch, dozing on the seat beside her, woke up with a start.

"*Mein Gott*, Angela, what's happening?"

"There's something I have to do, Mr Aranovitch."

Her phone rang. She flicked it on to 'hands free'. Mrs Willoughby's voice screeched out of the small speaker.

"Where are you?"

"Nearly home."

"You said two pm. I'm standing at the window and I can't see you…"

Mrs W's voice trailed off. Angie wondered how much schnapps she'd imbibed. "The traffic's terrible," she said.

"I have laid out the pills, boiled the kettle, warmed the water bottles, located the fish pie, I mean, warmed the fish pie, located the waterbottles… hic."

"And we have to make a detour…"

"Put the heating back on…"

"…Through Regent's Park."

"No, put my back out putting the heating back on…"

"There's something I have to do, something that can't

wait."

"There's always a ladies room in a hostelry, hic. Why don't you stop at one of those?"

Angie felt as if she was being squeezed into submission by a steam press. "I will only stop for a moment."

"Bravo, Angela!" Mr Aranovitch grinned at her.

"Is that Valentino Aranovitch's voice I'm hearing?"

Angie could feel her resolve waver. "I can't go into details, Mrs Willoughby."

"You don't seem to realise that I have the borough's adult-safeguarding team, several errant rabbits, the care quality commission, the malfunctioning microwave, and the board to worry about. And the fish pie will become all dried up."

Angie was totally sick of jumping to every command Mrs Willoughby uttered. The woman was unpleasant, ineffective, impossible and sozzled. It was time to stand up to her.

"In that case, Mrs Willoughby, tell them we'll be at Ravensville Mansions overlooking Regent's Park."

"Ravensville? Did you say Ravensville?"

"Yes. In fact, why don't you come and collect your wards from here. Goodbye."

She flicked the phone off, and turned into Avenue Road.

Mr Aranovitch made a victory sign.

"Thank you."

She was feeling rather pleased with herself too. The sun emerged from behind clouds and shone brightly.

"When we get back to Vetchling Grove, there's something else I want you to do," said Mr Aranovitch, now sitting upright on the seat beside her.

"Of course."

"It's about Sid."

"Sid?"

"You have to rescue him from that hellhole."

He wasn't going to suggest she took Sid home, was he? "And then what?"

"Take him to the river and set him free."

Angie thought of strapping the fish bowl onto her bicycle, pedalling to London Bridge and emptying it into the cold grey Thames. She saw a small flash of gold fly through the air and land way below her with a tiny splash. "But he won't survive very long in the wild," she said.

"Five minutes in the wild is worth a lifetime in an old-age home. Especially that one."

Angie couldn't argue with that.

The art-deco gates of Ravensville Mansions were open. A van was parked in the drive. She reversed carefully past it and parked right up against the brickwork, scraping the bumper slightly. If that bothered Mrs W, she could take over driving the wretched thing.

"I suppose Sid might make it until winter," she said.

"And what about these others?" Mr Aranovitch pointed at the old ladies dozing happily behind them. "Could we perhaps liberate them too?"

He wasn't asking her to tip them into the Thames too, was he? "But they can't swim."

The engine rattled as she fumbled with the ignition key. She found her hand was trembling.

He seized her other hand and squeezed it. "And you? Will you survive in the wilds, my dear?"

His eyes were twinkling. He seemed to know more about her than she knew herself. "This won't take a minute," she said, and planted a kiss on his cheek.

Mr Aranovitch snapped off his seat beat and stood to face the old ladies. "Time for one last song."

"Did you hear that, Lily?" said Mrs S.

Jingle Bells started up as Angie slipped out, closing the driver's door quietly behind her. She drew a deep breath and then turned towards the foyer, her heart pounding so hard it threatened to escape. There was only one question that mattered to her.

She peered at the glass front of the building. Only the porter was visible in the foyer. He was on the phone. She edged her way past the van. It was jigging slightly; there were voices raised from inside.

"Easy bloody does it."

"Keep holding those wires apart. Don't let the blue touch the red one, whatever you do."

"Okay, okay, I'm not."

"Have the frogs stopped?"

"No. But they've changed colour."

Angie didn't have time to find out what was going on. She strode on towards the steps and nearly got knocked over by a man in overalls. He was awfully familiar. He couldn't be that man at the zoo, could he? Yes, he could. She went cold. Stopped. Felt in her pocket for her purse. It was still there. Was this part of his patch?

Now there was a kerfuffle in the bushes on her left.

The branches shuddered then parted and a tall bony Middle-Eastern looking gentleman in a smoking jacket lurched out, looking distressed.

"My little angel…" he muttered, shaking his head tearfully.

"Oh, dear! Can I help?" she asked.

The man didn't respond. He stumbled over her foot, looking down. He must have lost something precious, she thought. There was something very familiar about his hawk beak and the way he swung his worry beads; but she couldn't place him. Perhaps he was a former inmate? Before Mr Aranovitch?

She put her arm out to steady him. "Do you need anything?"

"No," he said, pulling himself straight and staring down his beaky nose at her. "All my needs are met by my staff."

Illusions of grandeur were symptoms of dementia. He clearly needed her help.

"I think what you need is a cup of sweet tea. Come and sit down."

"Sit down?"

"There's a mini-bus right here."

She took his frail, thin arm and led him over to the bus. He followed, without saying a word.

"Come along." She helped him up the step. "Mr Aranovitch here will pour you a nice cup."

"I should be delighted," said Mr Aranovitch, producing one of the Vetchling royal flasks.

"Very kind!" said the elderly gentleman, his expression bewildered.

Mr Aranovitch was peering warmly at him. "We've met before, I believe," he said. "I never forget a face. Was it in Rome or Tbilisi?"

"Oh my God, you are right," said the elderly gentleman, perking up. "You were playing Bach on the flute, or was it the violin?"

Angie felt she could leave the two old men together; she headed back for the entrance of the building.

"I'm not expecting you to leave her for me," said a familiar voice from somewhere in the ericaceous border. It sounded awfully like Fiona.

What was she doing in the bushes?

Angie stopped. At the edge of the shrubbery was a discarded pair of high heels. They might be overturned and scuffed, but there was no mistaking it; they belonged to Fiona.

Angie felt sick.

What had she done with Jake?

"She knows about *you*," said another familiar voice. Who was that? She shook herself. Was she was dreaming? That was Ted's voice.

"How could she possibly know about me?" asked Fiona. "When I don't know *her*."

Fiona and Ted were together, here, in a bush.

"Ted!" she couldn't help shouting.

Branches parted and two faces peered out at her.

"Well, really!" Angie felt her fury rise like a Victoria sponge.

Ted was pale and speechless.

Fiona seemed apologetic. "It *is* Angie's turn," she said.

"*Angie?*"

Angie was gratified to see that he was gasping.

"I'm sorry, Angie," said Fiona. "You didn't answer your phone, so I couldn't explain that I have met someone new who…"

"New? Ted? There's nothing new about him."

"But..." Fiona seemed confused.

"You knew him all along."

"What the hell is going on?" Ted was shouting now. "I seem to be the only one here who doesn't know…"

"I don't know him from..."

"You've set this up..."

"Hold on a minute..." said Ted.

"Both of you."

"Set what up? It's only fair that I have Eddles. You have the awful Jake."

"Ted is my husband, dammit, don't pretend you don't know that." Angie felt as if her head was about to pop off.

"What?" Fiona's face was puckering. "This is your boring doctor?"

Angie could see she was genuinely shocked.

"Are you saying I'm boring…?"

"Don't say another word, darling," said Fiona.

"Yes, shut up, darling!" shouted Angie. "If you want her, you can bloody well have her."

After twenty years and two children, all he could do was gawp. And to think she'd been filled with remorse and guilt, and several other uncomfortable feelings. They could get on with it. There was only one person she wanted.

Angie stumbled away towards the front steps, pushing her way past the white van. Could Jake be here somewhere? Her heart felt as if it were trying to escape from her ribcage.

A taxi pulled up the street outside. Someone who sounded very like Mrs Willoughby was arguing with the driver. From the minibus came the strains of a violin. Mr Aranovitch was playing to his new friend. But another voice boomed over the music.

"This is the Vetchling Grove minibus, not a concert hall. Oh – we seemed to have gained a new member!"

Angie looked back to see Mrs Willoughby opening the door of the Vetchling van. She turned away and walked on towards the foyer.

"Jake?"

She didn't take any notice of that pickpocket climbing into the driver's seat of the van. She didn't reply to the shouted commands of Mrs Willoughby, or pay any attention to the fleeing raincoat of Mr Aranovitch as they disappeared through the wrought-iron gates.

She might have heard the removal van start and drive away. She certainly didn't hear the sudden shouts of other people emerging from the foyer.

"The van."

"He's stolen it."

"Arthur. My *aspirations* two by Piers Fettucini, it's priceless."

"Thief!"

Ray came sprinting out of the gate, followed by Fiona's husband. But it was too late for her to do anything to help any of them.

All she knew was that she'd managed to break rule number ten – 'whatever happens, don't fall in love'.

"Angie!" said the one person she wanted to hear.

He had dust on his jacket and a screwdriver sticking out of his top pocket. He grinned a huge, relieved smile, and opened his arms.

"You're here," they both found themselves saying.

Lightning Source UK Ltd.
Milton Keynes UK
UKOW04f0906030715

254499UK00002B/15/P